"You don't lik..." D0449646

Spencer had just spent the evening with Natasha. Was it wrong to need a little time to himself?

"I don't know you." Yet he recognized the way her eyes glistened in the firelight. They'd had that same glint the night before, under the light in Ellie's stall, just after she'd witnessed her first calf birth.

He could have sworn, that night, that the sheen was due to tears she was refusing to shed.

But tonight?

"You say that like you don't want to get to know me."

Apparently he was easy to read. But hey, he lived a simple life—a cowboy on a ranch. He didn't need subterfuge. Or societal graces.

It wasn't as if his cattle were going to get an edge on him because they could tell what he was thinking.

"I could pretend otherwise. With our business arrangement, and you here on my ranch, I probably should pretend. But no, I don't."

Dear Reader,

Welcome to the *Family Secrets* cooking show, and the episode where you're going to see everything that goes on behind the scenes, straight from the show's creator, producer and director herself, heroine Natasha Stevens.

Natasha's a strong woman. There are a lot of us making our way through this world. Some of us were just born that way. Most of us grew strong through the challenges life has imposed upon us, and the challenges we brought upon ourselves. Natasha's strength comes from a mother who would accept nothing less. It was formed in the womb. She knows no other way.

And then she meets two children—and a man—who expose the lie about everything she's always believed about herself. And Spencer is a cowboy to die for. To drool over. And yet...he's got a lie in his life, too. A big one. These are fictional people, but they're facing real-life situations. Problems that, when we face them, might make us give up hope.

But please don't give up on us. Because there is always hope. In my books, in Harlequin books, but in real life, too. In the real world in which we live. I know this for a fact. Because I, too, have felt hopeless, and have learned that if we don't give up, if we keep trying, and if we're willing to do the toughest job of all—listening to our true hearts—hope will be right there waiting for us.

I love to hear from my readers. Please find me at Facebook.com/tarataylorquinn and on Twitter, @tarataylorquinn. Or join my open Friendship board on Pinterest, Pinterest.com/tarataylorquinn/friendship!

All the best,

Tara

www.TaraTaylorQuinn.com

HEARTWARMING

The Cowboy's Twins

———

USA TODAY Bestselling Author

Tara Taylor Quinn

⟨H⟩**HARLEQUIN**®HEARTWARMING™

Recycling programs
for this product may
not exist in your area.

ISBN-13: 978-0-373-36819-8

The Cowboy's Twins

Copyright © 2017 by Tara Taylor Quinn

www.Harlequin.com

Printed in U.S.A.

Having written over seventy-five novels, **Tara Taylor Quinn** is a *USA TODAY* bestselling author with more than seven million copies sold. She is known for delivering emotional and psychologically astute novels of suspense and romance. Tara is a past president of Romance Writers of America. She has won a Readers' Choice Award and is a five-time finalist for an RWA RITA® Award, a finalist for a Reviewers' Choice Award and a Booksellers' Best Award. She has also appeared on TV across the country, including *CBS Sunday Morning*. She supports the National Domestic Violence Hotline. If you or someone you know might be a victim of domestic violence in the United States, please contact 1-800-799-7233.

Books by Tara Taylor Quinn

Harlequin Heartwarming

Family Secrets

For Love or Money
Her Soldier's Baby

The Historic Arapahoe

Once Upon a Friendship
Once Upon a Marriage

Harlequin Superromance

Where Secrets are Safe

Wife by Design
Once a Family
Husband by Choice
Child by Chance
Mother by Fate
The Good Father
Love by Association
His First Choice
The Promise He Made Her

Shelter Valley Stories

Sophie's Secret
Full Contact
It's Never Too Late
Second Time's the Charm
The Moment of Truth

It Happened in Comfort Cove

A Son's Tale
A Daughter's Story
The Truth About Comfort Cove

MIRA Books

The Friendship Pact
The Fourth Victim
The Third Secret
The Second Lie

Visit the Author Profile page
at Harlequin.com for more titles.

To my mother, Agnes Mary (Penny) Gumser, who spent my formative years putting me first, teaching me about the type of person I wanted to be. And who still, all these years later, is showing me, through every stage of life, how to listen with an open mind, to welcome with an open heart and to love with an open soul. I know joy exists because she first introduced me to it. And later, after a tragic death in our family, she showed me how to find it again.

CHAPTER ONE

The things you do for love...

Monitor receiver in hand, Spencer Longfellow took one last look at his sleeping seven-year-olds, slipped into his boots and quietly let himself out the back door, the line from an old song playing in his head.

The things you do for love...

Every single thing he did was for love. Love for his children. And love for his ranch.

He didn't much love the idea of waking up the glamorous city woman at two in the morning. But a deal was a deal.

And he needed the money she was paying him.

With a nod at Betsy, the wife of one of his most trusted full-time cowboys, he continued across the yard. Blanket and pillow in hand, Betsy was on her way to his couch, where she'd sleep until Spencer and Bryant, her husband, were back from the barn.

If they didn't make it back in time for

breakfast, she'd get the kids up, feed them and put them on the bus for him.

It was routine. One he'd grown up with on that very ranch.

Hating the extra five minutes it was taking him for the detour to the cabin he'd given Natasha Stevens to use during her visits to the ranch over the coming weeks, Spencer reminded himself, once again, of the money.

If you'd have asked him two years ago if he'd ever allow a TV crew access to any part of his two-thousand-acre ranch, he'd have issued an unequivocal *absolutely not*. But a lack of rain had all but wiped out his hay crop—right at the time the cattle business he was building, while hinting at a success that could climb even higher than his hopes, was still in the fledgling stage.

He was on the brink of turning the land of his ancestors into a lucrative venture that would ensure the financial security of not only the twins but also their children and grandchildren. All while remaining true to those members of the family who had come before. Using heritage to build on the legacy.

He just needed an influx of cash...

Passing a few dark cabins, he stepped quietly. Most of the guys who stayed on the ranch were single—and lived in the bunkhouse on the other side of the barns. A few, like Bryant, lived with their wives in cabins. Spencer was heading toward one of the larger ones—one outfitted with modern amenities including wired high-speed internet for those times when the wireless connection was in a mood.

A figure moved just outside the front door. Tall. Slender. She was in shadow, but there was no doubt in Spencer's mind, the second he saw movement down the steps, that the body belonged to Natasha Stevens.

"I've heard of cowboys sleeping in their clothes, to be ready to ride on a second's notice, but not a famous television producer," he said, meeting her a few yards from the cabin.

"You called five minutes ago," she said. He could tell she was grinning by the show of even, white teeth. "And I was prepared before I went to bed. It takes less than one minute to pull on jeans and a sweatshirt. Give me another one to pull on the boots…"

Her words trailed off as she kept pace beside him. He'd sped up to get to Ellie. And to keep his thoughts from lagging behind with visions of the city woman climbing out of bed and into jeans.

Natasha broke the silence in the crisp night

air, her voice night-soft in spite of the miles of vast land around them. "You said she was going to calf tonight. You were spot-on."

When it came to his precious cattle, he usually was. Came from breathing ranch air every day of your life. The whole heritage thing.

The closer they got to the big barn housing his dry cows, the faster he moved. As though he could outrun the fact that he was allowing a television crew to be a part of a live birth as part of footage that would be used on a cooking competition reality show.

He was a serious rancher who took pride in his work, not a drama monger looking for ratings. Not that he knew Natasha Stevens well enough to know if there was any drama, or monger, in her. It wasn't her fault that her presence there—and the fact that he'd succumbed to it for the money—made him feel cheap.

"How much do you know about cattle?" he asked her as lights came into view. Bryant was the only member of his staff who'd be with them that night.

"Assume I know nothing," she told him. He heard the click as she turned on her recording device—a compromise since he preferred not to be formally interviewed on camera. Reading from a teleprompter, as he'd be doing for his small portion of the filmed segments, was one thing. Answering questions without a script was another. He'd told her so, quite clearly, before he'd signed her contract.

To appease his conscience more than anything else, he gave her a brief rundown of America's top cattle breeds. If he was going to do this, he might as well make the best of it—get the promotion out of it she'd promised him.

"Ellie's classified as Purebred Wagyu," he told her. "You've heard of Kobe beef?"

"Of course. It's the best of the best..."

"Kobe's a type of Wagyu." He simplified it. "It's tender with abundant marbling. Historically the cows have been fed beer to amp up their appetite, which allows for premium maturity standards."

"Do you feed your cattle beer?"

He'd been experimenting with the process. Part of his new venture. If he could get a full herd of Purebred Wagyu grazing his lands, the twins would be set for life. At a cow per acre, that would be close to two thousand head at any given time. Being able to bring the Wagyu to production in less than a year per head…

But…he was way ahead of himself. Mostly he was raising Angus. Which were also premium steak producers.

"You're asking for my secrets," he told the show's host, producer and founder. "Did you know that one of the reasons Wagyu are historically so tender is that they were massaged as they grew?"

"Now you're messing with me."

"Nope," he told her. She didn't know him well yet. She'd figure out soon enough that when it came to his cattle, he never messed around.

Not ever.

"WAGYU'S MARBLING IS UNIQUE, not only because it adds juiciness and flavor to the beef, but also because the fat contains an acid that is friendly to heart health…"

Natasha's long legs made it easy for her to keep up with the handsome cowboy's strides. She just wasn't used to tromping across dusty ground in new cowboy boots in the middle of the night.

Though she'd lived on the West Coast for most of her adult life, she'd never succumbed to that particular footwear—having just purchased her new shiny red boots for the show. She'd figured boots were boots. Not so.

She clearly should have practiced walking in them before trotting across uneven ground in the dark. That she didn't think to do so earlier was definitely unlike her.

Truth be known, everything about this endeavor was unlike her. Taking her proven, successful show on the road? To a ranch?

What had she been thinking?

Their Palm Desert studio had been working wonderfully well for years.

Just because Angela had thought it would be a good idea hadn't been reason actually to do it. While she highly respected and relied on her stage manager, she disagreed with her often.

"…the marbling is also of particular note because it has the highest USDA rating, meaning it's veined throughout the meat. I've got pictures of the various grades. Remind me to get them to you."

"I'd like that, thank you." *That's right, focus.* At least Angela had found her a top-rate rancher in Spencer Longfellow.

Though she suspected her stage manager/ jack-of-all-trades assistant had chosen the dark-haired, dark-eyed rancher as much for his good looks—and his female audience draw—as anything else, Natasha respected his focus.

His drive.

His warm, virile energy was just something she'd work around. As soon as she got her footing.

His cattle quality lecture stopped as they reached the barn. Her first step from cool darkness to brightly lit warm barn was a shock. And probably why the cowboy at her side, dressed in jeans and a dark plaid button-up, taller than her five-feet-six by several inches, suddenly seemed so…desirable…to her.

In so many ways.

Giving herself a mental shake, she followed him across a hard dirt floor, past wooden doors and gated stalls housing other dry cows, she'd been told during her tour of the ranch earlier that day.

She didn't need a man. Or his strength. Didn't even want one. Her strength of character—okay, her innate need to run her own show, whether it be on television or in her home—was like a coffin in waiting for any relationship.

"Through here," Spencer said. Opened

wide a double size wooden door and moved so she could see inside.

Bryant, in jeans and a sweatshirt, sat in a corner of the stall, by the door. He nodded at her, sipping from a cup of coffee.

Ellie stood a few feet away, swinging her tail.

"Nothing yet?" Spencer asked, focused on his prize cow.

Pursing his lips, Bryant shook his head. She knew he was Spencer's age since they'd told her earlier in the day that they'd gone to high school together.

Having never seen a live birth before, of any kind, Natasha had only her imagination to feed expectation. A cow standing, seemingly calm, in a bed of hay wasn't anything close to what she'd come up with.

She wanted to ask if they were sure this was it...the moment of birth...but was able to clamp her lips together, holding her tongue hostage. They knew their business.

And if someone had made a wrong call on this one, they'd all know it soon enough.

"Come in." Spencer held the door open wider and motioned to her. "Over here." He pointed to the corner opposite of Bryant. "Stand, or sit in the hay," he said. "You should be fine, but with animals, one never knows. Stay alert. And be prepared to get out of the way."

She nodded, not sure if he was irritated by her presence or merely concerned with the birthing process.

Ellie's tail swished. Lifted. Natasha stared, wondering if she was about to see a calf appear, but saw only a slight oozing.

She glanced away.

"If you need to leave, do so." Spencer's words were harsh. But his gaze, when she caught him catching her slight discomfort, was warm. His grin even more so. "It's all part of nature," he said. "But it could take some getting used to."

She supposed, since he was doing so, they were allowed to talk.

"Did you have to get used to it?" she asked. For the show. Get to know the rancher. Not just the ranch. Humanize it. She knew what her audience would respond to.

"Not so much." He shrugged, glancing back at Ellie.

"Spence was barely out of diapers the first time he was present for calving," Bryant said. "Ain't that right, bro?"

"Yep."

Natasha wanted more. A lot more. Because her viewers would want more.

Down on his haunches, he seemed to be studying the cow's hindquarters. She heaved. Natasha saw a speck of black behind her tail. And then it was gone.

"What…" She broke off. Both men were staring at the cow. Bryant, next to Spencer now, rubbed her belly.

Bryant glanced back at Natasha. "That was a hoof," he said. "You'll see the front hooves first. Then the nose and head will appear. She works the hardest to get the front quarter birthed. Then, if all goes well, a lot of the rest will slide out."

"All is going to go just fine," Spencer said, standing. He moved to the cow's head. Petted her. "Good girl, Ellie. You're doing great." The tenderness in his voice struck her with an impact she didn't fully understand. "You're a good mama," he told her, continuing to stroke the upper flank of the cow.

Almost as though she understood, Ellie collapsed to the ground, lying on her side, as she heaved again.

CHAPTER TWO

HE DIDN'T WANT the woman there. Spencer took a deep breath. And didn't like what he smelled. A sixth sense told him something wasn't right.

And he knew what that something was. The city woman sitting in the corner, staring, while Ellie labored.

When she'd asked if she could watch, and record, the live birth, he'd agreed because there'd been no reason not to. Cows weren't like people. They dropped their young right out in the open and went on about their business.

One of her camera people had been by Ellie's stall earlier. She'd taken some footage of Ellie and Bryant. She'd be back to get some film of Ellie's calf when the work was done.

They'd air the cute stuff.

On her side now, Ellie heaved. The little black-tipped hooves appeared again. And disappeared again. He should be seeing them clearly out by now, full hooves, with a nose between them. Should be seeing more than a nose, based on when Bryant had told him Ellie had started to give birth.

She didn't need them there. It wasn't like he or his men could sit and watch over the hundreds of cows he'd have birthing every year once his operation was in full swing, but Ellie was special. She'd been his first Wagyu purchase. He'd laid down a mint for her. Massaged her himself, as the first Wagyu breeders had done so long ago. Technically the practice was no longer necessary, but he was doing absolutely everything he could to make this venture work. Overkill or not.

In a herd of hundreds, a few births would go wrong. He could lose a few calves. Maybe a mother.

He couldn't afford to lose Ellie.

Rubbing the side of her face, her neck, he said, "That's it, girl. You're doing good."

The words didn't matter. His tone of voice did.

Her nostrils flared, and she raised her head. Looked straight at him.

And that was when he knew that something was really wrong.

NATASHA DIDN'T NEED to understand anything about birthing to know that they had an emergency on their hands. Spencer had told her in the afternoon that his cows birthed their babies without assistance. That the process was natural and took about thirty minutes, and that the mama cow would immediately stand over her calf, clean him herself and get him to stand.

If all went well.

The pinched look on Spencer's face when he stood from his position beside the cow's head and moved lower told her that he was worried.

The flurry of activity and harsh, staccato conversation between him and Bryant that followed filled in the blanks.

The calf was not coming out hooves first. It was going to have to be turned.

Spencer was in charge. He obviously knew what he was doing. Ellie continued to heave. To make un-moo-like noises.

Natasha couldn't see much. Was watching out of mostly squinted eyes. The clear concern on Bryant's face told her that at least one of the bovine lives was in danger. Maybe both.

She had to restrain herself to keep from speaking. Asking. Looking for answers. A way to help.

Her way was not to sit back and watch.

"I turn him and he moves immediately back to position," Spencer hissed. She could see beads of sweat forming on his temples. The sides of his neck.

With energy pulsing through her, until she could almost feel its pressure against her skin, she itched to approach the cow's head, as Spencer had done. To rub gently. To comfort the beast.

He'd told her to stay put in the corner.

Would he need hot water? She thought about the buckets she'd seen on her way to the stall. About the big utility sinks along one wall of the barn.

Spencer barked orders as he worked inside the cow. Bryant complied, working the cow's bulging stomach.

She stood. Had to do something to help. To fix the problem. It was what she did. What she was good at. Taking charge. Helping. Fixing.

"Grab some gloves." Spencer's command was directed over his shoulder. She was the only person behind him. Seeing the crate of gloves along the wall, she grabbed a pair. Pulled them on.

They were far too big. There was no time to go shopping for smaller ones.

"While Bryant continues his pressure on the outside, I'm going to guide inside," Spencer told her. "I need you to grab the hooves as soon as they appear and pull with all your might."

She was strong. But *that* strong?

"If you can't budge the calf, don't worry. Just hold on until I can get there to pull him out."

Nodding, Natasha jumped into the fray. She grabbed when she was told to grab. Pulled. The calf didn't budge. Her arms ached. Using her entire body weight, she leaned back. And managed to keep the hooves outside the cow's body.

Everything happened in seconds after that. One minute Ellie was in obvious stress with Spencer on the ground by the struggling cow's tail. The next, Spencer was pushing Natasha aside, grabbing hooves, and had pulled a calf out into the world.

Her new red boots were going in the trash.

"I GET TO name her."

"Nuh-uh, I do."

Listening just outside the bathroom door

while his kids stood on identical stools at double sinks, supposedly brushing their teeth, Spencer smiled. Starting the day with only two hours of sleep would catch up with him.

Later.

For now, he had duties to tend to.

"No, Justin, that is not true. Daddy said that if she's a girl, I get to name her. And she's a girl."

Spencer couldn't help the smile growing wider on his face as he listened to the most articulate seven-year-old he'd ever known. Justin was a handful but didn't faze him a bit. Tabitha was going to be the death of him.

"Well, I get to pet her first…"

When he heard the intensity rising in his son's voice, Spencer entered the room to see two dark-haired little kids standing on stools, their brown gazes at war in the mirror. Neither of them had anything resembling toothbrushes in sight.

"You're supposed to be brushing your teeth."

"We did." Justin's immediate response was followed by a drop in his gaze. And then his chin met his chest. "No, we didn't," he corrected himself before Spencer could take the breath necessary to challenge the boy. "But… do we gotta?" Justin's eyes widened as he gave Spencer an imploring look. "They'll just get dirty again, and I'll brush it all away tonight."

Spencer pressed his lips together, hoping he looked stern.

The hardest part about being a single parent was having no one with whom to share the laughter.

"I want to see Bella before we have to catch the bus, and…"

"Who's Bella?" He allowed himself to be distracted. Just until he could demand brushing with the firmness it deserved.

"Ellie's baby. Justin thinks he's naming her," Tabitha said, opening the cabinet where their teeth-brushing paraphernalia was stored. She handed her brother his brush and then took her own. "But he's not, is he, Daddy? You said if she's a girl, I can name her."

He had said that. He couldn't remember when. Or why. But he vaguely remembered making the promise.

"Yes, I did. If she'd had a boy then Justin would name her."

Satisfied, Tabitha wet her brush and stuck it in her mouth.

"Toothpaste?" Spencer gave her *the* look. The one with eyebrows raised, warning that a child wasn't going to get away with something.

"I've got toothpaste, see?" Justin held out his brush, turning lips smeared with goo up at Spencer. And dripping a blob of blue on the linoleum floor while he was at it. Which was why Spencer had installed the linoleum over the old wood floors when he'd remodeled the bath for the twins to share. He didn't want to have to worry about spills and other little things.

Making a mental note to wipe up the blob later, Spencer nodded. He didn't care about drops on the floor. What he cared about was that the twins loved the ranch, their home, as much as he did.

That they felt the same sense of excitement—of security—that he'd always felt there.

"I'll tell you what," he said, doing a quick mental rearrangement of his morning. "You two finish brushing and grab your backpacks." He picked up Tabitha's hairbrush and started in on the morning ritual of getting the tangles out of her long, dark hair, remembering to be gentle on the ones that invariably rested at the base of his little girl's neck. She winced.

He winced, too. Waiting for the morning

when he could get through this part without hurting her.

"Lunches are made," he continued. "So if everyone is on his best behavior—" said for Justin's benefit "—we'll take a walk over to say good morning to Ellie."

"We'll miss our bus." Tabitha spoke with her brush in her mouth, leaving spots of toothpaste on the mirror as she met his gaze in the glass.

"I'll drive you to school this morning." He had no need for a trip to town but welcomed the idea of being away from the ranch for a couple of hours.

And he made no pretense to himself about the reason for that.

He wanted to spend as little time as possible with the city girl who'd invaded his space.

In more ways than one.

CHAPTER THREE

THE PEAL OF her old-fashioned ringtone woke Natasha from a sound sleep. Not sure where she was at first, Natasha reached an arm toward the side table, pulling herself to a sitting position.

Her mother called only when she had something important to say. And the ringtone was reserved exclusively for the woman who'd birthed her thirty-one years before.

Birthed. She knew, firsthand, what that meant.

By the time her eyes were fully open and focused on the paneled walls of the cabin's master bedroom, Natasha had regained full faculties. And memories of helping to bring a calf into the world came flooding back.

"Hi, Mom. What's up?" She forced cheer and wakefulness into her tone. Susan Stevens wouldn't approve of sleeping past six—no matter that she'd not made it back to bed until sometime after four that morning.

The red digital numbers glaring at her from the nightstand let her know that she was over two hours late getting up.

By her mother's standards. Which had been firmly indoctrinated as her own...

"How are you, dear?" Polite conversation meant that her mother was displeased. Or worse, disappointed. Now she felt like a real slough off.

Searching her brain for what she could possibly have done to earn this, she came back to the time. Had her mother already called once? Had she slept through the ring?

"I'm fine, Mom," she said, standing beside the bed to ensure that her blood was flowing and she sounded busy.

It was half past eleven in New York City. Her mother would have already handled a full calendar that morning and would be off the bench for the next hour and a half before her afternoon calendar began.

Susan wouldn't think ill of her for not taking her call. It was understood that they were both busy women. Missing a call was to be expected...

Which meant her own sleeping habits had nothing to do with her mother's displeasure.

Maybe a case had gone bad. As a superior

court judge on the criminal bench in a city like New York, Susan led a less-than-peaceful life.

She lived in a less-than-peaceful city.

So had Natasha…until…

"The new season of the show starts in a couple of days," Susan stated, as though Natasha didn't know her own schedule. Because she wanted Natasha to know that she knew. That she kept track.

Her way of saying that she cared.

"I'm already at the ranch," Natasha said, collapsing to the side of the bed. She told her mother about Ellie. About birthing the cow. And when Susan asked how she was going to integrate the experience into her show, a fifteen-minute conversation followed. A good, meaty, mind-melding conversation.

Between mother and daughter. Two high-powered women whose minds were simpatico.

"So…how's Stan?" Natasha asked, after their brainstorming morphed into a series of ideas, a plan, that pleased them both.

When she was up and ready, Bryant's wife was going to be doing a walk-through with her of the staging and kitchens that had been built in a tractor barn on the property. The pantry and green room. Now that she was awake, she was eager to get to it.

"That's what I called about…"

Back straightening, Natasha slowed her thinking. Had something happened to her mother's long-term companion? While not technically her father, Stan had been in their lives for over a decade, and…

"What's wrong? Is he ill?"

The appeals court judge had been in perfect health when she'd visited her mother over Christmas. But that had been…nine months ago.

"No…to the contrary, he's more physically fit than he's been in years," Susan said. A note in her mother's voice gave her concern. Or rather, a lack of any particular one did.

"He's taking an early retirement," Susan continued, her words even. Emotionless.

"But…he's only, what, fifty-one?" Her mother had thrown a high-powered fiftieth birthday bash for him. The guest list had included most anyone who was anyone in power in the city. Natasha had flown home to New York to oversee the caterer her mother had hired for the occasion.

"Fifty-two. And he's decided that he wants to sail around the world," she continued. Natasha sat frozen on the bed. She couldn't tell if her mother was being literal. Normally she'd have been able to tell.

"Wow." Not her best articulation, but she was shocked. To the bone. "I thought he'd die at ninety-five, still on the bench," she half murmured.

"I know. Me, too."

Just as her mother planned to do...

Unless... With a surge of...she didn't know what exactly—an emotion that felt a lot better than the disbelief and uncertainty weighing her down—she entertained the thought that had struck.

Could her mother be calling to tell Natasha that she was retiring, too? That she'd finally reached a point where she felt she'd done her duty to the world that had given her life—to the purpose for which she'd been born—and could just relax?

Where that thought came from, Natasha didn't know. She was certain it was unbidden. And unwelcome, too.

Her mother and she were not women who wanted to *just relax*. They weren't made for sitting around.

And yet...to think that Susan and Stan were moving on to the next stage of their lives together was…reassuring. In an odd, offhand sense…

"So, I just thought I should let you know…"

Wait. What? Wasn't there more? "Are you having a retirement party for him? Do you need me to cater?" Sense was coming back into focus.

"No. I won't be doing that." Susan sounded distracted now. Which made no sense again.

"My gosh, Mom, he's been employed by New York's legal system for thirty years. Has had an illustrious career. I can't imagine him not wanting a party to celebrate that. If nothing else, I'm sure there are a lot of people who'd be offended not to be a part of such a celebration."

"I'm sure you're right, Natasha. Which is why I'm certain he'll have a party such as you describe. I just won't be having it for him."

Oh. No. With a sudden thud, realization dawned. "Why not?" she asked, dreading the answer.

Her entire life, anytime anyone had tried to get too close to her and her mother, Susan had ended the relationship. Because invariably, the man had wanted her to become less of who she was and more like he'd needed her to be. Less powerful. More nurturing.

But Stan...

"We are no longer...friends."

They'd broken up, Natasha translated.

"Because he wanted to retire?"

That didn't sound like Susan. Even if she didn't want to join him in early relaxation, Susan wasn't one to ask anyone to be anything they were not. Because she couldn't be who she was not. Her mother was nothing if not fair...

"Because he wanted me to marry him. He wants to get married again. He said if I won't marry him, we're through."

Mouth open, Natasha just sat there. What was probably one of the most critical moments of her life, and she had nothing to offer in response.

Except a couple of inexplicable, seldom-present tears that slid slowly down her cheeks.

It was happening again.

Just as it always would.

For her mother.

For her.

Because, as the women they were, the women they'd been born to be, there was no other choice.

"SO, BRO, THAT'S one hot babe you've got staying with you," Bryant said. Spencer had stopped to tell his right-hand man that he was taking the kids to school. Bryant, who'd been after Spencer to take a look at some new side-by-sides for hands to use to check fence line, had invited himself to hook up the trailer to the back of Spencer's truck and ride along.

He'd talked Spencer into purchasing two of the all-purpose off-road vehicles. Which had used up more of his cash than he'd have liked. There was still a bundle put away. But that was all the security his kids had, and he didn't like dipping into it. Ever.

"She's not staying with me," he said now, still brewing over the side-by-side matter. Maybe he was being too much of a stickler by refusing to buy anything on credit. Maybe Bryant was right and he needed to loosen up a bit.

"You put her up in your old house..."

With a sideways glance at a man he wanted to punch on a regular basis—mostly because Bryant knew Spencer too well—he shrugged.

If he overreacted, Bryant would be on it like a newborn calf on her mother's teat.

What a night they'd had. The city woman had not puked as he'd been half expecting— hoping?—and she'd actually been a bit of a help there, toward the end. For a second...

"You got nothing to say for yourself?" Bryant's words prodded him. But not as much as the other man's grin. "You know when you say nothing, you're just telling me that I'm getting to you."

There came that urge to punch again.

"I'm not going to feed your lurid and completely drama-filled and ludicrous imagination," Spencer said, focusing on the road. He was kind of looking forward to getting the new vehicles off the back of the trailer he was pulling and giving them a go. So they'd be ready for a spin when the kids got home…

"She's in that house because it's the nicest one on the ranch." As it should be, since, as Bryant said, it had been his.

He'd built it himself when he and his mother had decided it was time for him to have a place of his own. He'd moved back into the big house only after his mother had passed. The year before he'd married Kaylee— another city girl.

And the biggest mistake of his life.

"And be a little more respectful, would you?" he continued, because Bryant had a way of putting him out of sorts like none other. "You don't go around referring to a successful television producer and star as a hot babe.

Next thing you know, Justin will be calling her that to her face."

His son adored Bryant—a lifetime cowboy if ever there was one—which mostly pleased Spencer no end. Justin was one of them.

He was also young. Impressionable. Had an overabundance of energy. And no mother.

"Point taken," Bryant said. And then turned a wicked grin on him. "But just between me and you…she's hot."

He didn't agree. "If you like that type of woman, maybe," he allowed so Bryant wouldn't think he was holding out on him. And start thinking he had something for auburn-haired model types.

Although…her hair was almost as long as Tabitha's. Perhaps the woman could give him a hint about the morning tangles…

With an eye on meeting his goal of a wince-less morning for his little girl, he figured it wouldn't hurt to ask.

"You like that type of woman." Bryant's words dropped to the floor of the truck with such force Spencer could have sworn he felt it.

He wasn't going to validate them with an answer.

"All kidding aside, Spence, we both know

what type of woman gets to you. I'm only saying that if you keep it light, joke about it, she's not going to do a number on you."

Though he'd cooperated because Spencer had asked him to do so, Bryant had been against him signing the contract with *Family Secrets* from the beginning. Was this why?

He gave his best friend a quick once-over.

"No worries, bro," he said, feeling easy again. He sat back and put the pedal to the floor as they crossed miles of empty California desert. "Glamorous women might be tempting, but Kaylee cured me of ever…and I mean *ever*…wanting to be with one again."

He spoke with total confidence. The second his wife had left her dust behind her as she'd driven off the farm—leaving him with full custody of their two-year-old twins— he'd been cured of any attraction he might have had.

Glancing at Bryant one more time, he grinned.

It was good to know that he had a friend— more like brother—who had his back.

CHAPTER FOUR

"JUSTIN! JUSSSTIIIIN! YOU come out of there right now."

In the middle of spooning a batch of chocolate chip cookie dough onto a tray in one of the kitchens on her newly staged set, Natasha froze.

Her staff, including Angela, had all been dismissed to other tasks. At the moment, "staff" meant a handful of techies, two camera operators and her stage manager/right hand/assistant. All of whom—except for Angela, who'd driven back to Palm Desert—had been sent off to town to squeeze in what R & R they could before working almost around the clock for the next few days.

Filming the show on location was taking more out of all of them than they had expected. She had to make sure they enjoyed their lives, too.

Losing employees was not something she took lightly.

The *Family Secrets* crew were her family. And…

"Justin, I mean it. Come out now."

The first command had come in the form of a stern whisper. The second in a more stern, loud whisper. The identity of the commander was a mystery.

Whoever Justin was, or wherever he was, remained unknown to her, as well.

But she had a theory.

She'd heard that Spencer Longfellow had a couple of children. And the whisperer was definitely of the child variety.

From what she'd understood—and she'd been pretty clear about gaining complete understanding on this point—the Longfellow children were the only human minors on the ranch. She'd have chosen to film elsewhere if that were not the case. And had almost chosen to move on down the road when she'd heard about the rancher's kids.

While she had nothing against children, Natasha needed to be able to work undisturbed. And to have her contestants and staff able to do the same. A lot was at stake for the winner of the show. Her show offered external economic value to the winner, and to contestants as well, and it was paramount that she provide a fair competition environment.

Filming on location was already going to create certain levels of stress and inconvenience, and they couldn't have added interruptions from little ones.

"Justinnn. I'm telling you." The voice was just above a whisper now. And closer. "Daddy said to stay out of this barn. Period."

Other than the voice, she heard nothing. No movement. Shuffling. Breathing. Or any other indication of life. Hair tied back, she wiped a hand on the full-body apron covering her jeans and black Lycra pullover. Thought about calling the children out, giving them a warning and sending them on their way.

A mental flash followed right on the heels of that thought. A picture of her mother all alone. She shook it away.

Hoping that if she ignored the interlopers, they'd mind their father and vacate the barn, she continued to scoop spoonfuls of batter from bowl to pan. She had a system. One pan's worth of cookies was cooling on foil, one pan was baking, and she needed to have the third ready to go in the oven when the others came out. Efficient.

Technically, she was checking out the kitchens. Testing the equipment. Making certain that everything was in place, worked and was fully stocked so that each contestant had an equally fair chance.

Normally that meant something simple. Prepared by someone on staff. And it had been that day, as well. For the first six kitchens. The last two hadn't been ready—some last-minute electrical hookups—and she'd sent her staff on to enjoy their free afternoon and evening.

That was technically the situation. And all true.

But also true was that today she'd needed comfort. And was taking it in the form of chocolate chip cookies.

With one eye on the timer and the rest of her attention on the bowl, Natasha figured she'd finish panning her cookie dough with about ten seconds to spare. More foil was laid out, ready for the cookies coming out. She could see it in her peripheral vision.

Except…something was wrong with the symmetry.

She gave the foil-covered counter a full-on glance.

And noticed a cookie missing from the far corner.

Only one.

Split between two children? Or had Justin glommed it all for himself?

She'd never had a brother. Wasn't up on little-boy things.

But...she'd known two mothers with sons recently. Contestants on her last two series. And had been drawn to both the mothers and their sons.

Been personally touched by them. By their stories...

Shaking her head, Natasha finished spooning dough. In spite of her hurried efforts, the timer went off before the spoon was sitting in an emptied bowl. But only a second before.

Transitioning trays was easy. Mitts on both hands, one out, one in, close door, set timer. And then, with freshly baked tray still in hand, she faced the counter.

Two cookies were now missing.

"Justin? Tabitha?" Spencer hurried from the back door into the yard. He'd been later than he'd expected, coming in from checking on the calf. Fifty percent of calf deaths within the first forty-five days of life came from birthing difficulties. Getting enough colostrum from the mother's milk—which provided the antibodies a calf needed to survive—had to happen within the first twenty-four hours. And Ellie's calf wasn't nursing enough. He'd left Bryant tube-feeding her colostrum.

"Justin!" He raised his voice as he ran into the yard. He'd missed the school bus dropping the kids off. They knew to leave their backpacks in the hall and go immediately to Betsy if he wasn't there.

The backpacks were in the hall. "Tabitha?" He was on his way to the cabin Bryant and Betsy shared, but his number one man had already told him that the kids weren't there. He'd called Betsy's cell the second Spencer had noticed the time.

"I've been all over the yard." Betsy ran up to him. "Over to the tree house, and down by the creek."

"Would you mind going up to the house?" he asked now, his chin tight as he fought back the thread of fear piercing his heart. If something happened to those two... "Just stay there in case they return? Or call or something?"

His kids didn't have cell phones. But they were going to. Flip phones. With no data capability. Just so they could call him.

"I'm going to check the other barns," he

told her, knowing as he did so that the kids wouldn't be there. Not together. The barns were off-limits unless they were with Spencer or Bryant, or had permission from one or the other.

Justin might get sidetracked by something and disobey him. Tabitha…never.

There were six big barns within walking distance of the main house. He headed toward the horse barn first. Tabitha wanted her own horse. Bad.

He was going to have to take care of that. Sometime. When she was big enough that the thought of her falling off didn't choke the breath out of him. She'd asked him again that morning how old she had to be.

He'd given her his standard answer: *"Older than you are now."*

Nodding at Will, the twenty-one-year-old who kept up the stables for him and fed the horses Spencer boarded to help make some extra cash, he walked up to the stall Will was mucking out. "You seen the kids?" he asked.

"Nope." Will kept right on raking. "Not today. But I heard about a foal that's going to be available for sale," he said, giving Spencer an over-the-shoulder glance.

"I'm not in the market for a foal."

"She won't be ready to ride for at least another year," Will said.

He had to find his kids. Not talk about horses. "If you see the kids, tell them to get back to the house, pronto," he said on his way out.

"My grandpa says you were riding by the time you were five!" the young man called.

Spencer ignored him. Because he had his children's safety on his mind. And because he was not ready to risk Tabitha's life on a horse. No matter how good a trainer Will Sorrenson might be turning out to be.

The tractor barn was empty of human life. He took a turn from there and, at a jog now, went down the row of cottages—some empty, some occupied—that housed married cowboys. And on to the bunkhouse. Justin had been known to wander in there a time or two, in spite of Spencer's strict instructions that he not do so.

If he'd taken his sister in there, he was going to get the first hiding of his young life.

The bunkhouse was empty, too. As it should have been. Most of his men were out on the range this week—their absence scheduled purposely to coincide with filming.

And that was when it hit him. He'd told the

kids that absolutely, under no circumstances were they to go near the outer barn that had been changed into a television studio for the next six weeks.

But they were seven. And it was TV.

Not sure if he was praying that the kids were there or not, he sped up, his boots kicking up dust on the dry ground as he switched course.

"Today I'm giving you my best peanut butter and jelly sandwich." Cocking his head, Spencer picked up his pace even more as he heard his daughter's voice coming out loud and clear from a location that was still some distance away.

A mixture of stunning relief—they were safe!—and tense disappointment—they'd not only disobeyed him, they'd involved the one place on the farm he wanted them the least—flooded him. No one had prepared him for the emotional roller coaster of parenting.

"I have the best bread—white—and I have two pieces of it…" He'd always served his kids wheat bread because it was healthier, but Betsy had white bread at home, and when they ate there…

His step grew heavier, frustration growing right along with dread. He'd heard that the *Family Secrets* crew had gone into town for the afternoon and evening—and had been relieved to have the place to himself. If Tabitha had found a way to make a mic work, he could only imagine the damage Justin had done.

Was doing.

"I have peanut butter—just the butter part, no peanuts."

She liked it smooth.

"And jelly—we use grape because Daddy likes it best, not jam with the lumps in it." The note of authority in her childish voice was growing in leaps and bounds.

Spencer started to leap, too, or at least it felt that way as he took the last few yards at a dead run.

He couldn't afford to repair an entire studio.

Nor did *Family Secrets* have time to build another one. Contestants were due to arrive the next day.

Rounding the corner in the barn, his worst imaginings became reality. There was Justin, sitting at what could only be some kind of sound board—or control center. His hands were on knobs. Turning.

"I take a knife, this kind, because I'm not

allowed to use the sharp ones..." Tabitha's voice was loud and clear—far too loud and clear—coming from somewhere on the other side of a temporary wall. He didn't want to think of the mess she was making.

He'd seen her "cook."

Justin hadn't noticed him yet, and Spencer had to rein himself in before he approached his recalcitrant son. The boy had gone too far this time.

He was going to be meting out some serious discipline.

As soon as he trusted himself not to lash out first.

His good day had just gone really, really bad.

"JUSTIN GERALD LONGFELLOW, please take your hand off that board. Now."

Natasha froze. And watched as seven-year-old Tabitha, with a rather large glob of peanut butter dangling from her table knife, stopped moving, as well. Rising from her seat in the middle row of the bleachers in their makeshift studio, Natasha kept her eye on the child but spoke into the headset she was wearing.

"Justin, are you okay?" She hadn't recognized the voice she'd just heard issuing an order to the boy in what could only be termed a threatening tone.

But then, the only men she'd spoken to on the farm, other than her own crew members, were Spencer Longfellow and the cowboy, Bryant.

"No, ma'am." She'd known the child only for about an hour, but long enough to tell her that the vulnerable tone in his voice was not common.

"Who are you talking to?" The male voice came again. But Natasha recognized it that time.

"Spencer?" she called as she rounded the corner of the wall in back of the stage. Locating the control booth behind the stage had not been anyone's first choice, but for remodeling cost effectiveness and electric concerns, they'd made the decision to put it there. Monitors allowed views of the stage from every angle. Monitors that were not currently turned on.

"Natasha?" The cowboy in dusty, faded jeans, a red plaid shirt and the inevitable boots stood there, his gaze piercing as he looked between her and his son.

"I'm so sorry..." Words came tumbling out of her mouth. "It didn't occur to me that

I should have told you I was keeping them awhile," she said. "It should have. I apologize."

His frown deepened. The opposite of the effect for which she'd been aiming.

"Tabitha? You can join us." Spencer's tone, though not as fierce, still remained unrelenting.

The little girl, knife still in hand, though free of peanut butter, came around the corner of the stage. She didn't walk down the steps.

And Natasha's heart gave a little twitch. She'd told both children they weren't to climb those stairs unattended because the safety rail had been defective—the wrong size had been sent—and the new one wasn't being installed until the morning.

Moving forward, she took Tabitha's hand and held on while the girl slowly descended the four steps to the linoleum laid temporarily on the barn's dirt floor.

"I'm sorry, too, Daddy," Tabitha said. But while Justin's face was pointed at the floor, his sister's nose pointed straight at their father. Natasha's heart noted that, too.

What in the heck was wrong with her, getting emotional all of a sudden? These children were interlopers who'd interrupted her only afternoon with solo access to the studio. She had much to do to satisfy herself that the set was ready to welcome contestants the next day.

And...

"I'm disappointed in you," Spencer said, the words clearly delivered to his daughter. Her lower lip quivered.

"Wait." Natasha couldn't stand back, in spite of her self-admonition to do so. "It's not her fault..."

She knew she'd made a mistake before his gaze landed on her.

"I'm sorry," she said.

"What did I tell you two about this barn?" he asked.

"Not to go here," Tabitha answered, still looking right at him.

"Justin?"

With his chin to his chest, the boy mumbled, "Stay away."

"You have Ms. Stevens apologizing for you, but I'm fairly certain that she didn't pick you up and carry you to this barn, did she?"

"No." Justin spoke, though he didn't look up to see that his father was pinning him with that stare.

"You walked here."

"Yes."

"Even though I told you not to." He glanced at Tabitha then, too.

"We didn't walk, Daddy," she said, her big brown eyes solemn as she shook her head of long, tangled hair.

"You didn't."

"No, Daddy, we ran."

"You ran over here?" The little girl had his full attention. "Even though you know I expressly forbade you to be here?"

"Yes."

"Why?"

In that second, Natasha's feelings of protectiveness toward the children changed to sympathy for the man standing there in front of them. He was clearly perplexed.

And alone in his parenting responsibilities.

She could only imagine… No, she couldn't even imagine trying to run a ranch and be the sole parent of two hooligans with acres and acres spread before them…tempting them…

"Because I was chasing Justin."

Spencer's brow cleared. For the second it took him to face his son. Down on his haunches, he placed his face within inches of the boy's.

"Is this true, Justin?" Spencer's tone was

soft now but, Natasha imagined, no less menacing to his seven-year-old son.

"Course. Tabitha doesn't lie…"

Implying that the boy did?

"You deliberately disobeyed me," Spencer reiterated.

The boy nodded.

"You weren't chasing a butterfly…there was no frog hopping in this direction…you didn't think you'd heard a cow…you weren't lost…"

The ease with which the words came gave Natasha the idea they were all excuses Spencer had heard before.

"No."

"Then why?"

She supposed he had to do this. Had to call the boy out in front of her so he'd learn his lesson. Still, she wished he'd take his disciplining home.

"I smelled the cookies."

Spencer's gaze turned unexpectedly in her direction, catching the grin that had sprung to her face. She wiped it away. Immediately. But suspected she hadn't been quick enough.

"You were baking cookies?" he asked. And the twinkle in his eye made her heart twitch again.

CHAPTER FIVE

SPENCER STILL WASN'T sure how it happened, but he ended up staying at the studio, eating the best chocolate chip cookies he'd ever had and watching while his children continued to help Natasha Stevens with the independent sound check she'd been running.

She'd explained that her crew ran the official checks. And that since the very beginning, she had run one of her own, as well. Because it set her mind at ease to know first-hand that everything was running properly.

Tabitha had been the one to explain that she and Justin were working for her for free as punishment for trespassing and stealing cookies.

And then he'd been hoodwinked into inviting her to share their dinner with them. He'd promised them hamburgers, camp potatoes and grilled corn because it was Friday night and they didn't have school the next day. He'd also promised roasted marshmallows over the fire pit.

With her crew gone for the night, it had seemed churlish to make a big deal out of his kids' invitation to her to their Friday soiree.

He just hadn't expected her to hang around after the kids went to bed.

He'd left the fire burning, because it was a nice night, and he'd intended to come back out with his tablet and get some work done.

The kids had said good-night to her. He'd nodded his goodbye.

And yet when, fifteen minutes later, tablet in hand, he'd carried a cup of coffee out to the fire pit, there she was, still sitting in the sling chair she'd occupied during dinner. Elbows on her knees, she was leaning forward, her hands folded, and dangling by the warmth of the fire. The formfitting, long-sleeve black shirt she was wearing outlined a perfect female form.

Attraction flared for the instant it took him to clamp down hard on it.

"I didn't expect you still to be here." He tried to come off as cordial, enough so that she could think he was pleasantly surprised to find himself still in possession of her company.

But even to his own ears, he sounded surly.

"I was enjoying the fire," she told him. "I can't remember the last time I had the chance to sit by a campfire."

"People don't have fire pits in Palm Desert?" He knew they did. A buddy he'd graduated with had one in his backyard, right next to his pool. Spencer had taken the kids there for a Fourth of July party the year before. Justin had put his hot dog in the pool to see if it would float…

"I don't have one," she said.

Taking a seat, he set his tablet on his knee. Tapped it. Waited for her to go. He watched stock prices every day. Wanted to see what the farm markets were doing. And then place a couple of orders.

He purposely did not make conversation. Enough was enough.

"You don't like me, do you?"

He'd just spent the evening with her. Was it wrong to need a little time to himself?

"I don't know you." Yet he recognized the way her eyes glistened in the firelight. They'd had that same glint the night before, under the light in Ellie's stall, just after Natasha had witnessed her first calf birth.

He could have sworn, that night, that the sheen was due to tears she was refusing to shed.

But tonight?

"You say that like you don't want to get to know me."

Apparently he was easy to read. But, hey, he lived a simple life—a cowboy on a ranch. He didn't need subterfuge. Or societal graces.

It wasn't like his cattle were going to get an edge on him because they could tell what he was thinking.

"I could pretend otherwise. Our business arrangement, you here on my ranch, I probably should pretend. But no, I don't."

She gave a soft chuckle. And he started to relax. At least she wasn't overly sensitive. Not that it would really matter to her if a country boy ranch owner didn't like her.

"Mind my asking why?"

He minded that her smile made her look even more beautiful—softer—in the night air. And he minded that she wasn't leaving him to enjoy the rare moment of solace in his day.

"It's nothing against you," he quickly assured her. He needed her money. And because of that, truly wanted her experience on his ranch to be a good one.

He just didn't want to be the one to show her a good time.

There were plenty of others who'd jump at the job.

"I didn't think it was."

She picked up a bottle of water at her feet—which was when he noticed she'd helped herself to a fresh one—uncapped it, took a sip and, slowly, with fingers that were long and slim, turned the cap back into place.

He wanted to kiss those fingers. Heat rose up his neck. How could a guy be embarrassed when he was the only one who knew of his humiliating thoughts?

He had to get rid of her. In a way that let her know, quite clearly, that she shouldn't come back. He'd designated the part of his property that was temporarily hers. She had plenty of room. She needed to stay there. In spite of whatever else his kids might pull.

"You're a city woman," he said now, feeling stronger already as it occurred to him that if he was boorish, she'd have no way of knowing it wasn't his norm. Seemed an easy enough way to ensure that she'd stay clear of him.

And what better way of convincing her than a version of the truth?

"You don't like me because I carry my New York upbringing with me?"

"What?" He frowned. What had he missed?

"You said *city woman*. I thought you were referring to the fact that I grew up in New York City."

"How would I possibly know that?"

She shrugged. And chuckled again. A nice sound. Not a derisive or sarcastic one. "My bio is public knowledge," she told him. "I just assumed, since the show was going to be filmed here, that you'd read up on it."

He'd read about the show's success. Had purposely shied away from any personal information about the show's founder, producer and on-air host.

Thankful for the darkness, he sat back from the firelight, hiding his expression from her gaze.

"So, what do you have against city women?"

"Nothing."

"You just dislike them all? For no reason?"

His version of boorish was clearly not working.

Maybe honesty would do it. Changing tactics, he said, "I don't dislike city women. I just don't get friendly with them."

Eventually, after more than a couple of minutes passed without a response, and without her leaving, Spencer looked away from the fire to see her studying him.

"What?"

She shook her head. "I'm just trying to figure you out," she said.

"What's that supposed to mean?"

"You seem like such a smart—and, judging by the way you deal with your kids, fair—man. Yet you'd have me believe that you arbitrarily disregard much of the female population simply because they live in the city."

"What's with you?" He leaned forward now, too, exposing his face to the firelight. "You get some perverse delight putting a damper on my evening?"

"No." She didn't smile, and his gut clenched. He wanted her gone. He didn't really want to hurt her. From what he'd seen, she was a genuinely nice person.

And a miracle worker with his kids that afternoon. Justin had called her *ma'am*. He couldn't get the sound of his son's reply to her out of his brain. What had she done with his boy? And how did he get it done, too?

"I'm taking advantage of your good nature, and your fire, to give me an excuse not to go back out to the cabin earlier than I have to."

Her words knocked him back. Almost literally. Wow. Talk about getting what you give out. The whole honesty idea…it had been a bad one.

"Life on a ranch can get lonesome," he said, "especially if you aren't used to it."

"I actually kind of like the quiet," she said, surprising him again. Why had he ever thought he was a natural with women?

"Something wrong with the cabin? It's the largest, and most newly remodeled, but we've got others a little closer together…"

"It's fine." She shook her head. "I'm being ridiculous. I don't know what's wrong with me today."

He didn't know her well enough to make a guess. Not that he wanted to.

"It's just… I had a call from my mother this morning…" She glanced at him again. But differently. Uncertainty didn't look right on her. Or normal.

"Is something wrong?"

"No. At least, according to her it isn't."

Okay. So now things were starting to make sense. She was out of her element, away from her friends, stuck in the middle of nowhere. And she'd had bad news.

Now, *that* he could wrap his mind around. And deal with, too. After all, except for when city women cramped his space, he really was a nice guy.

"You want to talk about it?"

"No." She laughed, but there was no amusement now. "I generally keep my own counsel." She picked up her water bottle. "It's probably just some manifestation of jitters because my first show on the road has its official start tomorrow…"

"I'm a good listener." Wait. He was getting exactly what he wanted. Her taking her departure. "It's not like you're ever going to see me again," he reminded her. "After our six weeks are up, that is."

The first week of filming was just preliminary stuff. Introductions. Some interviews. She'd given him a complete schedule so he'd know. Then, starting the next Saturday, four weeks of competition would follow. The sixth week was the final round, a cook-off between any and all contestants who won the preliminary rounds. That winner would receive, among other things, a contract to have one of his or her recipes mass-produced and packaged with national retail distribution.

Dropping her water bottle onto her lap, she relaxed against her chair. "My mom called to tell me that she was breaking up with her boyfriend."

"She's not married?" He gave himself a mental kick as soon as the words slipped out. Of course, if she had a boyfriend, she wouldn't be married. He really did need to get out more.

"No."

"How long has she been divorced?"

"She isn't divorced. She's never been married."

"Oh." The ensuing silence felt awkward, and he said, "Not that I'm judging. Just…"

"My father was a fellow law student at Georgetown. He had an interest in her, in hooking up, but not in marriage and children. Not until he'd established himself in Massachusetts law and politics."

Okay, now he was out of his league.

"The thing is, my mom said she wouldn't have married him if he'd offered. She claims that, like him, she'd had goals and didn't want to be tied down, either."

Wait… "I kind of know firsthand that when you're a parent, that's exactly what happens. Your wants and needs take second place to your children's…"

"At home, yes. Emotionally, maybe. But

not professionally. Look at you. You've got this ranch. It's obvious that you love it. And that you give it, professionally, everything it needs."

"I inherited the ranch. You know, from my parents. Who inherited it from their parents…"

Legally, anyway. Legally he'd inherited it from his parents. Sort of.

Legally the ranch was all his. That was what mattered. Why he'd suddenly thought of old news, he had no idea. And had no intention of doing so again.

Longfellow Ranch was his without question. Fairly. Legally. And morally, too. Just as it would one day belong to Justin and Tabitha…

"My mom had career goals. She cared more about them, has always cared more about them, than she's ever cared about a partner relationship."

He'd invited the conversation. Proclaimed his listening skills. Finding no response to her statement, he nodded.

"She's strong-minded. Knows what she wants. But it's not so much a selfish thing as it is that…she's right. She's accomplished everything she's set out to do. Including raising me in an environment where I never, ever had to doubt her love for me."

Now she had his attention. Having not had that kind of assurance in his own formative years, he wanted more than anything to get it right for his kids.

"Because she paid someone to watch out for you?"

"No. Because she was always there for me. And anytime I was otherwise involved, she focused one hundred percent on her career."

"Which is?"

"She's a trial court judge in New York City."

Wow. He was so far out of his league, he was surprised he was still sitting there with her.

"It suits her, being the boss. Making the decisions. She's good at it. Happy doing it. And I know in my heart, if she'd had to live side by side with another adult all her life, compromising her needs and ideals to fit another's, she'd have been miserable."

"But she had a boyfriend."

"Another judge, in appeals court. They were suited because there was no need for compromise. They both had their lives. And happened to enjoy doing the same things. It was perfect. At least, I thought so..."

Now he had to wonder: What did it do to a girl, growing up with such a strong female influence, and no male influence whatso-ever?

Unless... Had the boyfriend been around all those years? She clearly cared about the guy.

"How long were they together?"

"Ten years."

"Were there boyfriends before that?"

"Not that she actually brought home."

Her eyes had that sheen again.

Prompting within him another tug that he didn't like.

"So, what happened?" Best to get through this and move on down the road. She did, that is. She needed to move on down the path to her cabin. And the next evening, when that week's filming was over, ideally she would drive her SUV and her crew right back to Palm Desert until the following Friday. "Did they have a fight? Was he unfaithful to her?"

"He asked her to marry him."

And they broke up.

Spencer studied her in the firelight. Could

see her struggle. If he let himself, he was pretty sure he'd feel her pain.

And do something stupid, like give her a hug.

Yep. He was having a seriously bad day.

CHAPTER SIX

FEELING ABOUT AS stupid and awkward as she'd ever felt, Natasha stood up. She'd outstayed her welcome by a long shot and needed to take her demons to her temporary home.

"Thanks for dinner," she said, water bottle in hand. "You've got great kids."

Yeah, they'd disobeyed his direct orders, for a chocolate chip cookie. But they'd taken responsibility for their actions.

When he stood, too, she tensed a bit. In a not altogether horrible way. Except that that in itself was horrible.

She was not going to like this guy. He was as different from her as night was from day. And had made his dislike of her quite clear.

When he wasn't busy being sweet.

"I'll walk you back" was all he said.

"I know the way. It's fine."

"It's dark. And your people aren't back yet. Because we turned that part of the yard over to you, it's pretty much deserted until they return. I'll just see you to your door."

Because she was, as she'd just acknowledged to herself, completely out of her element, she accepted his offer rather than take a more normal course of action and assert her independence.

She could hear voices in the distance and see lights shining from the bunkhouse complex. He'd said that they had a kitchen over there—which the ranch hands were responsible for keeping stocked—and that, depending on the season, he employed up to fifteen men in addition to Bryant. He was still running hay while he built his cattle operation and needed men skilled in both business ventures.

He'd already answered any lay ranch questions she might have come up with on their walk in the dark.

When her hand brushed his, she sidestepped. And he noticed. Maybe he'd been more on target than she'd realized earlier. The silence was getting to her.

She was undersensitized.

"Can I ask a personal question?" It was better than stumbling in the dark.

"Yeah. I might not answer."

"What happened to Justin and Tabitha's

mother?" None of them had mentioned her all day. Even over dinner. They'd laughed and told her about some of their other cook-outs. Told her about a time when they'd been having a picnic at a lake on their property— Spencer had inserted that it was just a pond— and Justin, who'd been standing on the shore, had seen a fish and had tried to catch it with his bare hands. He'd fallen into the water instead. It had been only a couple of feet deep, but that was when they'd both had to start swimming lessons. Every day. Until they could each make it across the small lake on their own.

They'd taken several steps since she'd asked her question. He hadn't responded. As he'd warned he might not.

Her door was in sight. He walked her to the stoop. Waited while she took out her key.

"She left," he said when she'd opened her mouth to say good-night.

"What? Who?"

"Their mother. They were two. And don't remember her."

"She's never been back? She doesn't come to see them?"

"Nope."

She wanted to know why. In the worst way, she wanted to know.

But he wasn't her friend. Wasn't even a friendly acquaintance.

So she didn't ask.

THE RESTLESSNESS PURSUING Natasha as Spencer walked away might have caught up with her once she was alone inside the cabin, except that her phone rang.

"Do you have any idea how long this stretch is in the dark?" her assistant said in lieu of *hello*.

"The same sixty miles it is in the daytime, I expect," she said, grinning. Angela had a cryptic way about her, an almost impenetrable independent shell, but she was as hardworking and loyal as they came.

She was also fabulous at her job.

"It's really dark."

"I know. I drove it myself a couple of weeks ago, going the opposite direction."

"You could have warned me."

"I believe I did."

"Yeah, well, you could have made me listen…"

Sitting in the rocker by the unlit fireplace, Natasha relaxed. Really relaxed. This was her life.

Angela was her "people."

"How were things at the hotel?" she asked, knowing that she and Angela could just as easily have had this conversation in the morning when they met at Natasha's cabin for an early breakfast. She'd invited Angela to stay with her. Her stage manager had opted to take a smaller cabin by herself, closer to the crew.

"Good," she said. "Great, really. All eight contestants were at the cocktail party, and everyone was pumped up for the road trip." While most of their crew had just gone into the small local town half an hour from the ranch, Angela had driven into Palm Desert. While there, she'd stopped by the hotel that had a contract with *Family Secrets* for contestant accommodation.

"The bus is confirmed for a nine a.m. pickup, which will have everyone here by eleven. We can give them the abbreviated tour of the ranch and have them on stage inspecting their kitchens by noon. The bus will be bringing the catered lunch. We should be filming segments by twelve thirty and have them out of here no later than two, which will have them back to the hotel around four, giving them a full evening to enjoy Palm Desert."

They'd made it a condition of the show that

contestants' flights back home had to be Sunday, not Saturday evening as sometimes happened when they filmed in the Palm Desert studio.

They talked a bit more about the logistics of the next day's events. About the interviews Natasha planned to do that would be a bit different from every other show's because she wanted to tie the unique ranch setting in to something personal for every contestant. Something to convince viewers to root for each one. That was her job. To draw in the viewers who continued, after five years of watching four five-week segments a year, to make the show such an unexpected success.

Mostly she was talking to keep Angela awake, to keep her company, while she made the seemingly endless trek back across the desert.

She was talking so she didn't think about being a city girl. About a rancher who didn't like city girls. About two little motherless kids who'd loved her chocolate chip cookies. About the glob of peanut butter she'd cleaned up off the floor of the stage, and the smears off the counter, when she'd done her final walk-through just before dinner that evening.

Her mind wandered through all of those

thoughts, though, as Angela ran through lists they'd both been over already for the first official event in their very first show on the road. Angela listed which crew members would be staying behind at the ranch Saturday night to clean up and ready the set for the first competition the next week.

"You've got dinner with Chandler Grey tomorrow night," her assistant reminded her when they'd exhausted the next day's details.

She'd shockingly forgotten about the business meal back home in Palm Desert with one of their cable network's executives.

Her mind appeared to have taken a long trek away from home, out here on the ranch.

"I'm looking forward to it," she said with real enthusiasm. She'd been away only for a couple of days, but it seemed like weeks. She missed the city. Missed her condominium.

Missed her usual unflappable calm.

"I think he has the hots for you," Angela was saying now.

"He's married."

"Separated. I hear his wife was unfaithful."

She still wasn't interested.

"You haven't been on a date in months." Angela was really digging deep for conversation now.

While her assistant wasn't in a committed relationship, either, she went out several times a week. Mostly with the same guy. Natasha's theory was that if he asked Angela to be exclusive, she would be. If he asked her to marry him, she'd do that, too—not that she volunteered either theory to Angela.

"I'm not the marrying kind, and men my age are looking for commitment." That wasn't entirely true. There were plenty of men who were willing just to have fun, but she wasn't interested in their kind of fun.

The show was her life. It fulfilled her. And made her so happy she didn't ever even question her personal choices.

She knew what drove her. Knew her goals. She knew who she was. And knew what she could and could not let others expect from her. She knew what promises she could and could not make.

"I know Johnny hurt you, Natasha, but it's been almost a year…"

Johnny Campbell. Her "Stan." The man she'd thought would be her companion for life. They were best friends. Good together. Neither of them were interested in cohabitating or giving up their autonomy.

He was a stockbroker, a mover and shaker

who worked unending hours. He'd been *her* stockbroker. Until she found out he'd been stealing from her. Telling her he was investing her money when what he'd been doing was gambling with it.

Thankfully she'd found out during one of his winning streaks and hadn't lost as much as she might have.

"I'm not still hurting over Johnny," she said now, a bit surprised to feel how completely true those words were. "I'm open to dating on occasion. I just haven't met anyone who tempts me to spend time with him more than the show tempts me to spend time with it."

Also true.

She was thirty-one, not twenty, and knew that her chances of finding a companionship as open-ended as the one she'd shared with Johnny were dwindling.

She just didn't dwell on the fact. She wasn't going to let panic or fear for her future change her mind about what she knew she needed in her present.

Like her mother, she was too bossy, too impatient, too strong and independent to be good in a commitment like marriage.

As she sat there, talking Angela all the way back to the ranch, she found peace with her day. Her mother's breakup with Stan…it was okay. Because her mother was truly okay with it. She'd made the choice that was best for her, the one she could live with, be good at, be happy with. Which made it the right choice.

Whew.

Getting ready for bed an hour later, Natasha was humming to herself. The day had been rough. Touch and go for a second or two there. But she'd made it through.

And was ready to embrace her world in the morning.

SPENCER WAS UP before dawn. He checked on Ellie. Had a meeting with Bryant to ensure that he had no immediate problems on the ranch. The ranch hands were handling several tasks that day—fixing a fence that was showing wear, checking a couple of cows from the stock herd who were close to calving, seeing to a bull that had been seen limping on one of the camera monitors, receiving a large load of hay that was being shipped…

And Spencer was packing a lunch of peanut butter and jelly sandwiches on wheat bread with potato chips and apple slices. As soon as the twins were up, they were heading out for a day of four-wheeling. Spencer driving and the twins strapped in beside him. Far enough away from the compound that Justin couldn't somehow create havoc among the ranch visitors that day.

He had the TV filming schedule. And though his kids were tired, he kept them off-roading, laughing over dips in hills and taking small mountains like pros, until well after the tour bus had been scheduled to roll off his property with all *Family Secrets* contestants on board.

Making a mental note to give Bryant the rundown on the state of more fence lines he'd inspected that day, he fed the kids an early dinner and left them with Betsy while he went to check on the rest of the ranch. On Ellie.

Because it was on his property, and ultimately his responsibility, he stopped by the barn-turned-television-set. A handful of crew members remained, busily moving around the stage with clipboards, setting up cameras, working with lighting, cleaning mini-refrigerators in the kitchen.

He didn't see Natasha, which was fine. He wasn't looking for her.

The only reason she'd been on his mind all day was the money she was paying him. He needed her contestants able to cook in his barn, her filming to go well and her crew willing to work with what they had and be able to produce the quality show her network and viewers expected out of *Family Secrets*.

In the end, after collecting the kids and putting them to bed, he headed out to the farthest cabin in the compound. Just to be a good host. And put his mind at ease that all had gone well.

The cabin was completely dark, and Natasha's SUV was no longer parked beside it. He'd thought she, like her crew, would be spending one more night on the ranch before heading back to the city for the week.

Apparently he'd been wrong.

She'd already left—without bothering to say goodbye.

CHAPTER SEVEN

SPENCER GOT UP Sunday morning with a new lease on life. Natasha Stevens was gone. Her crew would be pulling out sometime that day. He and his family, his people, would have the place to themselves. Business as usual.

Blue skies and sunshine greeted him as he glanced out the kitchen window while whipping up batter for pancakes. Betsy had offered to cook for him and the kids. She'd suggested he hire a girl from town to do so as well when he'd said he couldn't have his best friend's wife waiting on him.

He'd conceded only to having someone come in twice a week to clean.

The rest was up to him. His kids were going to be fed and nourished by him—their father. Their parent. Tabitha and Justin were going to have a solid foundation. A sense of who they were, where they'd come from. A sense of home and belonging.

To add icing on that cake, he grabbed a bag

of chocolate chips and mixed a pile of them into the pancake batter. The griddle was heating. As soon as the twins appeared, he'd pour the batter—enough for the eight pancakes the griddle would hold.

In the meantime, because it was taking them longer than usual to get down to Sunday breakfast, he grabbed some oranges from the refrigerator—it would be another couple of months before the ones on the tree in the yard were ripe—and juiced enough for three glasses.

Still waiting, he warmed the syrup. Put butter on the table. Three forks. Extra napkins.

Lined up the plates on the counter.

Decided to go ahead and pour the glasses of milk his kids usually drank with their breakfast so they'd have strong bones.

And then he climbed the stairs. They'd taken way too long now, making their beds, getting into their clothes and brushing their teeth. And been too quiet, too.

Justin's room was first. He wasn't there. His bed was made. About as sloppily as usual, but made. The bathroom between his room and Tabitha's was empty, as well. The counter was wet, and there was a glob of toothpaste in the sink.

"Hey, slowpokes, what's..." His words fell away as he entered Tabitha's room. Her pink-and-white polka-dot ruffled pillow sham was on top of the pillow. The matching comforter evenly spread over the bed and wrinkle-free. And his daughter was nowhere to be seen.

"Tabitha? Justin?" he called to them as he checked his own room across the hall. He poked his head in the guest room as he ran past, then took the stairs down at a trot.

"Justin?" He always heard them on the stairs.

And had been listening while he prepared breakfast. It was routine. A normal day like every other day.

They weren't in the family room. Or the living room. Not in his office, where they weren't allowed to be without him present. Not in the dining room. Or the laundry room.

"Tabitha!" He raised his voice as he exited the house. What was up with his kids? Twice in less than forty-eight hours they'd disappeared. Twice he'd lost them.

It wasn't like him.

Or them.

"Tabitha! Justin!" he called, heading toward the calf barn while pulling out his phone and dialing Betsy.

People were going to start thinking he was a bad dad or something.

They'd made their beds. Brushed their teeth. There'd been no sign of a struggle. But he hadn't heard them on the stairs. Or heard them talking, either.

How could that have happened? Unless… he'd been so distracted by thoughts of the woman he'd refused to think about…

Or… Had they been purposefully quiet? It was the only way Justin kept quiet. By trying really, really hard.

Had his kids snuck out on him?

At seven years old?

Taking a quick turn, he headed toward the temporary television studio he wished he'd never agreed to allow on his property. He'd had great plans for the day. More four-wheeling. A visit to the horse barn for Tabitha. Hot dogs on the grill. Maybe some fishing. It all faded away, usurped by punishment.

He didn't discipline his kids often. Betsy said not enough. He did what he needed to do. As long as they followed his rules, they were allowed to be free thinkers. To develop their own individual personalities.

Until this weekend, the plan had worked. Almost unfailingly. With some Justin exceptions.

It was time to get a dog. An outdoor dog. One that Justin would have to feed. One who would bark in the yard anytime there was movement—as in kid movement. One who would follow the kids wherever they went. One he could whistle for and, by his response, would tell Spencer where his children were.

Scrap the entire rest of the day's plans. No full day of fun for the kids. They were going into town to get a dog. And then the kids were going to be yard-bound.

They hated that—not being allowed outside the perimeter he'd designated as the yard for punishment purposes.

He could see the activity at the studio before he was close enough to hear distinct voices. No cooking had happened the day before, but for all of the upcoming weeks, prepared dishes would be transported out on the bus with the contestants, along with any perishable pantry food—bound for homeless shelters, Natasha had told him during one of their original interviews.

Whatever else was going on, he didn't know. He could see big black equipment boxes going out on the buses. Probably because his barn didn't have the security of a television studio.

What he couldn't see, as he strode closer, was his children.

Angela, Natasha's second-in-command, stage manager, assistant and, he'd concluded, friend, met him before he'd reached the studio.

"You need something, cowboy?" she asked with a grin. The woman had a curious, flamboyant style, dressed in clothes that were as tight as they could be, and yet he was comfortable with her. Like, what he saw was what he got. He liked that. And liked that he wasn't the least bit tempted to get to know her any better.

She also seemed completely unflappable.

"My kids," he said, continuing toward her.

"Justin and Tabitha?" Her frown slowed his step. "They aren't here."

He stopped. "You're sure?" They'd hidden from Natasha on Friday. But just for a little while.

Justin could be crafty. But he was only seven. And he had a very black-and-white, mind-the-rules Tabitha with him.

"Positive. I've done a final check of the

space. We're out of here in the next five minutes."

Good. He needed his life back to normal. But…

"Well, thank you." He smiled. And then, because he wanted to know how long he got to enjoy his freedom from invasion, he asked, "When will you and Natasha be back?"

"I'll be here Thursday," she said. "With the crew."

Yes, that was what he'd meant. Just because the boss lady had been there first this past week didn't mean she would be again.

"…I'm not sure when Natasha's going to be here," Angela was saying. "My guess would be Friday. She'll want to check things over before Saturday's show. I'll ask her and give you a call."

"That's not necessary."

"I figured you'd want to know for whoever's cleaning her cabin…" He didn't like the quirk of Angela's head, the way she was studying him.

"It'll be done Wednesday," he told her, backing up. His cleaning lady was handling it all for him. And he had to find his kids.

"Well, I'll let you know when her plans—"

Shaking his head, he said, "Don't worry

about it. I have to find my kids. Have a good trip back." And he was around the corner, out of her sight.

"Tabitha! Justin!" He jogged. He called. Checked the barns between the studio and the house, intending to head toward the stream by way of the bunkhouse.

"Justin, don't!" Tabitha's stern shriek stopped him as he passed the house.

"You know Daddy says you can't put your dirty finger in the bowl *before* he cooks."

They were in the kitchen?

He was inside before his daughter could make another attempt to corral her wayward brother.

Catching Justin in the act.

The boy jerked his hand back and would have splattered breakfast all over the ceramic tile floor except that Spencer, knowing his son well, was there to catch it.

"Go wash up," he told his son.

"I already washed when I brushed…"

"And you had your finger in pancake batter. Go." He didn't raise his voice.

As soon as his son was out of the room, he gave Tabitha a very firm stare. "Where were you?"

She looked away. "I'm right here, Daddy."

"I went upstairs looking for you."

That brought her big brown eyes back to him. "We wanted Natasha to have pancakes. Justin says she's a good cook, and our Sunday pancakes are the best."

Sunday was always pancake day. Because the kids didn't have school and he had the time to make them. Because it was a tradition left from his childhood. Because traditions were important.

Sometimes they were everything.

"You went to Natasha's cabin?" he asked now.

"Yes." Tabitha nodded. "But she wasn't home."

"She left last night."

"She didn't tell us 'bye."

Yes, well, that was for the best. But he wasn't going to have his kids' feelings hurt.

"She's not our friend, Tabitha. When other workers come to the ranch, they don't tell you goodbye, either."

"She is, Daddy."

"Is what? A worker?"

Tabitha's tangled hair flopped around her shoulders with each vehement shake of her head. "She's my friend."

"No, sweetie, she's just someone who's working here…"

The shake of her head stopped him. "She is."

Tabitha was his reasonable child. "Honey, it's—"

"I know, Daddy. She is. I know 'cause I asked her, and she said yes."

"You asked if she was your friend?"

"I asked could we be friends."

His day just shot to Hades. He had no idea how to handle this one.

Because he needed time to figure it out, he changed the subject. "So, you and Justin, you wanted to invite Natasha to breakfast," he said, his gaze as calculating as he could make it while looking at the cutest thing he'd ever seen on earth.

"Yes."

"Why didn't you come to me about it?"

"You were a little mean to her, Daddy. She's *our* friend. If you asked, she mighta' told you no."

He was the parent. Disciplining his child. So why did he feel like he'd just been chastised?

"You thought you two would just show up here with her? Without letting me know?"

"No." Her face solemn, she shook her head again. "We were going to run back fast and tell you before she got here so that you could make enough. Or at least, Justin was going to while I walked with her."

His little mite thought of everything.

And was going to pose far more of a threat to his peace of mind than her brother ever would.

As though they were done with their conversation, she pulled out her chair and scooted her little body up onto it, her chin still only inches from the table.

He'd been against getting rid of the booster seats, but both kids had insisted when they'd started school that they were too old for boosters.

Spencer spooned batter onto the griddle, realizing too late that he'd turned it off before he'd left the house. He turned it back on, figuring it was good they weren't going to have a professional chef joining them that morning.

He waited until Justin returned. The boy picked up his glass of juice and took a drink before sitting down.

"So… Tabitha." He included both of them in his glance. "Did you and your brother purposely keep quiet as you came downstairs this morning?"

She nodded.

"And you snuck out the side door so I

wouldn't hear you leave." It was off the laundry room. And rarely used.

She nodded again.

"You snuck out behind my back." He stated the crime in clear terms so they were all on the same page.

This time he received two very solemn nods in reply.

"You know that means you will be punished."

Tabitha's eyes filled with tears, but she blinked them away. Justin sighed and looked down at the table.

"We were going to go four-wheeling and fishing today. And visit the horses. Instead, as soon as we get back from town, you will be confined to the yard until bedtime."

"Why we goin' into town?" Justin asked, while Tabitha's lower lip trembled.

"To get a dog. You two aren't going to be free to roam alone anymore. You've betrayed my trust twice in one weekend and…"

"A dog?" Justin's grin just about split his face.

"A dog!" Tabitha's squeal might have hurt his ears if he hadn't loved the happiness it embodied so much.

"Yes, a dog," he said sternly. A watchdog. To watch his kids.

"Yippee!" Justin jumped up so fast his milk sloshed over the top of his glass.

The boy threw his arms around Spencer's hips. Tabitha's were already there. His little girl looked up at him, melting him with those eyes.

"Thank you, Daddy. You know, I really wanted a dog."

"I wanted one, too," Justin said. "I always wanted one. Didn't I, Daddy?"

Spencer hugged his kids. But before he could answer the question, he heard a sizzle from the griddle. Had to tend to the pancakes.

"We're getting a watchdog," he said. "An outside dog. To watch the two of you. Every minute of every day."

This was not a present for them. It was for him.

The rest of the day was going to be a punishment, just as he'd determined.

Watchdog. Yard arrest. Hot dogs on the grill. And that was it.

CHAPTER EIGHT

NATASHA WASN'T SURE what she was thinking when she approached the box left at her private entrance at the Palm Desert studio on Tuesday. She and about twenty other people had keys to that entrance. It was well used.

But only by people with keys.

The box, left at that particular door, was odd.

Looking over the top of it as she drew closer, she searched for an addressee. Or sign of where the box had come from.

Found neither.

It looked like a box for moving books.

Nudging it with her foot to see how heavy it was, she jumped as it seemed to move again without her help. She stepped back. Heard scratching. Looked behind her in the mostly vacant parking lot. Workaholic that she was, she was often the first one in in the morning.

She thought about calling Angela. Or waiting for one of the two full-time janitors to arrive—building janitors, not the crew she hired specifically for her show.

"Meeooww."

The sound was faint. Tiny. But when she recognized it, she stepped up. Opened the folded closure of the box top and peered inside.

Four tiny, wide-eyed, motherless kittens stared up at her.

"Meeooow."

"WHAT ARE YOU going to do with them?" Angela, mouth open, stared into the box in Natasha's office later that morning. She'd been in a meeting with their accountant, handling paperwork for the week's contestant travel vouchers that she would personally disperse, when Natasha had come in that morning.

"The three gray ones are already spoken for," Natasha told her assistant, quite proud of herself. She named the three studio personnel who'd claimed them.

"What about this little black guy?"

"I'm told he's a girl."

Angela looked at her. Back at the cat. And then at Natasha again. "You aren't keeping her."

She wasn't. Of course. But…

She'd been off for weeks. Off her game. Off her...something.

It had all started the previous Thanksgiving, when one of her contestants had brought her four-year-old with Down syndrome to the set. He'd been such a happy little guy...bringing something...more...when he'd stumbled up on stage, brushed off his hands and announced that he was fine.

Then, in the very next segment of shows, there'd been the contestant who'd been searching for the son she'd given up for adoption. The drive compelling her, it had topped everything...

Her mother and Stan had broken up.

But she'd helped birth a calf. Bringing an animal into the world. It had felt so great...

"Of course I'm not keeping it," she said aloud when she noticed her assistant staring at her.

Dressed in her usual flamboyant leggings and short, blousy top, Angela bent to the box and came up with the black kitten.

"Cats are the one pet you can leave alone at home for long periods," Angela said.

Natasha was pretty sure she'd found a home for the last kitten.

"She's cute." Angela's smile as she lifted

the little black girl to her face confirmed Natasha's suspicions.

Her assistant, who, like her, lived alone, didn't usually show the softer side that Natasha knew lay carefully protected deep inside her.

But...

"I'm taking her," Natasha blurted.

She'd find another cat for her assistant. Buy it for her.

Standing, she approached the woman and kitten, reaching out to give the tiny head a pet. She could buy herself another cat, too.

But this one...she'd rescued it. Kind of like helping to birth a calf...

Grinning, Angela handed the kitten over. "I had that one figured out when I came in the door," Angela said. "I just had to nudge you enough to get you up to speed."

Angela knew her well.

Maybe too well.

"...AND THERE'S THE meeting with the studio executives this afternoon at four in the upstairs conference room." Still holding the kitten—Natasha had decided she was maybe going to name her Ellie after the mother of the calf she'd helped birth—Angela sat in the chair across from Natasha's desk, going over the day's schedule with her.

Her tablet on her lap, Angela had also discussed various technical issues from the weekend, the previous day's interview she'd had with a new janitorial service that would charge half the amount to travel to the ranch with them, and a conversation she'd overheard between cohosts of a studio-owned relationship advice call-in show—*Love Moments*. They'd been arguing, and the future of the show, according to Angela, didn't look good.

"By the way." Angela looked up from her tablet at Natasha. "How'd your dinner with Chandler Grey go the other night?"

"Fine." She described the new restaurant they'd been to. Indian cuisine. "You know how much I love saffron," she said.

"I meant Chandler, not the food." Angela's droll tone left Natasha in no doubt of her assistant's intolerance for obvious subterfuge.

"Fine," she said again, shrugging. *Maybe Lily instead of Ellie.* Though raven-black, the little girl looked like a Lily to her. "He just wanted to hear how the first week went, busing everyone, the taping, since it's the first we've been out of the studio. If you remember, he was really encouraging when we first told him we were taking a show on the road."

"He could have learned all about it with a phone call."

"I guess. I think he was going to offer some of the studio's equipment if we needed anything more. They do remote filming all the time."

"Again, a phone call could have done that."

"He's not into me, Angela."

"Of course he is."

"He was circumspect in every way."

"Did he walk you to your car?"

"We walked to our cars together. He didn't so much as brush a hand against mine. And said good-night as he was walking away."

Frowning, Angela cocked her head. "He's into you. I just think you should know that."

Angela wasn't teasing now. So…maybe there was some truth to her stage manager's assessment. Angela's quick mind, her ability to assess situations in seconds, was part of what made her invaluable to the show.

But whether she was right or not was irrelevant as far as Natasha's feelings were concerned.

Because one thing was quite clear to her.

She most definitely was not into Chandler Grey.

Separated or not.

BY THE TIME he'd put his kids on the school bus Tuesday morning, Spencer was ready to ban the name Natasha from the ranch. It would be against the law to speak it. To write it. Even to think it.

He was coming up with a punishment for the kids in the event that they broke this law—ranging from no cookies for a week to having to make a list of every animal name on the farm, and then move on to people if necessary—when he realized that he was, perhaps, overreacting.

Still, the tension the name wrought within him was real. And for a valid reason.

His kids had talked of nothing but the television producer since she'd invaded their premises—their home—for dinner the previous Friday night.

It wasn't good for them to get too attached. Because while she'd be spending a good bit of time on the ranch over the next five weeks—ample time for the children to begin to rely on her in their lives—she was going to be completely gone after that.

Natasha Stevens was a city girl. He'd seen his children through one city-girl abandonment, luckily with reasonable success. He wasn't taking that chance again.

"Woof!" Heading up the drive on his way to meet Bryant in the cow barn—he had another pregnant cow ready to go—he turned, looking at the back door of the house—the sliding glass door that led to the deck. And inside to the crate pushed up to the window by Justin just before he left for school.

Because the day before, when left alone for hours, the dog inside had managed to get her snout through the kennel bars and chew a hole in the drywall.

Daisy Wolf stood inside the crate, tail wagging, big brown eyes pleading.

The half-Lab, half-shepherd mix would be a great watchdog. Soon. An outdoor dog. Soon. For now, she was a twelve-pound puppy who, Tabitha insisted, wanted to be part of the family.

Making a slight detour, he let the dog out of her kennel, tied a rope to the collar around her neck and introduced her to her first day of work on the ranch.

NATASHA MADE HER way up to the executive conference room just in time for the meeting to begin. Unlike most of the shows filmed in the studio, *Family Secrets* was independently owned and run. By her. Other than her contract stipulations with the studio, she didn't answer to anyone.

And felt a bit out of place, like a distant relative at a family dinner, for these monthly meetings. She was there to be kept apprised of all legal and practical activities as some of them pertained to her space.

And she was there to be kept apprised of the studio's overall numbers and operations, as the success of the station had much to do with the success of her show.

She was a rare bird. Kind of like one of the studio executives, except that she had ownership in only one show.

Taking her usual seat, she was surprised when all conversation immediately ceased. All eyes turned to her.

Of the five other business executives there, one being fifty-year-old Chandler Grey, only one was female. Shelley Hale, a very young thirty, had recently inherited her seat on the board after the death of her father in a boating accident.

Natasha, in a black skirt and matching jacket, was the most professionally dressed among them. All four men looked as though they'd just stepped off the golf course.

Chandler Grey, seated across from her,

smiled, folded his hands on the conference table and leaned forward. "Before we get into this month's regular meeting, we have something to discuss with you, Natasha."

A sick feeling crept from her toes to her forehead. There was no reason for it. She wasn't up for contract renewal. Her show continually held the station's highest rating spot.

She should be filled with anticipation…

And felt like she was in a medical consultation with a team of doctors who had her life in their hands.

"We're merging with Travel America," he said, as though telling her what they'd ordered in for lunch. She was familiar with the station, of course. Anyone who watched cable television would have been. Its format was very different from their current one. Instead of live shows, reality TV and cooking, they produced travel documentaries. All day. Every day.

"They've got a strong niche market, as do we, and also appear to have reached the top of their growth potential. Our last quarter's numbers indicate that we may have, as well. The merger is designed to cross-pollinate viewership to escalate growth potential for both of us."

Great. Fine. Possibly a sound business decision for both stations. But where did it leave *Family Secrets*?

"We're going to be merging programming styles and content." Bob Parker, the station's CEO, took over from Chandler. As if in slow motion, Natasha's gaze turned to Bob. In his mid- to late fifties, Bob had been the one she'd first pitched to, back when she'd been a host on a popular cooking show network and wanted to be her own boss.

He'd always been kind to her. Professionally decent.

Was that about to change?

Her mind spun, not out of control, but with options. *Family Secrets* was a proven success. Someone else would pick her up. Her previous network had offered more than once. But she'd have to give up her autonomy, give up some creative control.

Her stomach knotted.

"We'll be keeping some of our best-performing shows, with changes to help them fit into the new programming style," he continued, and she nodded. Told herself to hang on.

"Unfortunately, others that don't fit will have to go."

These *others* were owned by the station, but loved by those who starred in, hosted, wrote and produced them. Did they know, already, what she was about to be told?

"I feel certain that many of them will be picked up by other networks or independent stations…" Chandler Grey said.

Surely this wasn't her kiss-off. Her contract ended in December, but they could buy her out.

She might lose the faith of some viewers. Or just plain lose them if they didn't know to follow her elsewhere. She'd have to hire a PR firm. Mid-October audition shows were already scheduled across the United States. This year's Thanksgiving Day show contest was already open, and recipe entries were flooding in more than ever before after the previous year's huge success. The show was filmed live right there in the Palm Desert studio. Costs to change any of that could become prohibitive very quickly…

"The deal with Travel America was signed on Friday," Bob continued.

So Chandler had known during their Saturday dinner…

And never let on.

So much for having the hots for her…

"But because of your unique position of owning the rights to your show, we waited to make an announcement until we could speak with you personally."

Did the board know that Chandler Grey had taken her to dinner? Had it been at their behest?

Thank God she'd retained the rights to her show. The risk—and financial commitment—had been greater. But the show was hers. These guys could cancel it from their network, but they didn't control its existence. Or its destiny.

One thing was for certain. She was not going to lose her show. Names started to line up in her mind's eye. Heavy hitters she would call as she looked for a new home that would allow her full ownership. They'd all require a move—most to LA.

An inconvenience, but not a problem.

This was all potential inconvenience. Perhaps major inconvenience. It wasn't life-threatening. The main thing was, the show stood in a firmly secure position within the industry. As long as that remained the case, she was good.

Bob Parker pierced her with his gaze. "The bottom line here is that we—" he glanced at the other board members around the table, all of whom were watching her and nodding "—want you to join us…"

He went on to explain how her show would fit the new format with only one change. She'd be required to film at least three of her four segments a year on location. The draw of her show's ratings was what had helped entice Travel America. The board was willing to help offset the cost of travel so that Natasha would not be out revenue due to their change. On the other end, she stood to gain increased revenue with the potential new viewers.

Natasha heard it all. Cataloged it all. She made mental notes to share with Angela and, later, her mother.

She listened. Straight-faced. Giving away nothing.

And through it all, one thing kept running through her mind, over and over, more loudly than anything else.

They wanted her to join them. She and her show still had a home.

CHAPTER NINE

THEY MADE IT all the way to the breakfast table on Wednesday without Natasha Stevens's name coming up. Tabitha broke the streak that morning with her announcement that it would be only two more days until Natasha's return. She looked to Spencer for confirmation.

He shrugged, told Tabitha he didn't know when Natasha would be back and distracted both kids with a mention of the forlorn face looking at them from behind kennel bars. Daisy Wolf couldn't be freed until they'd finished eating.

The more time they took to eat, the less time they'd have to feed the puppy and take her out to the yard to do her after-breakfast business.

"I can't wait for Natasha to meet Daisy," Tabitha said then, and Spencer could have kicked himself for not stopping while he was ahead.

He explained that the television producer

was going to be too busy working to meet a dog, but Tabitha just looked at him with pity. As though he didn't understand what she seemed to know.

He was the one who understood. Far too much.

His daughter was lonely for female companionship. And was bonding with the wrong woman.

He'd known there'd come a time when he needed to get serious about finding a more permanent relationship for himself—to think about marrying again.

For Tabitha's sake—and Justin's, too. But also for himself. He didn't want to grow old alone. And he knew he was going to be far choosier this time out. No more going for the attraction high, the new love adrenaline, the excitement. He'd had those and knew quite painfully what happened when the novelty wore off.

So, starting that day, he was going to get serious about finding the woman with whom he wanted to spend the rest of his life. He'd dated several fine candidates over the past couple of years. Local women who loved ranch life. Who "got" it. He just had to narrow down the field. Choose one. And invite her to the ranch to see if she got along with his kids.

By nightfall.

He could have her over for dinner that very night. That should knock talk of Natasha Stevens right off the table.

Which would get thoughts of her out of his mind, as well. Kind of difficult to forget a woman your kids kept mentioning.

He weighed options all morning as he and Bryant took a side-by-side out to rope one of his prize bulls and get him into the front pasture to impregnate the half-dozen cows who were ready. They weren't Wagyu, but they were purebred Angus. Part of a herd that he'd raised and grain-fed since they were born.

By lunch, he'd decided on Jolene as their dinner guest. They'd been out a dozen times, at least. Line dancing, mostly. She wasn't dating anyone, not that he knew of. They got on well together. The oldest of eight, she was used to kids, comfortable around them. Of all of the women he'd spent time with since his wife left, she was the one who consistently asked about his kids.

And who didn't seem to be any more in love with him than he was with her.

Her job at the local farm and feed store

had her well prepared for ranch life. And yet it wasn't a job that would be horribly difficult to leave. Not like, say, being a television producer.

He shook his head as he took a big hunk out of the peanut butter and jelly sandwich he was eating while standing at his kitchen counter. Then he washed it down with half a glass of milk and took out his phone.

Jolene was in his contacts under Friends. She was pretty enough to look at, just not really his cup of tea. A year or two older than him, she was a little loud for his taste, but Lord knew he wasn't perfect, either. She was kind.

More important, he trusted her.

He knew she'd always wanted to be married and have a family—just hadn't ever met the right guy. Her biological clock was ticking.

And he liked slow dancing with her. They fit well.

He dialed. Invited her for dinner. Agreed that it made most sense for her to drive her truck out, rather than have him lugging his kids into town to collect her.

He set a time. And hung up. Good. He felt good. The next important step in their lives had been taken.

Satisfied, he finished his sandwich, leashed Daisy and took her back to work with him.

The afternoon was half-gone before he remembered that he hadn't taken anything out of the freezer for dinner.

He hoped Jolene liked grilled hot dogs. They had half a pack left from Sunday that needed to be eaten.

Justin and Tabitha were always happy with grilled hot dogs.

And if this next leg of their family's journey was going to be successful, Justin and Tabitha had to be happy.

ACCORDING TO THE VET, Lily was healthy. No worms, parasites or ear mites. She needed milk to drink. A mixture of canned and dry food, and a litter box. Natasha handled all of the details on Wednesday after work. She'd already called one of her previous interns to take care of Lily while she was gone for Saturday's taping. She'd leave Friday morning and be home either late Saturday or early Sunday morning, depending on how long the postshow interviews went.

And how the taping itself went. Part of the deal with the rancher was that he'd appear with her at the beginning of each show to welcome the contestants to his ranch and talk about some aspect of beef raising or egg laying.

While he wasn't an official judge, he'd also be tasting every dish at the end of each show.

He was a novice. Which could necessitate retakes Saturday night after the contestants were bused back to their hotel.

When her stomach tingled with anticipation at that thought, she quickly switched gears as she drove home with her new little girl in a crate beside her. She thought of the list of questions she and Angela had created for him to go with this first week's competition category—vegetables you might find in a cowboy bunkhouse. All of the contestants for this show had been vetted as ones with family recipes from the ranch.

And she thought about Tabitha and Justin. Because they were safe. And sweet. And because thinking about them made her smile.

Justin's antics. Tabitha's discipline.

They were a hoot. Which would make good television viewing... Picking up her cell as she pulled into the garage of her luxurious and spacious condominium, she scrolled for the cell number Spencer Longfellow had given her after he'd signed the contract to lease part of his ranch to *Family Secrets* for six weeks. Clicked to Bluetooth, and was carrying Lily's crate into the house, the pet-store bag filled with the kitten's necessities over her arm, by the time she heard the first ring.

He picked up on the third.

She was breathless for a second. Because she'd been carrying in so many things at once.

"Hi, it's Natasha," she said, letting Lily out of her crate and grinning as the kitten pounced. And then again. In circles around herself. "Natasha Stevens," she said into the silence that had fallen on the other end of the line. "Is this a bad time?"

"No." How could a guy sound so good to her while also sounding as though he could have done without her interruption?

He'd taken a large sum of her money. He owed her what she'd paid him for.

"I've got several points to discuss with you," she said, all business as she took his answer at face value when what she'd almost done was offer to call him in the morning.

The morning might be too late. In the morning Angela would be filling a judging slot that had come open unexpectedly due to an outbreak of head lice in the local elementary school.

"I'm listening."

She wanted to know where he was. It was after four. The kids would be home. And were probably out running wild on the farm someplace.

Having a blast.

For them. A blast for them. Fishing in the creek and catching frogs did not sound the least bit entertaining to her.

"First, I wanted to confirm the schedule that Angela emailed to you. We've got from ten until noon on Friday set aside for rehearsal with you."

"I got it."

Angela had sent him a basic on-air fact sheet—what to wear, what not to wear. Information about the makeup team that would be on site, making sure that he looked natural under stage lights, that sort of thing.

She wondered what the twins had been up to that week. A nonessential thought.

"Do you have any questions?" she asked.

"No. There was a number to call if I did."

His nonchalance got her dander up.

"I hope you're taking this seriously." *Family Secrets* might not mean a lot to him, but it was a million-dollar producer and…her life.

"I won't let you down, Natasha." His voice

had changed completely. Dropped to an almost seductive tone. Except that there was nothing the least bit personal between the two of them. "I give you my word."

She reminded him about the possibility of retakes on Saturday evening and tried to hear whatever was in the background of his call. Silence. That was it. No children's shrieks or laughter.

"I have a favor to ask," she said instead. "In the form of a business offer." The time-sensitive portion of her call.

There was no plan. There had been no discussions with Angela, no spreadsheet entries or well-thought-out procedures. She was winging it. Which was so unlike her.

But if she didn't ask now, it would be too late. The idea had only just occurred to her. She was the boss.

Some of her best ideas had come on the fly...

"Don't you think we should get through our first business venture first before discussing another?" he asked.

Was that a chuckle she heard in his voice? And a responding grin on her face? Huh?

"My proposal has to do with this current

venture," she said, taking care that the words were imbued with pure professionalism.

"What do you need?"

"*Family Secrets* hires different judges for each of the five weeks of competition—the four regular competition segments and the final round. We have a pool of vetted judges here locally from which we pull, offering our contestants exposure to many chefs and dining connoisseurs, and gaining them a plethora of feedback as well..."

When she heard herself sounding like a commercial, she paused. Where was her usual poise? The calm and professional demeanor she could count on in the tensest and most chaotic situations? First she was getting girlie on him. Then overboard fake.

If she hadn't known better, she would have surmised that the cowboy made her nervous.

"Our judges are professional chefs, restaurant owners and culinary instructors. In addition, because no secret family recipe would remain a family favorite if kids didn't like it, each week we have a juvenile judge at the table. It's one of the traits that set us apart from every other cooking show out there."

She gave him time to jump in. He didn't.

"We've made arrangements for a child

judge, with chaperone, to travel to the ranch each week by town car with the rest of the judges. They've all worked together before. They all know each other."

"Makes sense."

Lily was pawing at a dust bunny under the dining room table.

"Yes, well, we've had an outbreak of head lice in the local schools, and both my judge and alternate for this week have infestation within their families. Obviously I can't take a chance of exposing anyone else…"

Did he get where she was going with this? And why was she hesitating?

"I'd like to use Tabitha and Justin, Spencer. At least for the next two weeks. One of them one week and the other the next."

"No."

She blinked. Reached for the kitten. Held her close to her cheek. "Excuse me?"

"I said no."

"You haven't even heard my offer."

"I've told my kids they are not to go anywhere near that barn for the duration of your occupancy."

"I'm sure they'd understand the exception."

"No."

"It would be a great opportunity for them."

He was being rude.

She should just let it go.

Any other time she would have let it go. Finding parents who were thrilled to have their kids on national TV was not difficult.

"There's no telling what Justin might do," he said now, kind of grudgingly, she thought.

Did he feel bad about how much of a jerk he was being?

She had no basis for the thought. But hung on to it anyway.

"I'm not worried about him," she assured the single dad who had a lot on his plate. "Other than the final show, we aren't live. We can retape any necessary portions. Besides, part of the family feel is the fact that you never know what's going to come out of a kid's mouth. It's part of the show's charm, their unpredictability. I don't know why I didn't think of this before, but with you, a rancher, cohosting, so to speak, it's fitting that ranch children be among the judges."

His ranch children. Because she'd met them. And had had them on her mind often since. Usually things stayed with her only if they were important.

"I don't think it's a good idea…"

"Why not? It would be a great experience

for them. They were both excited to be in the studio." She was pushing. And didn't like it.

"Precisely," he said, his decisive tone coming over the line loud and clear. "Tabitha and Justin are, as you say, ranch kids. There's no point in getting them exposed to the glitz and glamour of television life, or having them longing for something so far removed from their existence that there's no way to marry the two."

She was talking about one show apiece. Filmed at their home. Not marriage. Or even a vacation to a real studio with city lights and famous people.

"I pay well."

"They're a little young to worry about wages."

She named her going stipend for one week's judging. "Parents of several of my regulars have set up college funds with the moneys," she added. "We deposit to them directly, which simplifies things for family tax disclosures."

"Why are you doing this?"

Pushing him. Though he didn't spell it out, she knew what he meant.

"I don't know."

This time she didn't attempt to fill the pause that fell between them.

She put the kitten down. Gave her a tiny gray toy mouse. Reached for the five-pound bag of litter.

"I'll talk to them," he said.

In a completely businesslike tone, Natasha told him that she'd appreciate a call back that evening.

She didn't gloat. She didn't even smile.

But she felt better.

CHAPTER TEN

THE KIDS TOLD Jolene all about Natasha. As in, that was all they talked about. He suggested they introduce their dinner guest to Daisy Wolf. Tabitha related, in full detail, the reason for the dog's purchase. To watch them because they'd run off twice to see Natasha.

When he served dinner—hot dogs and macaroni salad out on the picnic table—Justin determined that the dinner they'd had with Natasha was better.

As much as he felt the need to, he couldn't really fault his kids. They were polite. Friendly. Jolene was like any number of other people they'd met in town, at school and around the ranch during their lives.

They were seven.

And enamored of a person unlike them.

The crowning moment came when Jolene asked Tabitha if she'd like her to read her a bedtime story and the little girl said, "No, thanks."

"They don't like me," the pretty brunette said as Spencer left the kids getting ready for bed to walk her to her truck.

"They like you fine."

"They like Natasha." He saw the question in Jolene's eyes as she gazed up at him. He hadn't told her about his quest to find a wife. Or that she was his first choice of candidate. But he had a feeling she'd known that the evening was an attempt to explore a changed relationship between them. And wanted to know if it had also been the last attempt.

He shrugged off her concern. "They've never met anyone from television before. We'll do this again when the studio thing is done. You'll see. They'll be all over you."

At least, he hoped they would be. He liked having Jolene in his home. She fit without taking up too much space. Was as comfortable to be around as his favorite furniture.

Her adult conversation had been a welcome addition to his dinner table.

And neither of them had any misconceptions. They weren't and never would be in love. They were practical people trying to get what they wanted and needed out of life. People focused on being happy where they were.

"When will the taping be done?"

She hadn't asked about *Family Secrets* filming on location at his ranch. He figured she, like the rest of the town, had heard about it through the grapevine.

"Five weeks."

They'd reached her truck. As she stopped by the door, he noticed the mud-caked state of one of her boots. Well-worn brown boots. Nothing like the fancy red ones Ellie had birthed all over.

"So, I shouldn't expect a call from you until then?" Her blue eyes gazed up at him. He had a feeling she was waiting to see if he'd kiss her good-night. Had a feeling she wasn't any more excited about the prospect than he was.

Truth was, he didn't even feel tempted. Not with his kids waiting inside for him to tuck them into bed.

Her question, asking him if she shouldn't expect a call for a while, hung there, waiting to be answered.

He didn't know what she should expect. Hadn't really figured out how this whole find-a-wife thing was going to work in terms of his daily routine.

"I'll call you," he said, putting a great deal of effort into the smile he gave her.

It must have been okay. She smiled as she climbed into her truck.

"Drive carefully." He tapped the hood of the truck as he stepped away. And stood watching until there was nothing left of her visit but dust on the drive.

He wasn't sure he'd just had dinner with his future wife. Jolene was a sweet woman. She didn't love him any more than he loved her, but she deserved to be loved. She was still young enough to find someone. Maybe it wasn't fair to ask her to settle.

One of the guys in town had been talking about some woman he'd met through an online dating service. Just to keep his bases covered, maybe he should sign up for one of those, too. Making it perfectly clear that he was looking for a life companion. Not a lover.

Satisfied, his step picked up as he went upstairs to call a family meeting with the twins. They had a business venture to discuss. One wherein he explained work ethics to his children. You could not be friends with your boss.

So if they went to work for Natasha Stevens, they absolutely could not invite her to dinner, or to do anything else with them, ever again.

He had this. The kids whooped and hollered about being on television. What kid wouldn't?

They listened solemnly as he explained the rest.

All went perfectly according to plan, and he was pleased that he'd maintained control. Right up until Tabitha called for him as he was leaving her room after tucking her in.

He turned back. "Yeah?"

"We don't have those work rules here, huh?"

Frowning, his sense of goodwill froze. "What do you mean?" He walked back in the room, hoping to keep the conversation— and any latent fallout—just between the two of them.

"Weelll…" She peered up at him from her pillow, her hands folded primly on top of the covers over her belly, as he sat on the edge of her bed. "You said bosses and workers couldn't be friends…"

"Yes, that's right." Relief swept over him. He'd gotten through. They had their program.

"But Bryant is your friend."

The word that sprang to his lips couldn't be spoken. At least not in front of her. He saved it for later. "Well, that's different," he said. Leaned over, kissed her on the forehead and told her good-night.

THOUGH NATASHA DIDN'T really expect a call from Spencer Longfellow that night, she held off calling Angela. They always spoke some-time in the evening—Wednesday would be later rather than earlier.

Lily's litter box had a new home in the laundry room, behind the door, next to the trash can. The kitten had already used it. She'd also snagged the comforter when she'd followed Natasha into the bedroom. Natasha had been halfway out of work clothes and into leggings and a T-shirt when she'd noticed the kitten hanging from the end of the bed by her claws, unable to move.

The comforter was a couple of years old. Though she'd been happy with it, it could stand replacing. Lily, on the other hand, she had a feeling she'd keep awhile. It was nice, having another living being in her space.

Perhaps her mother should get a cat. She sug-gested as much when she called to tell Susan Stevens about the changes at the studio—about the traveling she'd be doing. Her mother thought the merger sounded positive. And thought the travel would do Natasha good.

Validating the conclusions Natasha had al-ready drawn.

Life was good. Better than good. It was as close to perfect as anything imperfect could get.

She glanced at the clock. An hour past the twins' bedtime.

He wasn't going to call...

To PROVE TO himself that he had no feelings of anticipation or any other sort regarding Natasha Stevens, Spencer went about his evening as normal. He made the kids' lunches for the next day. He took out chicken to thaw for dinner the next night. Worked in his office for an hour.

And signed up for a dating service.

Anytime Natasha sprang to mind—which, he told himself, happened only because of the conversation he'd had with the twins—he'd think about Jolene in his home earlier that evening. Think about whatever woman might be waiting for the opportunity he had to offer.

Having no idea how late city-slicker television producers worked in the evenings, he waited until after nine to call her.

"Hello?"

Her voice, soft and husky, sounded like she'd been asleep. Was she alone?

She wasn't married. He knew that much

from earlier discussions. But she could have been living with someone. Or on a date.

Before his mind could travel that far-too-dangerous road, he asked, "Did I wake you?"

"No, I've still got another hour's work ahead of me," she told him. "I'm in my office."

"Still at the studio?" He tried to picture her there. Failed. And figured it was for the best.

"My home office." He couldn't picture her there, either, but wanted to.

"Me, too," he said, leaning back in his leather desk chair to survey the old but spacious and elegant room his ancestors had used before him. Floor-to-ceiling bookcases lined one full wall. Books covered every inch of those shelves. He'd referenced only the ones related to farming.

In the dim light, he couldn't even read the titles. One lamp was lit. One that had been around longer than he had. On a side table by the leather wingback chair he could remember his father sitting in. Barely.

He'd been six when his father and another man had been killed in a crop dusting accident.

"One of the downsides of being self-employed," Natasha was saying. "No one to tell you to take the evening off."

"Ah, but there's no one to tell you you can't take an afternoon off and do something crazy just for the heck of it," he said. Having had Jolene there, having plan B in place, too, had relaxed him. Enough so that he was almost enjoying this conversation.

"When was the last time you did that?" Natasha challenged him. He wondered if she was still in business clothes. Did the woman even own a pair of sweats?

She had jeans. At least one pair. Designer, he figured. He'd seen them the night Ellie calved. And expected they'd be her stage costume for the shows she taped on his ranch.

He'd watched some of her other shows. Online. Before he'd signed his deal with her. She'd looked like a classy model ready for an evening out to dinner in expensive clothes and higher heels than any woman would ever wear on a ranch.

"On a weekday?" They were talking about an impromptu day off. Not how attractive one or the other of them might be.

The thought bothered him. He'd been thinking about her show attire. Right? So...

yeah, she was attractive. The fact that he'd noticed made him a normal guy.

"Any day," she said, a curious note in her voice. Almost…playful?

When he thought of Natasha Stevens, many descriptions came to mind. *Playful* wasn't one of them.

"I took Saturday off," he said, surprised that she didn't know that. Apparently she hadn't noticed his absence.

He'd thought…maybe…she'd left without saying goodbye because he'd been gone when she'd had to depart. That theory had just been debunked.

"Ah, but did you do something spur-of-the-moment fun?"

"Yep. I went four-wheeling." So he'd also looked at some fence. It had been there, hard not to see.

"What about the twins?"

"They were with me." They'd had a great day. If you could discount the preoccupation all three of them had had with the woman who'd invaded their space.

Frowning, he put an elbow on his desk, looked at the spreadsheet on his computer screen—hay profits for the first nine months of the year. They were doing better than he'd projected. But, with the California drought, still not that great.

"What about you?" he asked her. He had more work to do. But wasn't sure he'd get back to it that night. The numbers weren't going anywhere. "When's the last time you took a day off?"

"I can't remember." Her nonchalant tone made him a little sad for her.

"Hypothetically, what would an afternoon of craziness look like for you?" Not a business question. Not necessarily a friendship one, either. He was curious, was all.

He'd never met a television star.

"I don't know how crazy it would be, but I'd love an afternoon lying at the pool of some posh resort. Or lying on the beach. Of course, assuming I can be still long enough to get a day out of it. I used to like to in-line skate."

He'd been busy picturing her in a swimsuit in the sun. Switched gears abruptly. "I don't see you as the sporty type."

She was in shape, of course. Just far too elegant to sweat.

"I grew up in Manhattan," she reminded him. "I used to skate as my mode of transportation."

Kaylee, the kids' mother, had been a dancer

when she was younger—among other things. She'd been good at tennis and golf, too.

"Do you play tennis?" he asked.

"Some. I had lessons."

"And golf?" He was just shoring up his defenses. Without really having anything to be defensive about. He wasn't in the least bit of danger of falling for the cooking show host.

"Nope. No patience for the hours it takes to complete one game."

He'd been golfing a time or two. He'd gone with Kaylee's father back when the older man had thought he and Kaylee had been just friends. Kaylee's dad had been pleasant, but he'd left no doubt that Spencer's playing was not up to par. He'd spent their time on the golf course telling Spencer about the life Kaylee had waiting for her back in Washington. The plans that had been made long before she'd even graduated from high school.

The powerful marriage she would make. The secure future that would guarantee her a life of luxury and make her a very wealthy, powerful woman.

"My ex-wife played tennis, but she was good at golf, too," he said, finding it important to lump Natasha and Kaylee together.

"Did you grow up with her?"

"Kaylee? No. I met her in college."

"You went to college?"

He'd barely had a chance to roll his eyes when she blurted, "Oh, Spencer, I'm so sorry. That didn't come out right. I'm surprised because I assumed, from things you said, that you'd never been off the ranch. Not because I think you're lacking at all in the education department. Or lacking in intelligence, either."

He grinned, kind of liking this new side of her. Thought about letting their relationship continue in this vein, with her feeling contrite and him having the upper hand.

But had a feeling she wouldn't allow it for long.

"I'm not offended, Natasha. I did tell you I've never lived anywhere but here at the ranch. I commuted to college in Palm Desert." Why was he still grinning?

"Every day?"

"Four days a week. I have a couple of associate's degrees in agricultural-related fields."

The ranch was everything to him. He'd had to educate himself in order to do the land justice, to know that he could carry on the family tradition. That he'd be worthy of the honor and not let down the family legacy.

"And that's where you met your ex-wife? In Palm Desert."

"Yes." The less said about Kaylee, the better.

Jolene knew about her, of course. A lot of people in town did. But not because they'd seen all that much of her. Kaylee had made the almost two-hour trip to Palm Desert even to grocery shop.

"Is she still here?"

Kaylee and Natasha had a lot in common. Both from East Coast families who wielded modern-day power. Establishing all that the two women had in common was an exercise that would serve him well.

"Last I heard from her, five years ago, she was back in Washington, DC. Reunited with her family, I'm assuming."

"Reunited with them? Did they go somewhere?"

"They disowned her when she married me."

Because there was a danger of pity filling her silence, he forged on. "Her folks are lobbyists. She's their only child, and they had big plans for her."

"So, why College of the Desert? I'd think

a community college across the country an obscure choice for her."

The fact that her parents made plans for her had seemed to roll right off Natasha. Because having powerful parents and a powerful future was commonplace in their world. College of the Desert was the anomaly.

"She was studying art. Fashion. Her favorite designer lives in Palm Desert. Has her studio there. Kaylee worked for her."

Palm Springs, sister city to Palm Desert, was one of the nation's fashion capitals, he'd learned during his years with his ex-wife.

Nothing he'd ever need to know when he was married to Jolene, or anyone else willing to be his farm companion.

Expecting Natasha to ask about the designer, and to recognize the name when she heard it, Spencer was thinking about impressing her with the wedding reception the woman had hosted for him and Kaylee…

"So, you never met her parents?"

"Her dad flew out a couple of times. I met him." At some point he'd realized that Kaylee's father had flown out for one reason and one reason only. Because she'd been talking about him, too much. Because her parents were growing concerned about her friendship with the only somewhat wealthy young rancher. He'd flown out to put a stop to things.

"He stayed at the ranch, then?"

He'd refused to make the drive, not that they'd been on houseguest basis at any point.

"No."

"The whole time you were married…"

Her soft tone was getting to him. The last thing he needed from Natasha Stevens was pity.

"…we neither saw nor heard from them," he finished for her, not even trying to be anything but abrupt.

"Even after she was expecting the twins?"

"She didn't tell them." At least, not at the time.

"They don't know they're grandparents?"

"Yes, they know now. I wouldn't agree to sign our final divorce papers, giving me full custody, until they knew." He'd actually expected them to care.

"Did you get a decent settlement?"

What the… "No." Justin would be quaking in his seat at that tone. Spencer didn't care what it did to Natasha. She could handle it.

"I didn't want their money." True enough. He'd also had more put away than they'd thought. Spencer had been left with plenty of security. He just wasn't going to steal from it to get his cattle operation going. That security belonged to his children... "I wanted nothing from her but my children," he continued. "I wanted to make certain that everyone involved knew I was signing away our rights to any part of their money, current or future, in exchange for full custody of Justin and Tabitha. Everyone on the same page. Everything clear."

He wanted it clear to Natasha, too. He and his kids were Kaylee's little embarrassment. Her walk on the wild side. The thing her parents wanted swept under the rug. He might be a rancher in the sticks, but he knew how it all worked. And his kids were not going to be subjected to such treatment again.

Ever.

CHAPTER ELEVEN

TAKING HER PHONE and a cup of hot chamomile tea with her to the walled-in backyard of her condo, Natasha wandered over to the play pool she'd had installed before she moved in. The yard wasn't huge. The kidney-shaped pool and hot tub weren't, either.

But the effect—with the flowering landscaping, pavers and lighting—was paradise.

"I make a mean chili," Spencer was saying as, still holding the phone to her ear, she relaxed into one of two padded loungers by the pool. Cool night air caressed her skin, cooled her cheeks. She breathed in and closed her eyes. "I've won the local chili cook-off two years in a row."

She'd known he did most of his family's cooking. The subject had come up sometime during their initial interviews. But that hadn't meant he was good at it.

After her college gaffe, she hadn't been about to ask.

"I'd like to taste it," she said now. Thinking chili sounded wonderful for a Friday-night dinner on the ranch.

They'd somehow made it past the awkward moments and had been chatting for almost half an hour. He still hadn't told her his decision regarding the twins as judges on her show. She wasn't pushing him.

Wasn't in any hurry to get off the phone, either, in spite of the fact that Angela would wait up until she called. Since she hadn't called earlier in the evening.

She'd been riding uncharacteristically rough seas of emotions, what with her mother's breakup and the station's merger. It felt good to have a conversation that didn't affect her life in any way.

Spencer Longfellow was not only a surprisingly great conversationalist but also absolutely no threat to any part of her life. Their lives, the wants and needs that drove them, were so different, never had the cliché *ships passing in the night* been more apt.

Glad for the sweater she'd thrown on, she leaned back, lifted her face to the night sky. And then immediately brought her gaze back to the pool again. She was too wired to go without visual stimulation.

He'd fallen silent. And hadn't offered to make his chili for her during her time on the ranch.

"You still there?" she finally asked.

"I am."

"Did I say something wrong?"

"No…sorry." He was practically whispering. "Sorry," he said again at a normal volume. "I heard noise upstairs and went to check it out."

"Everything okay?"

"Yeah." He chuckled. "Justin was playing with some cars on the floor of his bedroom. I could hear them rolling…"

"I take it he's supposed to be asleep. Did you bust him?" She grinned, feeling good as she sat at her pool, enjoying the atmosphere.

"No. The little guy has trouble sleeping sometimes. He's always been that way. He'd play in his crib as a toddler, too. And then fall asleep in the middle of whatever he was doing. I once found him sitting up asleep in the corner of his crib with a cloth book open on his feet."

That pang she'd felt when she'd seen a little boy with Down syndrome stroke his mother's cheek on her show the previous year…it was back.

"So you just let him play."

"Not at first. I used to stay on him. Take things away over and over…"

Made sense to her.

"But all that did was make bedtime a horror story. And make us both tired in the morning. When I let him work out his energy in quiet play, he's asleep much sooner and sleeps soundly."

"But you still go check on him when you know he's up…" Parenting was complex. Which was why she steered clear of it. She liked to be in charge. In control. And you couldn't control another human being.

"No, I went up because I heard Tabitha get out of bed. That one is usually asleep the second her head hits the pillow."

A vision sprang to mind of the long-haired cutie standing on her stage, so seriously describing her peanut butter sandwich. Natasha was smiling as she said, "What was she doing?"

"Talking to her brother."

"Telling him to get back to bed?"

"No, asking him what he was going to do if he hated food he tasted. Since they aren't supposed to say mean things to people and hurt their feelings."

She blinked. Sat upright, her gaze frozen on a reflection of the moon on the water near the edge of her pool.

"You didn't say... I... You're letting them do the show?"

"I have a feeling I'm going to regret this in a big way, but...yes."

They talked for another couple of minutes, and then Natasha had to go. With the twins doing the show, she had work to do.

Natasha knew the surge of pleasure she felt was beyond the scope of mere professional satisfaction. Of having the judging problem solved.

Which was why, when she called Angela to let her know the news, she paid close attention to the amount of inflection she allowed in her voice.

She had an issue to deal with where the Longfellow children were concerned. Or... where her life was concerned.

She was aware, and dealing with it. She was spending way too much time thinking about the kids. Lily was the solution. The kitten would be a family of her own. They just needed a tincture of time for bonding, for emotions to settle into place.

What she didn't need was her stage manager circling around her, watching, judging and drawing completely erroneous conclusions.

THE ONLY REASON Spencer was watching for Natasha's SUV to pull onto the ranch Friday morning, the only reason he was waiting for her arrival, was that he needed to get a few things fleshed out with her while the twins were at school.

He'd called Jolene the night before. Suggested that they go dancing Saturday night. Maybe to get things back to what they'd been—friends who made great dance partners. But maybe they could test other waters, as well. Betsy had agreed to watch the kids. He'd also already had one response to the profile he'd put up online. And planned to answer it sometime that weekend. Working toward his plan grounded him. Made him more comfortable facing his interactions with Natasha Stevens.

The security camera at the gate a half mile from the house showed him when she turned onto his property. Which gave him time to meet her at her cabin as she pulled up. Based on her previous visits, he'd known she'd stop at the cabin first, where she always left her car.

He also expected that once she got over to the studio, she'd be surrounded by her crew for the rest of the day.

"Can I have a word with you?" he asked, meeting her at her vehicle. While he owned the cabin, its premises were off-limits to him while she was in occupancy.

In jeans and a form-hugging dark blue tank top partially covered by a sheer tapered white shirt, she looked...not completely out of place on the ranch that morning. Her long auburn hair, though still curled and attention-grabbing, was up in a simple ponytail.

"Sure. Walk with me."

Pulling a duffel bag from the passenger seat beside her, she took one step, and he noticed her shoes—changing his mind about the whole fitting-in thing. They were tennis shoes. Of sorts. But instead of flat soles, hers had two-inch heels.

He took her duffel while she grabbed a garment bag from the backseat. He headed toward the front porch by her side.

Caught a whiff of the perfume he'd come to associate with her, making him feel things he had no business feeling.

He had ranching to do.

"I've set very particular behavior guidelines for Tabitha and Justin." He dropped her bag just inside the door of the cabin and repositioned himself outside, several feet away.

She nodded. "We've got things to go over," she told him. "And I need some coffee. Why don't you come in and let me get my notes, and we can get this nailed down so that you feel comfortable."

He was going to feel more comfortable as soon as he delivered his news.

The woman he'd chatted with on the phone Wednesday night was nowhere in sight. Relieved, Spencer followed the all-business television producer inside.

SHE KNEW RIGHT where his old mugs were. Grabbed the coffee carafe he'd used during the years he'd been commuting between Palm Desert and the ranch and pulled a filter out of the drawer where he'd always kept them.

The big house already had a full supply of…everything…when he'd moved up there. Made sense to leave his old place furnished and stocked.

Still, it made him a tad bit…antsy…seeing her so familiar with his things.

While the coffee dripped, she pulled a pad out of her purse and set it on the table. A tablet and a couple of folders followed from a satchel she'd left on the old leather couch. Her hands reminded him of Kaylee's. The fingers were slender, soft-looking. Unblemished by the scars and calluses that came from working with cinches and harnesses, angry chickens and their coops. Tractors. Natasha's hands were pearly, not weathered.

He needed weathered hands in his life.

HE TOOK HIS coffee black. She liked hers with goodies in it. Different goodies for different moods. Or times of day.

Natasha added a little cream to her mug, put in a dash of nutmeg and sat down.

"Tabitha and Justin can't be on your show."

She continued with the sip she'd been taking. Swallowed. Held her mug with both hands in front of her chin.

The rancher, in his plaid button-down shirt and jeans that fit him sinfully well, could have been a fantasy from the big screen.

Unfortunately, he wasn't.

"What do you mean, they can't be on my show? Why not?" If they had some other obligation, fine, but she was only a day out. He shouldn't have taken this long to tell her. He should have called…

"Because it won't be good for them."

Wait. "You're changing your mind?" she asked, one eye on the folder off to her left. The kids' contracts were inside. Unsigned.

"I am."

"But...you can't."

"Of course I can." His tone was even. The expression on his face congenial.

He wasn't a stupid man. He had to know...

"The show's tomorrow." Angela could find another young judge. Someone local. But vetting would take time—putting them in more of a scramble than either she or Natasha liked.

"I know. And I'm sorry."

He didn't look sorry.

Her sudden sense of disappointment had no place at this meeting. Frustration, yes. Maybe a dash of anger for his inconsideration. But...

"A little advance notice might have been nice."

"I didn't decide until this morning."

She was upset with him. And yet...he was a man who seemed perfectly at peace with himself. With his decisions.

She respected that.

"Why'd you change your mind?" What did it matter? She needed to call Angela. And then get on with the business of prepping him for their run-through later that morning.

"Because doing the show goes against the behavioral guidelines I've given the kids. Those lines will blur soon enough, as they face life's challenges. But ideally not until they're a little older—old enough that they'll be able to rely on their own judgment. For now, their rules are their boundaries, which are the source of their security."

"What'd you do, stay up all night reading a parenting book?"

She hadn't meant the words to come out of her mouth. Was shocked that they had. Natasha always weighed her words.

It was the second time she'd had an outburst where Spencer was concerned. And probably only the second time she'd unintentionally blurted out anything in her adult life.

"I'm sorry," she said when he sat there looking at her. Not with pity. Not condescendingly. As though he was telling her everything was okay.

But it wasn't.

She'd lost her judges. She'd spoken without thinking. She was upset beyond what the situation called for.

"What boundaries are we talking about?"

she asked in her most measured tone. She sipped coffee. Wished it was something calming, like chamomile tea.

"I've told them that if they can't say something nice about someone, they shouldn't say anything at all. And that they are never to use their words in a way that they know will hurt someone's feelings. They understand that just because they don't like something doesn't mean it's bad. That they have to be respectful of the fact that someone else might like it."

Was this guy for real?

Was she being foolish in wanting to believe so?

What did it matter, either way? He was a blip in her life.

"I have very clear boundaries for my judges, too," she told him, pleased with how businesslike she sounded.

The loop he'd thrown her for was minimal compared to some she'd had. Like last season, when there had been numerous security meetings and checks because someone had threatened one of her finalist contestants.

His raised eyebrow invited her to continue without any promises that there was room to change his mind.

"The judges are not there to make or break

a cook. Or even to determine if someone *is* a good cook. They have to say something nice before they can criticize. Any criticism has to be offered in a kind way, and then only if it's constructive..."

"You don't deal with children much, do you?"

"If you'd let me——"

"There's no way a seven-year-old is going to figure out what constructive criticism is. Even Tabitha would make herself sick trying, and then burst into tears..."

"I don't deal with children much, no," Natasha said, surprised to feel a grin coming on. "Angela usually handles this end of things. But if you'd let me finish, you'd have heard me say that our kid judges never say negative things to the contestants. If they like what they eat, they say so. If they don't, they say why only if they want to. Their feedback is presented in such a way that the child is only teaching the chef about what kids like and don't like. They're doing them a favor, not criticizing or being mean.

"They don't even know whose dish they're judging. They're given their own plate with all four dishes in separate compartments, marked simply A, B, C, D. They have to indicate which ones they like, which ones they don't like. And which two they like best. If they don't want to speak beyond that, they don't have to.

"Three choices about each dish. The contestants can see them eating. Can see the expressions on their faces as they taste the food. I might not spend a lot of time with kids, but I do remember being one..."

He was watching her lips, a peculiar light in his eye.

And then he smiled.

"What?" she asked, though she'd been smiling, too.

"You've saved my bacon."

Now she frowned. "How'd I do that?"

"I had no idea how I was going to break it to my kids that I'd changed my mind. Now I don't have to."

Her negotiating skills had always been good.

CHAPTER TWELVE

SPENCER DREW THE line at a trial makeup run. Natasha had stressed that her technicians needed to get his lighting right. He figured if they were professionals, they'd adjust. He had work to do as soon as he finished in the temporary studio, and he was definitely not going anywhere without showering after having makeup on his face.

He stood at her podium. Read from the teleprompter. Found that apparatus kind of amazing—made of some nearly invisible acrylic, he could look through it, see crew members in the audience and yet also see the words he was supposed to say as though he wasn't reading them.

For that day's purposes, he didn't have to read any actual lines. That would come later, after lighting and voice checks. Then they would make certain he knew what he was doing and could actually pull off the show.

Natasha was…impressive. With a firm

voice that was somehow also kind, she was all business. Though she considered and took suggestions, there was no doubt that she was the boss and that everyone knew it.

There was also no doubt that her staff loved her.

And that she returned the affection.

On set, she glowed. Even when the stage lights were off. She exuded confidence—in front of the camera and in the audience, too.

She wasn't just working. She was doing what she loved.

Made him antsy to return to his cattle. To brand and repair fences. To get on a horse and ride his ranch. He didn't ranch just because he'd inherited the family business. He ranched because he loved it.

"She's pretty amazing, isn't she?" Angela, whose low-cut top, short skirt and high boots didn't attract his eye nearly as much as Natasha's covered skin, pointed toward her boss.

"She's good at what she does," he said, waiting on the side of the stage for a technical problem with one of the cameras to be resolved. Felt odd to stand around while others worked.

Like he was somehow...less.

"You have a girlfriend?" Angela was watching her boss. But he felt the intensity of her question.

Was she hitting on him?

"No," he said. Natasha was in conversation with her head camera operator. He thought of Jolene. Of the online dating profile he had yet to explore. "Maybe. Yes."

He was pretty sure the show host wouldn't be pleased about her assistant talking him up.

Angela's chuckle brought his gaze back to her in time to see her looking between him and Natasha. "Which is it, cowboy? Yes or no?"

Detecting definite flirtation in her tone, he prepared to extricate himself politely, yet he didn't feel any vibes coming off her toward him.

"It's…complicated," he told her. Why not just say yes? He might not have chosen the woman yet, but he was firmly on the marriage plan.

But until the woman had agreed to his plan, it seemed a bit presumptuous to spread the news.

"You committed to anyone?"

She hadn't made eye contact. Or moved closer to him. None of the usual flirt tells.

"My kids."

The stage manager opened her mouth as though about to say more, but Natasha called out to her, and she was off.

Leaving Spencer to watch the boss lady without anyone to notice or make anything of it.

NATASHA WAS SURPRISED, and maybe a tad bit disappointed, when Bryant's wife, Betsy, brought the kids to the studio Friday afternoon for their appointment with her.

Part of her agreement with Spencer was that the kids be treated like employees. That they understood they were doing a job for which they would receive pay.

Coming up with a contract for them to sign had been Angela's idea over lunch. She'd delivered the finished product to Natasha's makeshift desk in what was normally some kind of tack room but had been cleaned out for her use.

She'd hoped to show it to Spencer—okay, hoped to please him with the seriousness with which she was taking this situation—but instead she showed it to Betsy, asking the younger woman for her approval first.

With the document only two lines long, in words both kids could read, there wasn't much to approve. The point was in having them sign their names to their promise to do the job they were being paid to do.

"This is good," Betsy said, with a quiet, well-groomed child on each side of her.

For the first time, Natasha doubted her plan to include the twins in her show. All of her other judges had agents—a prerequisite to doing the show. And contracts through them. They all had prior time in her studio, watching the show. "Do you kids want to do this?" she asked.

Neither of them had so much as said hi. Or smiled. Justin hadn't fidgeted. They both looked at Betsy to answer her question.

Maybe she'd miscalculated. What did she really know about children, after all, except what she could remember about being one?

Kneeling down in the dirt, she met each one eye to eye.

"Do you want to be a judge on my show?"

"Heck yeah!" Justin put a fist up in the air, just missing Natasha's nose.

"Tabitha?"

"I do want to judge," the little girl said.

"It's just…you don't seem very happy being here. Not like you were before." She included them both in her gaze.

Justin's look in his sister's direction, as though asking her what to do, caught at Natasha in a way she'd never have believed could happen.

The little boy might treat his sister like an irritating bug sometimes, but obviously there was a lot more to the pair's relationship than she'd seen.

"Daddy said that when you work for someone, you can't be a friend," Tabitha said. Clearly. With a little-girl inflection on the very adult words.

Natasha looked up at Betsy, who shrugged, and then back to the kids. "So that's what this is about? You not telling me hello? That's why you don't seem to be happy here?"

Justin's nod was as exuberant as his air punch.

"I told him about Bryant, though," Tabitha said, puffing up with importance. She looked at Betsy, grinned when the jeans-clad woman smiled at her, and then turned back to Natasha. "Bryant is Daddy's worker *and* his best friend."

Hiding a wide grin of her own, Natasha had to ask, "And what did your daddy say to that?"

Maybe it was wrong, putting his kids on

the spot, encouraging what could be construed as disloyalty to him. And yet...

As he said, she *was* paying them to work for her. And their personalities were a huge part of *why* she'd hired them.

"He said, 'That's different. Good night, sleep tight.'" The solemn look on Tabitha's face implanted itself on Natasha's heart.

Betsy turned away, presumably to hide another smile. Natasha wasn't feeling amused anymore. Why didn't Spencer Longfellow want her to be friends with his children?

Why did that hurt her feelings?

"Well, if you're both absolutely certain that you want to do this job, then please take a seat." She indicated two folding chairs in front of her desk.

One miniature cowboy boot clunking against the leg of the card table serving as her desk, Justin took the seat closest to the door, leaving Tabitha, in jeans, a Western shirt and tennis shoes, to walk around him to the other seat, with Betsy standing behind them. Natasha took an identical chair on the other side of the table.

"Now." She folded her hands, placed them in front of her and leaned forward. "First we'll talk about the job. Then, if you still want to do it, I'll have you each sign your official contract, and you'll be workers, okay?"

They both nodded.

And she hired them.

NATASHA DEBATED, FRIDAY EVENING, whether or not she was going to stay alone in her cabin or act upon a very strong desire to seek out the rancher she was going to have to share friendly on-air chatter with the next morning.

Angela's script had them trading some verging-on-sexy banter. She had them flirting. In a family viewer kind of way.

The cowboy and the television star. She got it. Was used to playing her part—the professional chef turned reality TV show host.

There was just nothing in any of it that explained why he didn't want her around his kids. Had she made some horrible faux pas?

Ultimately, it was the fact that she was so bothered that propelled her toward the main compound—and the big house—just after eight. She'd waited until after dinner—telling herself she couldn't possibly be disappointed she hadn't been invited to dinner a second time since she hadn't expected to be.

She waited until after the kids' bedtime.

She put on her new cowboy boots—red

again—because she needed practice walking in them. In clean skinny jeans from one of her favorite designers and a red button-down shirt, she pretended she was taking a casual stroll as she went looking around at some of the other cottages. Most were inhabited by her crew but vacant for the evening as they were in town again. She looked for lights in the distance beyond them, something to break up the darkness, found none.

She'd heard that Ellie and her calf had been moved back out to pasture. One for lactating cows and their young. That half a dozen other cows had given birth the past week. She'd heard about the pasture filled with cows Spencer had specifically chosen to mate with one of his prized bulls.

She'd heard that cows were in heat every twenty-four days or so. More like a human cycle than a dog's.

She'd heard it all from Betsy. They'd walked together toward her cabin earlier that evening. Betsy had been coming from dropping the kids off at the big house.

The world was so silent, she could actually hear the breeze. Not a wind—she could hear that just fine at home—but a soft flutter of air that barely brushed her skin. As she walked closer to the house, the breeze was joined by what she thought was music. She couldn't make out the song or where it was coming from, but as she drew closer, she made out the guitar. And the male voice.

Figuring she'd stumbled into the vicinity of a cowboy campfire someplace over by the bunkhouse, she slowed her step, enjoying the music.

She'd been to the best operas in New York. To every Broadway play of note, and off-Broadway shows, too. Her mother had bought them season tickets to the symphony for her thirteenth birthday.

She knew music. Loved it. Was often moved by it. Turned to it for solace. For company.

But she'd never been a country-music listener.

Close enough to hear the words now, she followed the story of a young couple who would see each other when the work was done. By the time the single crooner reached the last verse, she was standing still, listening as the male partner in that couple, now an old man, pleaded with his wife, who had just passed away, to wait for him...promising to be there as soon as his work was done.

Such simple words.

A simple tune.

And yet there she was, standing alone in the dark, with tears dripping down her cheeks.

SPENCER DIDN'T KNOW anyone was in the vicinity until he'd finished the song. One of his favorites. And the theme song for his marriage plan. He wanted that kind of forever. The kind where you and your partner were always there for each other.

And where you understood that a farmer had chores that would always need to be done.

The kind of relationship where there was also the understanding that loyalty and family were what mattered most in life.

The kind that honored affection and the pursuit of happiness more than the pursuit of wealth.

He could see Natasha in the distance. Used to the night sky, to his land and the vast California desert beyond it, he figured he could see much better than she could.

Not sure where she was going, and not wanting to draw her to his sanctuary—the old truck that had once belonged to his father and had sat for so long it had somehow become yard art—he held the guitar on his thigh with one arm draped over the top of the instrument.

He had more to work through, more lyrics to live as they slid by his lips, but they'd wait until he was alone.

Dinner had been nothing but talk of Natasha. Bath time, the same. Natasha this, Natasha that. He'd searched for ways to distract his children, to no avail.

Maybe he should have had Jolene over for dinner again. Had already put it on his calendar to issue an invitation to a woman for the following Friday night. Jolene or someone from online. Maybe he'd take the kids out to eat in town to meet her.

The television host—seeming to him like an invader from outer space—had changed course. Instead of the studio barn still far in the distance, she headed toward his house. She'd reach him first, at the far corner of the yard, sitting on the hood of his father's old truck.

He could try to escape, to sneak around the side of the house before she'd seen him. He could sit very still and hope that, in the darkness, she didn't notice him.

Figuring the second was the more mature

option, he watched her approach. Only her outline was fully visible to him. The shape of her. The way she moved. All of it drew his eye. Fascinating him, like she was some otherworldly creature.

Her hair was down, long, curling around her shoulders before cascading down her back. Looking at it made his throat dry. So he stopped. Turned his gaze to the night sky. Searched for answers he'd never once discovered there.

But found peace in the constellations he could see so clearly. He knew every one of them, thanks to his father. Justin and Tabitha knew them, too. You could always find your way, the direction to home, if you knew where the Big Dipper was, his father had told him when he'd been no more than four. He'd never had cause to test the theory, but he'd passed it on to his kids just the same.

That was family. Tradition.

Kind of like Natasha's show. Family secret recipes. The honoring of one of the most important family traditions—the feeding of the family. Gathering for a meal.

"It was you," she called.

He'd heard her getting closer. Just hoped that if he ignored her she'd move on past—

thought maybe if he didn't look at her, she wouldn't see him.

Or, at least she'd have the grace to pretend she hadn't.

But he'd known better. The second she'd turned toward his house, he'd known that she was seeking him out.

He just didn't know why.

And half suspected he wanted it to be for something other than work.

They'd gone over everything they could possibly go over for the show the next day. From what Betsy had said, Tabitha was completely prepared for her short portion in the day.

His daughter had proven the truth of that by rehearsing all night. With Justin critiquing her.

"Play something else," Natasha said, leaning her backside against the rusty bumper of the old truck. Her back to him, she crossed her arms, as though settling in for a concert.

Or a wait.

He strummed a few chords. Intending to end it there. He took a breath, readying to tell her he was done and heading in, to make some excuse, and caught a whiff of her. That seductive city-girl perfume.

He had no original tunes. Just his renditions of the tried and true. One came to mind. A song from the point of view of a woman, a cowgirl, watching as her man fell prey to the wiles of a city woman. She was watching from a distance as he charmed the other woman, noticing that she couldn't do a two-step or shoot pool. The woman would never be able to do the things she could do—so, ultimately, he was never going to be happy. Driven by something deep inside him, Spencer began to strum the tune.

And then to sing it.

He had to put it out there. Had to make it known that she was all wrong for him.

So that he didn't do something completely wrong and start liking her. He'd been down that road. Taken his kids with him.

His family wasn't going to suffer another debilitating crash.

CHAPTER THIRTEEN

"You DISAPPROVE OF ME." Natasha, leaning back against the grille of the truck, looked out into the night as Spencer's song came to an end.

His choice of song—about a city girl not fitting into country life—had been deliberate.

"No."

"You don't like me."

"I like you fine."

"But there's something wrong with me..."

It was cool if he didn't want to know her any better, if he didn't feel a curiosity about her equal to that she felt about him. But to think she wasn't fit company for his children...

"Of course there's nothing wrong with you." He leaned on his guitar as he'd been doing when she'd approached. She could see him in her peripheral vision. And that was enough.

Spencer Longfellow emanated *man*. She

was beginning to understand why the stereo-typical cowboy character starred in so many marketing campaigns. If all cowboys were like him…

How he felt about her didn't matter. Whether or not she saw Tabitha and Justin outside the studio didn't matter, either. It wasn't like their lives would ever cross again.

Unless the ranch became a permanent travel studio—one segment a year—based on new contract parameters requiring her to produce at least four segments a year, three of them off-site.

They'd already invested in building a studio on the ranch. If she could continue using it, she'd need to find only two more locations. Or maybe one more permanent and one traveling…

"Tabitha wants to meet Lily," she said. Which would be difficult, considering that she wasn't fit company for the child outside her role of boss.

"Your new kitten. Yes, I heard."

"Your new puppy, Daisy Wolf, was out on the ranch with you this afternoon."

"That's right."

"Justin was glad, because that meant he wasn't being watched, and could he please have a turn up on the stage without anyone there like Tabitha had last week?"

"They went missing twice in a week."

"Because of me, yes."

"A dog will alert me to their whereabouts. And chase or fight off many of the dangers that could befall them. If she's trained right, she'll even pull them out of the creek if necessary."

Someone should have made him father of the year. Seriously.

"I didn't hear about Justin on the stage," he said.

A fact that clearly bothered him.

"His time was brief." She wasn't going to say more. But wanted him to trust her with the twins. They were adorable. And seemed to get something good from her. "Turned out he wanted to see if the new wood was as slippery as it looked. He made one dash and home-base slide before he lost privileges."

"That's my boy." His voice sounded like he was smiling.

"I handled the situation in an appropriate manner."

"I have no doubt."

"So why don't you want me around them?" She turned to look at him then, examining his features in the night. Funny how her eyes adjusted to the darkness even without the help of city lights. It was almost as though she could see more out there, farther.

Spencer glanced at her, too. And then continued to hold her gaze. Assessing her?

Usually blessed with a pretty decent ability to read people, she couldn't figure him out at all. Unfortunate.

"I don't want *them* around *you*."

"Isn't that the same thing?"

"Not at all. I fully trust you to be with them, to keep them safe. I don't want them to need you."

"I don't understand."

"They're seven, Natasha. They throw their all into everything they do without thought of consequence or the future. You're here on and off for six weeks and then you'll be gone. Having you here is a great adventure for them. I don't want them to get too attached and then be devastated when you leave and never come back."

It was the "never come back" that got through to her. That, and the song he'd just sung. "Like your ex-wife." Her softly offered words dropped loudly into the night.

"Yes."

"Not every woman is like her."

"City women aren't made for ranch life."

There was plenty she could say to that. Like…no one was "made" for just one thing. People changed and grew and evolved. But she got what he was saying. He had a point.

"I'm not made for ranch life," she said, understanding so much. She'd never be content to live as he did, all day every day, or most days, on the ranch. She needed…more.

But this…interest…between them. It would never be more than something peripheral. Still…it could possibly be permanent. A friendship that formed and lasted a lifetime.

The idea pleased her.

A lot.

"I HAD THIS great-aunt growing up."

Leaning on his guitar, Spencer had to hand it to the woman who, with two hands on the hood of the truck behind her, had boosted herself up to sit beside him.

He'd laid down the law about her and his kids—in essence gave her the kiss-off in general—and she was still happy to shoot the breeze with him.

It wasn't a Friday night with his future wife. She wasn't marriage material for him. These minutes were a waste in that he wasn't spending them moving forward with his plans. But everyone needed time off now and then.

Natasha had said so that past week. During one of their phone conversations.

He'd insisted he took time off.

He was proving his point. That was all.

And she'd had a great-aunt...

"Your mom's aunt, I'm assuming?" Since her father hadn't played a part in her life.

"Yep. I never knew Mom's dad, my grandfather. Aunt Grace was his younger sister who kept in touch with my grandma even after they were no longer technically family. I adored her."

"Your grandma or your aunt?" She was talking about the aunt. He just liked messing with her.

"Both, actually," she said, her tone genuinely affectionate. For a second there he envied the two older women who were probably both dead.

Until he realized that he was making no sense.

"Many of my favorite childhood memories are times when Aunt Grace was visiting."

"She lived in Manhattan?"

"No."

The old truck was so firmly embedded in the earth it had inhabited for decades that it didn't actually move as she shook her head, but he felt as though it had.

"She lived in Florida," she told him. "She'd come up a few times a year, weather permitting, to shop, see shows…and me. She'd take me shopping. I saw my first Broadway play with her. She slept in the other twin bed in my room, and we'd lie awake in the dark and tell secrets."

He could tell by the tone of her voice that she was smiling. He smiled, too. "Sounds like a great set of memories."

"They are. You have no idea how many times over the years I draw on them to lift me up. The first time I got dumped—" she turned to him "—I was thirteen and thought my world had ended…" With a shrug, she faced forward again.

Lost in wondering what kind of idiot had dumped her, he heard her say, "When I got passed over for a spot at a girls' school I wanted to attend. The day my grandma died. The summer my best friend moved away. The night I had my car accident. I was nineteen and it was my fault…"

He realized she was listing bad times in her

life…figured out, a little slow on the uptake, that she was talking about instances where the memories of her great-aunt had pulled her through. Still lost on her at thirteen and being dumped, he quickly tried to pick up his pace.

Where had her car accident been? Had anyone—she—been hurt? How old had she been when her grandmother passed? He knew something about that kind of grief.

He'd barely started school when his father died.

What was her best friend's name? How old had they been when she'd moved away? Did they stay in touch?

He and Bryant had been buddies for longer than they'd been alive apart…

"So… I think…that your kids are safe with me," she told him. "I'm a city girl, yes. But I understand the value of loyalty and longevity."

Everything about him froze. His body. His emotions. His thoughts. He was a statue, looking down on himself. Taking a time-out.

Just as quickly, and without warning, he was hit with a flood of…things that complicated his life. Messed with his plans. Played with what he knew to be true.

"I won't leave them high and dry, Spencer." It sounded like an avowal of love. A ballad.

He shook his head.

"As a matter of fact, I have a plan that could put that in writing…"

He studied her in the darkness, half thinking he'd just imagined those last words.

"I told you before, the other night on the phone, that I had another proposition, but you wanted to wait until we finished this first phase before you heard me out. The thing is… my situation has changed a bit, and I need to get a sense of whether or not you'd even be willing to consider my idea. I need to begin looking elsewhere immediately if you're not interested."

Business. She was talking business. Not marriage.

Or anything else remotely personal.

"I'm listening." He said it to buy himself time until he could extricate himself from whatever hell he'd dropped into.

A hell that taunted him with whispers of heaven.

He listened as she told him about her station's merger. About her need to host three-quarters of her segments off-site from the Palm Desert studio.

"Where will you live?" The first question out of his mouth made no sense in the context of the conversation.

He was still buying time, right?

"In my condo in Palm Desert," she said. "My office will still be at the studio. It just means that for three of a season's four six-week segments, my crew and I will be on the road…"

She continued to talk. He was glad to know Palm Desert would remain her home base. For the twins' sake.

He could see potential for her to be true to her word where they were concerned.

And they were his only concern.

"…so you can see why it would be highly beneficial to me to have you as a permanent host," she was saying when he fully tuned in again.

No. Wait. What?

"I've already invested in the studio. And it's close enough to home to allow for easy midweek commuting. I'm willing to pass this savings from not having a long commute on to you," she told him. And named a price— almost double what she'd paid him for her six-week invasion in his life.

His mind calculated it into the number of

Wagyu cows he could purchase in one year. And the very few years it would take to grow a sizable enough herd to provide his heirs with financial security for generations.

"Then the twins would know, for sure, that I'll be back."

His heart rate increased. Uncomfortably. She was lovely.

He wanted her.

On his property. As a business associate.

And only for six weekends a year.

Once the agreement was in writing, he could focus on getting the rest of his life in order— on putting his marriage plan into motion— with no more distractions.

CHAPTER FOURTEEN

IN SHINY BLACK skinny jeans, a black-and-white Western shirt with jeweled studs and white cowgirl boots, Natasha ran her fingers through her long auburn curls Saturday morning, taking one last look at herself in her makeshift dressing room.

Would Spencer like how she looked? She leaned in. She might be used to getting her own way. Obviously she was bossy. But she was also kind. And caring. Did that show in her eyes?

Hazel eyes gazed back at her. She knew the color well and had grown up hating its indecisiveness. They weren't green. Or brown. And they didn't show her much else, either.

"Natasha?" Angela had followed her makeup artist, Lori, out of the room. Natasha should have followed them.

"I'm coming," she said, pressing her lips together to make certain that her lipstick was set. What did it matter how she looked to Spencer Longfellow?

He'd agreed to take a look at whatever business papers she had drawn up to solidify a yearly Longfellow Ranch segment of *Family Secrets*.

"Spencer's asking for you." Angela popped her head in the door, one of four, at the back of the barn they'd transformed. "He's not saying so, but I think he's nervous."

"Where are the twins?" As long as Justin and Tabitha were happy, he'd be happy.

Besides, she wanted a word with them before she got too busy.

"Justin's out front with Lionel, helping tape cords, just like you said."

"And Lionel knows that he's to keep the boy busy and then sit with him during the show?"

Their high school intern for the segment was a nice kid who was almost as energetic as Justin.

"Yep."

"And Tabitha?" Natasha glanced around as she walked toward the front of the barn, looking for the little girl, for Spencer, but also noticing every other aspect of their operation: lights, staging, cameras, kitchens, the pantry where all shared ingredients were stored. She'd checked every kitchen herself early that morning. And the supply truck had just arrived and been unloaded, so she could personally ensure that all contestants' ingredients matched the lists they'd submitted earlier in the week.

A couple of members of her staff smiled as she passed. Most were too busy to notice. Her people were hardworking. Focused.

And loyal, too. They were a family.

Her only family.

She loved them. They gave her the affection and respect due a matriarch.

"Tabitha's in wardrobe," Angela was saying. Spencer had insisted that the little girl wear one of her own dresses. Natasha had insisted that they'd find something for her in their stock.

Not because it was mandatory. Which she'd have told him if he'd asked. But he hadn't. And she hadn't said, because the day before, Tabitha had bounced in her chair when she'd heard she could choose her own "costume."

"There you are." Spencer came around the corner. Natasha nearly bumped into him. Reached out to steady herself by grabbing his arm.

And then held on too long.

She and Angela had made the decision to have the handsome rancher cohost his segment with her because they'd known he'd make viewers drool.

He wasn't supposed to make *her* feel like doing so.

"Nice jeans," she told him, stepping back to give him what she hoped was a professionally assessing look. He'd wanted to wear blue jeans—insisting that cowboys didn't wear black jeans when they worked. Showed too much dirt and got too hot.

After she'd explained that he needed to be in fancier clothes for television, he'd agreed to purchase a pair of black jeans.

He looked like they'd been made on him.

His boots were black, too. And the black, white and red shirt—a masculine complement to hers—was the one *Family Secrets* had purchased for him. His chest left no spare fabric.

Tending to a question from their lighting crew, Angela moved out of earshot.

"I'm a rancher, not a television host." Spencer's delivery was a bit harsh. But she saw the uncertainty in those dark eyes.

She hadn't been able to find any hint of emotion in her own mirrored gaze...

"And that's why you'll be so appealing to our viewers," she told him, smiling. Lori had applied the minimum of makeup, just as Natasha had specified. "You're being paid to be yourself, Spencer. If I wanted a professional actor, I'd have hired one."

His hooded glance, accompanied by a hint of a smile, sent tingles down her spine. Good ones.

"Are the contestants here?" His question gave no indication that he'd felt any frisson of his own. Or was aware that she had.

Call was still an hour away.

"Yes, they're all in the green room." The largest room the crew had constructed, it was on the other side of the barn and even had a linoleum floor.

"Natasha?" Angela called out to her and she had to rush off, but as she did so, she gave the cowboy's hand a squeeze.

And felt him squeeze back.

HE NEEDN'T HAVE been concerned. There was no audience. The taping started and stopped as necessary for all kinds of adjustments— not one of them due to the rancher guest host.

Walking out with Natasha, standing with her at the podium, was a bit of a rush—in a temporary kind of way.

When she grabbed his hand, holding it as they walked off stage—something that had very definitely *not* been rehearsed—he almost missed a beat. Until he realized that she was just ad-libbing the part they were playing. Cooking show host having chemistry with rancher guest host.

A fact made more clear as she dropped his hand the second they were out of the camera's view and rushed off without even a glance in his direction.

He was glad. The bit of a dip in adrenaline was due to the fact that he was off stage. Away from the lights, camera and action for a few moments.

He should have invited Jolene to the taping. The thought had never even occurred to him until that moment. Or maybe it would be a good first date if he liked the profile he read online. He'd get to it that weekend. Plenty of time to make plans before next week's segment.

They had four minutes off stage before going back on to welcome the contestants to their kitchens. To introduce them with pre-scripted bios scrolling on the teleprompter.

Four minutes assuming there were no glitches. Some lighting changes were happening behind the scenes. For the final airing, he'd been told, commercial messages would be dubbed into the break.

For Spencer's part, his job was to stand and wait for Natasha to come back to his side and walk on stage with him. So he stood.

And with so much time on his hands, he thought about, for the return journey, lacing his fingers through hers rather than the generic hand clasping she'd instigated on the way off.

She was paying him for spice.

And he was a man who always earned his keep.

NATASHA WAS MORE than sixty seconds late. Not a big deal considering they weren't live. But every member of the crew present stared as she slipped into her place beside Spencer. Angela, who was calling the show, gave her a pointed look, a raised brow as though asking if everything was okay.

Natasha turned away from the curious glance. "Tabitha's with Lori," she said hurriedly, putting her game face on as she waited for their cue. "She's in show riding clothes, white leather, red blouse, white boots…" Like Natasha's, the little girl had proudly pointed out, sticking the tiny boot out for inspection. "And in seventh heaven," she added.

Why wasn't Angela calling them? Glancing over, she saw her assistant still watching her. She'd forgotten to give her nod, signifying that she was ready.

Rectifying the situation, she said, "She's absolutely adorable."

Angela gave them their cue, which would afford them time to get into place at their podium on stage before the contestants filed from the green room for introductions. Spencer linked his fingers with hers.

She took that as a sign of his approval of her as a friend for his daughter.

ONCE THE CONTESTANTS were on stage, Spencer was to remain there with Natasha until the show's end. If, during these taped segments, he needed to leave for any reason, there was a small gap in the set where he could do so— and then return the same way. Contestants could also leave the stage via the fake wall without disrupting filming.

"So tell me, Spencer, how do you think this city girl did last week when you woke her in the middle of the night to birth a calf?"

The words weren't on the teleprompter. The look she gave him told him exactly what she was doing. Showing him that not all city girls were alike. Or something like that.

His spine tightened up. He was not going to start wanting things he would never have. No, to the contrary, Spencer Longfellow lived his life grateful for his blessings. His kids. The ranch.

But...he was a guy...on national television.

"You surprised me," he said, giving her a look that was more about physical attraction than cows—letting her wonder, if she chose to, what else he might be thinking.

For their audience, of course.

"So..." She grinned at the camera and then turned that look on him. "You're admitting that a city girl can fit in on a ranch if she has a mind to."

The lights were making his blood too warm.

They should have stuck to the script. He was going to put that forward as a condition of his continued cooperation. Maybe.

While he didn't like squirming, he kind of

liked being playful, for once in his life, because it was all an act.

"I'm admitting that your performance the other night was…pleasantly surprising."

Suddenly he wasn't talking about cattle. It was the night before. And they were back on his old man's truck. The way she'd talked to him, like they were equals, like she was talking to him simply because she enjoyed doing so…

"And with that, we're moving back to…"

With complete professionalism, Natasha broke the moment. The cameras cut away. And they weren't smiling at each other anymore.

Most of the time, unless Natasha was parrying with him, his job was to appear avidly interested in the cooking going on in the eight kitchens, arranged in two sets of four, on either side of the stage. While a camera remained on him at all times, only small clips of that footage would be used as the final show aired that evening. So he watched the cooks. And waited for his next cue.

Trying his best to ignore the woman standing so close he could smell flowers with every move she made.

So he noticed when she turned off her mic.

"What do you think?" Natasha asked, leaning toward him, her hand by her mouth, her gaze on the eight chefs trying to work their magic. To the camera, she could have been whispering about any one of the contestants.

He wanted to appear macho. Nonchalant. He grinned. Turned of his mic. "I think it's a hoot," he told her. "I had no idea so many people did so much work for a one-hour show."

"You've seen only a glimpse of it," she told him. Her glances were not for him. Or on him. Her smile didn't fit the words, either. She had her TV face on all the way.

He missed the woman who'd been sitting on his truck the night before, asking him to play a song for her.

But knew that the woman before him, reality TV star and producer, professional chef Natasha Stevens, was the real her.

"No one's going to believe there's something going on between us," he told her—mostly for his own benefit.

Dumb of him to think about her as a woman at all. She was his business partner. But as the show played on, as the mics went back on and he continued to trade lightly flirty banter with his cohost, he tried to think of her only with the respect and affection that came with the hope for financial remuneration.

And nothing more.

"What do you think of Chef Tammy?" Natasha was leaning in, her mic off again. His gaze traveled along the eight chefs before them. No name tags. Five were women ranging in age from twentysomething to sixtyish.

He'd introduced all five of them, leaving the male contestants to Natasha. He'd read the women's bios on camera for national television. He read. He hadn't paid attention to who was who. "Which one is she?"

Her grin could have been deprecatory. Or pleased. With that fake TV smile plastered on her lips, he couldn't be sure she'd really grinned at all.

"The blonde. Stage right, kitchen three."

Thankfully he was better at retaining directions than names. Tammy. The twentysomething. She was tall, leggy. Wore her jeans like a pro. Her big, glitzy belt buckle could have been merely an accessory, but he didn't think so. It looked like the result of a national win.

And he remembered. "Miss Rodeo Kentucky."

"Right."

He watched her dicing several different vegetables, one after the other, with perfect precision. "She seems to know what she's doing."

Natasha had offered him the chance to watch the previous week's taped interviews as a way to familiarize himself with the contestants. He'd found no point in the time suck. He didn't need to know any of them. He just needed to be able to read from the teleprompter.

"I was asking what you thought of her as a woman. She's single. A cowgirl. Right up your alley."

So much about the statement offended him. She thought he needed a matchmaker? Like he couldn't find a perfectly suitable woman on his own?

It was completely unprofessional of her. She might have even violated some workplace sexual harassment law.

Her mic back on, Natasha gave a softly spoken tutorial of reducing wine in a shallot sauce—describing the actions of the chef in stage left, kitchen two. Chef Michael, he heard her say.

Was Natasha under the impression Spencer was developing an interest in her? Was that why she'd been trying to pair him up with the pageant queen? If he'd even remotely given her that impression, he needed to set things straight.

"I was toying with the idea of some banter between the two of you," Natasha said, still smiling toward the contestants, her mic off again. "Ranch owner and rodeo queen…"

He glanced Tammy's way.

Natasha hadn't been warning him off?

Had he let on that he cared that she had been? Because he didn't really care. About her *or* what she thought. At all.

His life's plan showed all signs of growing quite nicely.

Giving her a quick glance, he was startled to find her watching him. He watched back. They hadn't gone over this eventuality.

She blinked. He felt like her lashes had brushed against his heart.

"Whatever you think is best," he said, panicking for a second that something was wrong with him. That the woman had some kind of powerful effect on him.

She nodded. And moved immediately into a little rehearsed ditty distinguishing feed corn from sweet corn. He hadn't even seen her take her mic live.

Anything that might have transpired between them had clearly been his imagination. He was in full control. He reminded himself to look hunk-like for the camera. He really didn't care whether or not Natasha Stevens found him attractive.

CHAPTER FIFTEEN

"...AND I HOPE very much that Daddy will not make me eat dinner because I am too full..." Tabitha's big brown eyes, only slightly accented by stage makeup, were solemnly serious as her face covered Natasha's television monitor.

During the taping of Tabitha's tasting, she'd asked the little girl what she wanted most in the world, an interview question she'd used many times to give her viewers a sense of connection with the young judges.

She, Angela and Damon, her top video editor, were piecing together the day's show in a makeshift sound room set up in the back corner of the *Family Secrets* barn on Longfellow Ranch. The quick turn from taping to on-air was something they had down to a science in their Palm Desert studio.

And the aspect she'd worried about the most when they'd made the decision to take the show on location.

It was now something they were going to have to get used to, to meet the contingencies of the new contract she'd signed Friday morning before heading to the ranch. Three-quarters of their shows would now be done this way if she was going to continue to have a firsthand part in the process.

They would put the footage in their cloud, accessible by a crew in the Palm Desert studio who could produce the final show.

She wasn't ready to give up control of that process.

The edits, the choices of what to include and what to delete from the show—that was the art of what they did. Those choices defined the entire viewing experience of the show. Defined the show itself.

"I want this shot," she said, sitting back for Damon to take note of the Tabitha frames she'd highlighted.

Spencer and the kids had left a couple of hours ago. She'd seen them walk out together. And then she'd gone to work.

Which was as it should be.

As she wanted it to be.

So why, when she left the barn studio that evening and saw a pickup pull into the lot, saw a woman get out and approach the big house, did she suddenly feel bereft?

HE'D HAD THE idea to invite Jolene to watch the show with them about halfway through the taping. Pretty much right after Natasha had asked him what he thought about Miss Rodeo Kentucky, if he recalled it right.

So certain that it was the right course of action, he'd actually slipped off stage during the second half of the show, just long enough to make a call and put the plan into motion.

That was him—the man who put plans into motion.

Because what he didn't do didn't get done. It wasn't like Spencer had anyone else to rely on to take care of his business.

Or the kids' business.

Other than paid employees, that is. And they weren't responsible for or involved in family affairs.

Bryant and Betsy came close. But on holidays, they were with their own families.

No, when it came to family, it was just him. Making a family for his children so they wouldn't grow up to be thirty, almost all alone in the world.

And while the evening could be deemed a

success—Tabitha and Justin talked to Jolene when she spoke to them—he felt, as he tucked them into bed half an hour late so they could stay up and watch the show, that he'd somehow let them down.

Or let someone down.

Shaking off the unusual pessimism, he went back downstairs to play guitar with a woman who was never going to be more than a friend to him. She'd just told him so, in so many words. The spark wasn't there. But she enjoyed her time with him. And would like to continue to see him.

Sometimes the best marriages were ones between friends. Or so he hoped.

If there were no false expectations, there would be no crushing disappointment, either.

His plan would work. Maybe with Jolene. Maybe not. But it would work.

Before he went to bed that night, he read the online profile that had been sent to him. He didn't respond. But remained hopeful that there would be others.

Just in case.

NATASHA LEFT THE ranch Saturday night. She'd packed clothes for Sunday. Had figured she'd see the kids in the morning, as both had mentioned that they'd gone looking for her before breakfast the week before.

The white pickup truck in the drive Saturday night had changed her mind.

Not that it bothered her. She just didn't want to intrude.

As Spencer had tried to tell her, his kids needed stability. Someone they could bond with, who would be around all of the time for them.

She was the great-aunt. There for a minute and then gone.

Still, as she worked all day Sunday and then started her week, she felt…incomplete. As though she'd left something important undone.

She hadn't. She knew that. And pressed forward. The times she thought about calling Spencer Longfellow, even going so far as to make up a business excuse to justify contacting him, she didn't do so. Instead, she talked to Lily. When she was home with the kitten. And talked to Angela at work.

About work. With a new year coming and two other off-site studios to create, she had more than enough to do. By Tuesday she and Angela had flights to six different cities in six different states scheduled for the month after the ranch segment finished.

They were starting off in places with television studios that already had kitchens in place. New York. Nashville. Orlando. New Orleans. Chicago. And, interestingly enough, Anchorage, Alaska. A lot of local stations hosted cooking shows. *Family Secrets* would just have to expand sets from one kitchen to eight.

Or…as they had at Longfellow Ranch, they could build their own set. But only if the space was one they could use for multiple years.

Tuesday afternoon, she met with her accountant. And then her lawyers. She had paperwork drawn up for a four-year contract with Longfellow Ranch to the specifications she and Spencer had discussed. The contract she'd signed with the studio was for four years. It was good business to keep things simple.

And Wednesday morning, when normally she would have been at the studio, she left Angela to manage *Family Secrets* business, got in her SUV and drove out to the ranch. If Spencer wasn't there she could leave the contract for him—give him time to have it vetted by his own lawyers, then sign it and have it notarized, so she could take it back to the city with her that weekend.

She could have mailed it. He could deliver it to her by return mail. But she wanted to look over the studio. She'd had it designed by an architectural firm that specialized in professional kitchens, but they'd cut corners, thinking that the space would be used for only six weeks. Most of the equipment was there on lease.

If they were going to make the arrangement permanent, she'd need changes. And wanted a chance to look things over herself, in complete quiet, before engaging in the rounds of meetings that would need to take place before any work could begin.

After the current segment, of course.

But with the amount of time these things took, she couldn't get started too soon.

She thought about calling Spencer—several times—as she drove. Even picked up her phone when she reached the little town closest to his ranch.

Instead, she found herself searching for a white pickup truck. With Longfellow Ranch mud on its tires.

As if she'd ever be able to distinguish that.

She didn't need to see Spencer. If she called, he'd think he had to stop what he was doing and come find her.

By their current agreement, she had rights to the studio barn at all times during the six weeks she'd rented it. She'd go straight there.

And if she saw him, she saw him.

If not, she'd leave the contract at the front door. Or maybe with Betsy...

She could always mail it from town...

Longfellow Ranch came into view before she'd made her final decision on what she'd do with the contract if she didn't see Spencer. Turning in to the main drive, she felt confident that her normal work attire of pants, pumps and contoured blouse would attest to the fact that she wasn't planning to spend time with a rancher on a ranch. That she was there as part of a regular workday.

About to take the turn that would lead her directly down to the studio barn, rather than driving the long way that would first take her by the ranch house, she changed her mind at the last minute.

Was that a town car at the main house? The vehicle was definitely black. And expensive-looking. Hoping there was nothing wrong, she drove slowly past. Thought about stopping in with the contract, but didn't.

If there was a problem at hand that she needed to know about, she or Angela would get a call.

On their business line.

She spent an hour at the studio, roaming around, getting the feel of the space, trying to focus and "flow," before she admitted to herself that she was there to see Spencer. Just to get him to sign the contract.

Once that was done, she could relax. A quarter of the next four years, one of the three location segments for each year, would be in the bag. Just having one down would be huge. She could relax, take the changes in stride.

Get back on her game.

Besides, she had a dinner meeting with her senior crew that evening. To discuss the upcoming format and travel changes that would be going into effect after the first of the year. She'd like to be able to tell them that they had one permanent location already locked in— one that wouldn't require them to be away from their families as much as others. She hoped everyone would be on board and able to stay with her, but if not, she needed to know as soon as possible.

No longer pretending that she was just as happy to leave Spencer's contract with Betsy, or at the house, she locked up the studio—without having taken a single note—and headed back up toward the house.

What she'd do if the black car was still there, she hadn't yet decided. But figured she'd at least give a knock on Spencer's front door.

As it happened, a woman came out of the house, followed by Spencer, just as she pulled up. Slender. Well dressed. Refined. The dark-haired woman was in pumps and a navy suit and looked older than Spencer.

But who was she to judge? A lot of young guys went for older women these days…

The woman didn't look happy.

Natasha couldn't imagine Spencer being at fault for that.

Stopping, she saw his head turn toward her. And though she acknowledged even in the moment that she'd probably imagined it, she thought his expression showed…delight. Before he hid it.

The other woman got in her car, started it and was already backing around to drive out by the time Natasha had parked.

Spencer met her halfway to his front door.

She glanced at the expensive black car leaving dust in its tracks. "An unhappy customer?" she asked.

It was none of her business.

But she paid attention when he shook his head. Paid attention to the frown he was wearing, as well.

Probably for her as much as the woman who'd just left.

"I came to bring you this," she said, handing him the envelope she'd pulled out of her satchel before leaving the SUV. "Have your lawyer take a look, sign it when you're ready and we'll be good to go."

She wasn't going to ask if he'd changed his mind. Didn't want to give him an easy out. She also knew him well enough to understand that he'd have no problem informing her if he had.

He took the envelope. Didn't open it. But slid it under his arm. As though he meant to do something with it. She took that as a good sign.

"I…was just out looking at the space," she said when he made no move to walk with her to the house. To invite her in. "As soon as the current segment is done, I'd like to have the architectural firm begin work on a more permanent set, with an eye possibly to designing other sites for me, as well. I'd like to keep the sets as similar as possible..."

She was babbling. So not her.

He nodded. Still frowning. Still not going in. But not walking away, either.

"What's wrong?" She was only a business associate. It wasn't her place to ask. But it was obvious he was bothered. And she wanted to help if she could.

He had the option to shoo her away.

Shaking his head a second time, he looked at Natasha. And kept looking.

CHAPTER SIXTEEN

HE NEEDED TO get married. The plan was in place. Jolene was in line, but Spencer still wasn't sure asking her to marry him was fair. He knew he was never going to marry for love again, but she still yearned for that chance.

She yearned for a family of her own, too.

He could give her that, at least.

With Natasha looking on, he'd also spoken with Tammy, Miss Rodeo Kentucky, on Saturday. Just to congratulate her on her honorable mention.

But she'd be back that weekend. He could try harder. Just to show Natasha for absolute certain that there was nothing between them.

The *Family Secrets* host stood in his yard—on a day she wasn't expected—and he couldn't find the words to get rid of her.

"Nothing's wrong." He considered it a step toward recovery—from what, he didn't know—when he managed to get the lie past his teeth.

He was burning from the inside out with the irrational need to get to town, haul his kids out of school and lock them on the ranch—where they'd be secure and happy—for the rest of their lives.

At the moment, everything seemed to be falling apart around him.

Everything seemed to be threatening what mattered most—his family unit.

Including himself, he acknowledged as he added, "Really, everything's fine." And continued to stand there, connecting gaze to gaze, as though she'd somehow understand what he couldn't.

"You don't expect me to believe that."

The warmth in those not-quite-brown, not-quite-green eyes called to him.

"That was Kaylee's mother." He just put it right out there.

"Who's Kaylee?" She wasn't grinning. No TV show personality present at all.

"My ex-wife." He'd told her once before, but didn't blame her for not remembering.

"That Kaylee." Her expression changed. "Tabitha and Justin's mom. I thought she wasn't in contact."

"That was their grandmother."

"Has something happened to Kaylee? Is she okay?"

"She's fine," he said. "She's married to a Washington mover and shaker." And he honestly didn't care—other than to wish her well. No angst. No defensiveness. No…sadness. If he'd ever really loved her, he no longer did.

"I'm sorry." Natasha's gaze shadowed. For a split second, he wanted that compassion.

"I'm not," he told her, meeting her gaze head-on. Closing Pandora's box. Natasha's compassion was not good for him. He held up the envelope she'd delivered. "I'll take this to town today. Have my lawyer take a look, and if all is well, I'll get it in the mail tonight."

Her glance at the envelope seemed a bit startled. As though she'd forgotten why she was there.

Which gave him a brief bout of pleasure.

She nodded. And then said, "Why would your ex-wife's mother drive all the way out here to tell you Kaylee got married? Didn't you say her folks had never been here?"

Jolene would never have asked the question. She wasn't that invasive.

"I did." He had to get rid of her. She was too dangerous.

"So…" Frowning, she cocked her head at

him. She was supposed to be taking the hint and heading out.

"You want a glass of iced tea?" His throat was dry. Hers might be, too. He could put her drink in a plastic cup that she could take with her for the drive across the desert.

"Sure." She walked with him to the house. Knew her way to the kitchen. Leaned against the counter while he put ice into two plastic cups left over from a cookout he'd had a while back.

He couldn't figure how a woman dressed like she belonged in a New York office could look so at home in his kitchen.

But he didn't let the perception fool him. He knew better.

Best not forget.

"Apparently, at the time of our divorce, Kaylee and her father failed to tell Claire Williamson, Kaylee's mother, that she had grandchildren. She's since found out and sought legal opinion as to the paperwork Kaylee signed giving up rights to her children and found that while Kaylee has no rights, she, as a grandmother, does. Apparently all fifty states uphold grandparent visitation rights." The words came out while he poured.

Now, that was grounds for compassion.

He didn't turn around to find out if he could sense any from Natasha.

"Top that with the fact that the man my ex-wife recently married is close to sixty and incapable of fathering any more children, and you have a woman with a plan."

He was still processing, but that was the gist of it.

"What plan?" Natasha was no longer leaning on the counter. She took the tea he'd poured for her and handed one to him before settling at the table. In Tabitha's spot.

So as not to be rude, he also sat down.

Ignoring her tea, Natasha leaned forward, placing her hand on his knee. "What plan, Spencer?"

He looked at her, so…there. In his space. His life. Just for the moment. But the moment was all he needed. "Kaylee never wanted kids," he said. He sipped tea. Set the cup down. Crossed his arms across his chest.

And didn't move his knee at all.

"She didn't say so," he clarified. "Not until the twins were on the way. She'd convinced herself she'd changed. That she really wanted me and the life I had to offer. But it hadn't taken long for the rural life to drive her nuts.

By the time she'd figured it out, she was pregnant."

That about summed up the problem.

"So…" he continued, "marrying a guy who's already had his family, and signing on for a life without children, seems perfectly right for her. I think she made a good choice. I'm happy for her."

She'd given him the best part of his life—Tabitha and Justin—so he wanted her happy, too.

"Claire doesn't agree."

He couldn't pretend. The twins' futures depended on him facing the truth here. Feeling as though everything inside of him had just gone weak, Spencer felt something that he supposed was panic.

He focused on the feeling.

"She wants them."

"What?" Jumping up, Natasha yelled the word. Spun around. Sat again. "She can't just come in here and threaten to take away your children! You're a great dad. They have a great life here. No court in the country is going to take those kids from you!"

If he hadn't been so out of his element, he might have smiled at her vehemence.

"She's not threatening to take me to court,"

he said. Not yet, anyway. "She wants to spend time with them. Let them get to know her. And then she wants them to visit her in Washington. Spend the summer there with her. Most particularly, she finds that Tabitha's situation is unhealthy, with no mothering influence in our home, and she wants Justin because it wouldn't be fair or right to break up a set of twins."

On the surface, it didn't sound completely outrageous. Or wouldn't if what Claire was offering weren't so at odds with what he already provided his kids. Summers on the ranch were a way of life that got in the blood and stuck there. Gluing you to a life of happiness, of belonging, and...because he was playing his cards right...lifelong security.

And no matter what it looked like on the surface, he knew where Claire was heading.

"You can't let her have them for such a long stretch. She'll try to acclimate them to that type of life, make them think they can't live without it..."

The steely glint in Natasha's eyes reminded him who she was—where she'd come from. She knew more about Kaylee's type of life than he did. Had grown up in the East Coast world of money and power.

She was telling him what he'd already figured out. Claire might say that she wanted only visits. But she was planning to wage battle with him over them. Not in the courts yet. Natasha was right. She probably wouldn't win there.

But if she could confuse the kids with different choices, spoil them with everything money could buy, she might be able to convince them that they wanted to live in Washington with their mother's family.

And *then* she'd go to court.

"Tabitha needs a woman's influence." He repeated the statement Claire had made most often during her ten minutes on the ranch.

The woman had come prepared with the perfect speech. Meant to sound loving, friendly and conciliatory while it was deadly.

"She has Betsy." Natasha punctuated the words with a nod of the head.

"She needs a mother."

"A lot of girls are raised by single fathers."

"The Williamsons have enough money to offer her the world. Ballet lessons. Horseback riding lessons. Pretty clothes and the 'moral and manners' guidance every young girl needs." He was paraphrasing, but that was the gist of it.

The horseback riding had been an arrow in his gut. So far, he'd been refusing to let Tabitha on a horse, but the chance to have one of her own was something she might be willing to sell her soul for.

A purchase he'd be putting in motion that afternoon. He'd give her the horse for Christmas.

"You have money, too."

Not like they did. Not enough to pay expensive lawyers in long legal battles and give his kids all of the fine things the Williamsons would provide, and still pay for college and have enough left to guarantee that the ranch would be secure for generations to come…

Weakness returned to attack his joints. He looked at her. "If she has legal visitation rights…" Claire needed only to make that one statement for him to know her game. And his vulnerability.

With all of the powerful people at their command, they could beat him at whatever war they waged.

They could hire investigators. Have means to look at dusty records. And if they looked deeply enough, long enough, they could find some dirt that might sway a judge into thinking he wasn't good enough…

His gaze landed on Natasha, like a last-ditch effort. If Jolene had been there, he was confident it would have landed on her.

"You need to get married," Natasha said in the same tone she'd used when outlining her business plan for a yearly Longfellow Ranch segment of her show. "Kaylee has signed away her rights to the children. If you're married, your wife will naturally assume those rights. Even better if she adopts them. No one is going to take a child from a loving family just because a grandparent wants him or her."

Yes. Heady with relief, he knew what she was saying was right.

He'd been worried over nothing.

Nodding, he grinned at her. "I have a plan already in motion to that effect," he told her.

"You do?" Natasha sat back, frowning.

"Yes. I've recently implemented a plan to find a wife. I hope to be married, or at least engaged, by Christmas." Originally the timeline had been the following summer. But Claire wanted the kids during their first break from school. That was Christmas.

"You plan to find a woman, date her, fall in love and marry in the next three months?"

"I have no intention of falling in love," he told her. "That's not what I'm looking for.

And I've got a couple of options in the works.
A woman I've known a long time who is a
good friend. And I've put out a request on the
internet, as well."

She blinked. "You aren't kidding."

"No." He shook his head. "I've never been
more serious."

"Is she, the woman you've known a long
time... Do I know her?"

"No."

"Does she drive a white pickup?"

He had a mind to ask how she knew that.
But didn't want to explore far enough to find
out. "Yes."

"Do the kids like her?"

"I'm working on it. They don't know her
very well."

"Does she like them?"

"I think so. Of course. But, as I said, they
don't know each other well yet. I've made it
a habit to keep my dating life separate from
them. I didn't want them confused. If it turns
out that she doesn't love them, I'll move on
to plan B."

For a businesswoman, she was looking
pretty shocked. Or horrified. Or something.
He thought she, of all people, would get it.

"But...you don't love her?"

"I love my children," he said very suc-
cinctly. "I would give my life for them."

"I know, but…"

"I love my ranch," he continued. He'd give
his life for it, too.

She nodded. "But…"

"I loved a woman, once."

"Kaylee."

"Yes."

"I understand your reluctance to try again,
but you can't judge all women by one, Spencer. You chose to marry someone who wasn't
right for you. That doesn't mean there's not a
woman out there who is the right one."

"I have children to think about. I won't
let their stability, their security, depend on
whether or not my heart flutters when I'm
around my partner. The twins need me to
respect her. To be fond of her. Good to her.
They need her to love them. To put them
first." He knew these things.

Knew what it was like to grow up without them.

If he got nothing else right in life, he was
going to do this one thing perfectly.

"Betsy and Bryant seem to love each
other," she pointed out.

He wasn't sure how she'd been able to

make that assessment, having been around the ranch only a few times.

"I'm not saying that marriage and love can't happen. I'm saying that I have no faith in my heart's ability to discern whether or not I love a woman, which means my odds of making a second mistake are high. I will not bet my children's future on those odds."

"What about your mother? You obviously loved her. You stayed on the ranch with her, took care of her. I know it's a different kind of love, but I'll bet your father loved her, too. In the way a man loves a wife."

"I felt deep affection for her." The woman he'd called his mother. "She wasn't one given to any real show of emotion," he said. "And so, in that vein, I can't tell you whether or not her marriage was based on love."

Natasha looked…strange.

"Really," he said, wanting to reassure her, "it's fine. We'll be fine. It's a good plan. And hey, as soon as I sign those papers—" he nodded to the envelope he'd dropped on the other end of the table when they'd come in "—you'll be around enough to keep an eye out and see that I'm on track."

Yes. It felt fine. Right.

His plan was good.

CHAPTER SEVENTEEN

NATASHA WORKED UNTIL midnight Wednesday. Making up for time away that morning. And getting ahead, too. She was up at five and in the office by six the next day, too, so she could finish up business. Her bag was packed and in the car. Arrangements were made for Lily.

With everything done, there was no reason not to head back to the ranch Thursday evening rather than lose valuable work time on Friday traveling across the desert. Spencer should have a signed contract for her. And she had work to do to make the barn studio a more permanent working space.

They'd need flooring and a real stage, not the wood-veneered metal breakdown one they were currently using. And she wanted a proper office.

Spencer didn't know she was coming. She didn't report to him. And didn't want to create an expectation that could be difficult to maintain. If she was going to lease the right to the studio on his property, she needed complete autonomy.

And yet, as she made her way to the ranch, she thought about him and his kids. The sunset over the mountains in the distance was glorious, bathing desert growth in shadows and color. Still, it didn't hold her attention as it once might have.

Nor did thoughts of the various contestants in the ranch segment. Normally she got to know her contestants like friends.

This time they were like pegs in a cribbage board. Necessary to the play, but otherwise anonymous.

The fact might have bothered her if she had the mental faculties to focus on it. Instead, she thought about... Spencer and his kids.

Had he told them they had a grandma who wanted to meet them?

Did he see the good in that for them? Aside from the danger of losing them to her. But he wasn't going to do that. He'd marry. The kids' home life would be secure, well-rounded. And they could have a grandma to spoil them occasionally.

Would her mother have spoiled any kids Natasha might have had?

She couldn't see it.

Maybe because she couldn't see herself with kids.

Pulling onto the ranch just after dark, she debated taking the road straight to the studio. Not because she planned to work there that night. But because then she could take the back way to her cabin without shining her headlights directly on the main house, disturbing Spencer.

Or letting him know she was there?

Mostly she wanted to avoid the sight of the white pickup truck parked out front...

The thought shocked her. Why would she care about that truck? She was the one who'd suggested Spencer get married.

She just hadn't thought...

Well, what had she thought?

When no ready answer presented itself, Natasha turned her SUV toward the main house. She was going to tackle this problem just as she did everything else in her path.

Head-on.

THE TRUCK WASN'T THERE. Lights were on in the front room. And in the back, too, from what she could tell through the big front window.

School-night bedtime was still half an hour away.

And there was no town car in the drive.

Not that she'd expected there would be. The kind of threat Claire Williamson posed would be months in the developing.

Spencer would be married long before then. Nothing was going to unravel for this little family.

Not that it was any of her concern.

She slowed as she neared the house. Kids lived there. Daisy Wolf was puppy enough to be unpredictable. And she didn't want to hurt anyone.

Still yards away, she saw the front door open, and a child came barreling out. Justin. What gave him away was how he tripped over his foot.

Tabitha was only one step behind her brother. "Natasha!"

She heard the kids' happy hollers even with her windows closed.

Spencer wouldn't want her to hurt his kids' feelings by driving on past, so she pulled to a stop. Rolled down her window. But then got out.

Someone had to stop Justin from hurling himself into the darkness. She caught him, feeling his arms around her neck, holding him tight so they didn't fall, before setting him back down. Tabitha's arms around her hips came out of nowhere. She held on to the girl to steady them both.

She held on longer because she wanted that hug more than she'd admit.

She wasn't a hugger. Never had been. This was unsettling.

"I been practicing every night, haven't I, Tabitha?" The boy was jumping up and down beside them even before Natasha let Tabitha go.

"Yes, and he is pretty good," Tabitha said, grinning. "But he doesn't like lots of stuff," she said, her expression serious. And then not as she asked, "You want to dunk doughnuts? We're dunking doughnuts with Daddy."

Natasha looked up. Spencer was halfway across the yard. His back to the lights coming from the house left his face in complete shadow, so it was impossible to tell what kind of mood he was in.

Or how displeased he'd be with her impromptu addition to family snack time.

"Natasha wants to dunk doughnuts, Daddy!" Justin said, his voice about three octaves above normal.

"She didn't say that yet, Justin. Do you want to dunk, Natasha?" Tabitha tugged on her hand.

"It's up to your daddy," she said, knowing that putting the onus on him wasn't the way to endear herself. But she wasn't going to disappoint these kids. They were just too cute.

And the light in her heart they left in their wake was proving impossible to resist.

"You dunk, you eat," Spencer said, reaching them. He didn't sound mad.

So she joined them.

SPENCER COULDN'T TELL what Natasha was thinking when she discovered that his doughnuts turned out to be little O's of oat cereal. When the twins had been little, the O's had been a lifesaver pretty much every day. In the truck on the way into town, on a high-chair tray while he cooked dinner, sitting in front of the television set watching football...

Now that they were "grown up," as Tabitha put it, they needed grown-up O's. She'd been trying to get him to buy sugared cereal when she'd made the announcement.

He'd come up with a distraction meant to be a onetime thing that had escalated into a family tradition. The first time, he'd had her dunk her plain oat O into a blob of jelly he'd had on a spoon. That had evolved to evenings of finding different things to dunk into. They had their favorites, which he'd occasionally put out on the table in little bowls. The three of them would dunk while they did their homework. Or colored. Or had family talks.

That night he'd given them bananas that he'd put in the blender with milk. Some chocolate syrup. And a bit of Betsy's strawberry jam.

The kids fought over who got to sit next to their guest. She put herself at the end of the table and had them sit opposite each other. He sat in his usual seat at the other end.

"You can't lick your fingers and put them back in the bowl," Tabitha explained as she leaned over the bowls of dunking sauces. "See, you do it like this…" She demonstrated how she dunked her O and then dropped it into her mouth without letting her fingers touch her lips.

"I do it like this." Justin, on his knees on the chair and with both elbows on the table, leaned forward and grabbed a piece of cereal. He dunked it, dropped it on his paper plate and then hooked it with a toothpick, putting it into his mouth.

Spencer locked his lips together. His kids, especially Justin, took offense when they thought he was laughing at them.

"Now you try," Tabitha said, pushing hair out of her face with the back of her hand. He was going to have to get that mop under control. No one on the farm cared if her hair was a tangled mess by the end of the day, but there was no way he was giving Claire that image to take to court.

For fifteen minutes, Natasha played along with the kids. She dunked. She ate. And when her fingers automatically touched her lips, Tabitha, who always watched, caught her and made her go wash her hands before she could dunk again.

Eventually they remembered that Spencer was there. And made him dunk, too. He was happy to comply.

Happy, period.

Happier than he'd been all week.

Funny what a little dunking doughnuts could do for a guy.

CHAPTER EIGHTEEN

NATASHA GOT UP to leave when Spencer announced that it was time for the kids to go to bed. She would have been out the door, except that he asked her to wait for him. So she cleaned up the table and washed the few dishes in the sink instead.

Her kitchen in the condo was elegant and stocked with tools befitting a professional chef. It had been a long time since she'd had her hands busy in an ordinary home kitchen.

"You didn't have to do those," Spencer said, coming into the kitchen just as she was drying her hands. "But thank you."

"You're welcome." She smiled at him. He smiled back.

"Oh…" he said after a long moment, breaking eye contact. "I wanted to give you this." Pulling an envelope out of his back pocket, he handed it to her. "I was going to mail it but then figured, with you being here over the weekend…"

So it was official? They were a permanent team? At least for the next four years?

The kids would be eleven then. She'd get to see them mature…

"Your lawyer found everything in order?" she asked in lieu of ripping open the envelope and seeing his signature right there next to hers—which was what her baser instincts were telling her to do.

"Just like you described." He nodded. Crossed his arms. Dropped them. Shoved his hands in his back pockets. Pulled them back out. Hooked his thumbs into his front pockets. And left them there.

"Good." She smiled again. He nodded. And she remembered something she'd wanted to point out to him.

"Once you get married and things are settled with the kids' home life, this whole Claire Williamson deal could turn out to be a good thing."

He pulled his head back. And she figured she could probably have used a bit of finesse in introducing the topic.

"How so?" he asked when she was beginning to think that they wouldn't be discussing the issue any further.

Or that she'd said the wrong thing and

would now have to fight her way back into his good graces so she could spend time with the kids that weekend.

Not that she'd have any extra time.

But maybe… Friday evening…

"It's just…if anything ever happened to you…" Family was a much better option for orphaned kids than a foster-care system that could be forced to split them up.

"The ranch would be theirs," he said, frowning.

"I know, but…if they're young…"

What was she doing? Talking to him about his death as though it were imminent?

He looked at her again. His expression cleared, and he nodded. "You're right," he said. "Although they would have their new mother…"

"Unless something happened to her, too."

His grin was incredulous. "You're a real grim reaper, aren't you?"

With a stomach doing flip-flops, she defended herself. "A responsible parent is ready for any scenario," she said. And then, without thinking, she added, "My mother told me who my guardian would be in the event that something happened to her so I'd be prepared…"

At the time it had been a friend of her mother's from college. Later, when the woman had married and moved to Texas and they'd drifted apart, it had been another judge. A woman her mother was still friends with.

"How old were you?" Spencer's glance was…inquisitive. As though he was seeing more than she was showing him.

"Eight."

"And you were okay with that?"

"No. Not at first. I worried like crazy about not having family of my own. But I got over it, and then I was fine with it."

Except that she'd still, on occasion, wished her mother would fall in love and get married.

She'd thought Stan was the one…

Was that why she'd been so upset when her mother had broken things off with him?

She dismissed the idea.

But could feel its lingering presence all the same.

"I was six when my father was killed." His words pulled her out of herself and back to the Longfellow Ranch kitchen.

"What happened?" she asked, standing there in the middle of the kitchen, facing him. She wouldn't have minded sitting down. But didn't want to take a chance that if she moved, he'd see her to the door instead.

Or quit talking to her. Spencer Longfellow was one private dude.

"Crop dusting accident," he said. And then turned around, leading the way out of the kitchen, through the living room, to the front door. "It's dark out there at night," he said, using his head to motion toward the front yard. "I'll walk you out."

She had no workable choice but to follow. Still, there was more she wanted from him. What, exactly, she wasn't sure. She just didn't want to leave yet.

"You're right, you know," he said as he waited for her at the bottom of the front porch steps and started slowly across the yard. "It will be good for the kids to know that they have family outside of me and their home here. Added security. It's good for me to know that."

Good. She was glad she'd been of help. She nodded. Took a few steps in her heels in the soft grass.

"Have you talked to your…prospective wife…since Claire was here?" She'd thought of little else the night before. Until she'd put her foot down and forbidden herself any more time spent on the topic.

"Jolene? She was here last night. For dinner."

Natasha's heel caught in the dirt. She stumbled. But before she could lose her balance, Spencer had a hold of her elbow. Kept his hand there as they continued the trek to her SUV. "How'd it go?" she asked.

"Okay."

She stopped. Looked up at him. Noting that he still had a hold of her arm. "You can be really infuriating, you know that?"

"What?" he asked, frowning again. She thought. In the darkness, she couldn't be sure. "What'd I do?"

"Okay," she imitated him. "What's okay?"

She felt as much as saw his shrug. "Okay's okay," he said.

"Did the twins have a good time?"

"They didn't have a bad time."

"Did she seem happy to be with them?"

It was really none of her business. But she'd do the same for one of her crew members, even though their personal lives were out of her realm of concern.

"Yeah. She really wants them to like her."

Of course she did. If she wanted him. And what woman wouldn't want the sexiest, most handsome cowboy in the state?

No, wait, that was *Family Secrets* speak. Still, the way Spencer filled out his jeans and his denim shirts, the way his hair covered the top of his brow and his eyes glowed with emotion…

Well, of course Jolene would want his kids to like her.

"Did you tell her about Claire?"

"No."

Natasha wanted to be surprised. Instead, she felt kind of special, sharing something intimate with him.

"Did you tell the kids?" She'd been thinking about that all day. And hadn't been able to make herself stop.

"Absolutely not. Not until I have a solid plan."

"I meant about Claire."

"So did I."

But… "Are you sure she'll give you enough time to…?"

"I told her to give me some time to think about it, and I'd see if we could work something out."

They were standing in the dark. His hand on her arm. Their faces inches apart. She couldn't really see into his eyes, but she was completely aware of the emotion emanating from him. Or between them.

As he told her far more than he had the morning before.

Because he was warming up to her? With the contract between them, would he finally start to trust her as a friend?

Why it mattered so much, she had no idea. It wasn't like Natasha was hurting for friends. But...she'd been out of sorts lately.

It would pass. It always did.

"YOU LIED TO her to buy time," Natasha was saying, a note of disappointment in her tone. Or at least, as he heard it.

"No." He shook his head. "I don't lie. I hurt feelings before I lie. Or keep my mouth shut. Not that I wouldn't lie to protect my kids, if I had no other choice, but..." What in the hell was he doing? Saying?

He sounded like a rambling idiot.

He had to get her to her car. Let her get on up the road to the life...work...phone calls... whatever...waiting for her. But he couldn't let her go thinking he was a liar.

"I always take time to process any big decision," he told her. "And right away I see that it would be better for the kids if I could somehow manage some kind of agreement between Kaylee's mother and myself, rather than have her take us to court where the kids would have to testify."

There. Now he could walk her the rest of the way to her car. As soon as she indicated that she believed him.

"You're a good man." Her words were no more than a whisper on the wind.

"I like to think so." Lord knew he worked hard to be.

And yet…in that second, he knew he was about not to be. And there was nothing he could, or would…

His head lowered. His lips touched hers.

Touched them again.

When he went down for the third time, he knew he was making a mistake.

Still, he didn't break away. He held her, pulling her close. Kissed her as though she was…his.

With a muffled…something…she pulled away from him. Gently, was how it seemed to him, and walked to her car, stumbling twice along the way.

He watched her get in. Start the ignition. Put the car in gear and back up enough to get her car on course to head up to the T in the road. He watched her turn right, and watched as her taillights disappeared in the direction of the cabin at the end of the road.

He stood there and watched the night pass, too. For more than an hour.

He didn't know what else to do.

He couldn't go back to the life he'd had planned when he'd left his house. Couldn't marry Jolene when he'd uncontrollably kissed another woman.

Could he?

Had the kiss been an aberration? A result of the panic he'd felt the other morning? Some kind of residual reaching out to the person who'd befriended him in his time of need?

Was he losing his mind?

He didn't have to love the woman he married—in fact, he was determined not to do so—but he needed to at least feel compelled to kiss her, didn't he?

Jolene had been to his home three times and he hadn't kissed her good-night, much less kissed her good-night like that.

He couldn't go back.

And he couldn't go forward, either. He needed to get married.

And the woman he'd just kissed—like that—could absolutely not be his wife.

CHAPTER NINETEEN

NATASHA TALKED TO Angela before bed. She wanted to have her mind fully focused on what mattered most—*Family Secrets*—and sleep well. It didn't happen that way. She didn't sleep well at all.

But when she stepped out of her SUV at the makeshift studio the next morning, in the jeans and wedge shoes she'd be wearing to work that day, she was fully on task. She had a signed contract connecting her to Spencer Longfellow for the next four years. *Family Secrets* needed him. Her job was to make it work.

Which meant making sure he was comfortable. At ease.

He was her cohost. Someone she was scripted to flirt with on air. Any thoughts of that off-air kiss were to be quashed. They led nowhere good.

She'd see him for their scheduled lighting check that afternoon. She might or might not see him when she took Justin through his rehearsal—depending on whether or not he sent the kids with Betsy, or someone else, again.

Beyond that, she couldn't worry.

The week's category was breakfast—ranch style. Betsy was providing the eggs, and Natasha passed her and Bryant as they filled the pantry with freshly gathered eggs from two large baskets.

She nodded, smiled, but didn't stop. Her crew had already arrived and were slowly gearing up for the busy day of lighting and test runs that happened before every show. Natasha would be wearing a tight red dress with Western embellishment—along with her white cowboy boots—the next day, and the lighting had to be adjusted accordingly.

Angela dropped Spencer's matching shirt on Natasha's desk just before eight that morning. They spent the next hour walking around the barn space, making plans for the remodel that would begin shortly after that first segment finished. She and Angela were going to be on the road for much of the six weeks after that, auditioning contestants, and now, scouting for other locations.

Filled with adrenaline, sizzling with energy, Natasha did what she did best—produce.

They needed the Longfellow Ranch business tied up before they left.

She needed to make certain that the intern she'd hired to watch Lily would continue to do so.

"I want to adjust our schedule just a bit," she told Angela as they met back at her office for a quick arugula salad. "Give me three days home a week. There's just too much going on with all of the changes, and we need to be on top of things in the office."

The need had occurred to her the night before. Thinking about Lily solidified the plan.

She couldn't let go of her home base. *Family Secrets* and the Palm Desert studio were her home. While the travel station moved in and power shifts happened, she had to be present to maintain control of her part of their world.

Angela nodded. Chewed. Made notes. She didn't comment. Didn't seem to notice anything different about her.

Natasha loved her for it.

THE SECOND THE kids were on the school bus Friday morning, Spencer headed over to the studio. He had to see Natasha. To apologize. And…he didn't know what.

Ask for his signature back? With the Williamson threat pending, he absolutely could not turn his back on a lucrative venture that in no way threatened the ranch, or his and his kids' life there. A venture that not only ensured that they could continue living the way they were but also gave his new beef venture national exposure. Free advertising for four years.

When he saw her SUV out in front of the barn-turned-studio, he still hadn't figured out his approach. But it didn't matter. She was busy, he was told, when he asked one of her crew members if he could see her.

She was busy when he checked back later that morning, as well. And again shortly after lunch. Apparently the woman was getting a heck of a lot more work done than he was that day.

It occurred to him to wonder if she'd told everyone that she didn't want to see him. She might have. He wasn't sure he'd blame her.

Yet it wasn't Natasha's way—to put things off. To run and hide.

He showed up for his two-thirty lighting check right on time. Didn't bother to go early.

And didn't have a speech prepared, either. After stewing for the first half of the day, he'd calmed down a bit. Natasha was carrying on business as usual.

He could do that, too. Piece of cake.

Except that as soon as he saw the auburn-haired TV star he wanted to get closer to her...

The temptation didn't last long. Seconds, maybe. He was a grown man with requisite self-control. He did not like being attracted to his new business partner.

"Hi." She came toward him with her game face on. "A couple of my guys told me you were asking for me earlier. Sorry, things have been crazy here this morning. A cable broke, the router was down..." She paused. "Anyway, I gave instructions to everyone that anytime you ask for me, I am to be found immediately."

He nodded, relaxing in spite of the tension between them. She hadn't been avoiding him. They could work with the rest of it.

Clearly she was as motivated to do so as he was.

They were momentarily alone—heading toward their dressing rooms to change into the next day's wardrobe.

"About last night..." He had to get it out, set things straight. Offer assurances. Reinstate boundaries...

The look she gave him appeared in no way pained, but her slight frown said she was confused. "Last..." Then her brow cleared. "Oh, the kiss, you mean." She chuckled. "Don't worry about it, Spencer. It happens."

What did that mean? *"It happens?"*

But why should he think it wouldn't? Not with him, of course. However...she was a television personality. And a rich and beautiful woman. A stolen kiss was clearly no big deal to her.

"It goes with the territory," she was saying. "We're flirting on air, convincing our viewers there's chemistry between us. We're human. It's natural that we'd be compelled to test the truth of our make-believe world..."

Now, that made sense. Good sense. He liked it. A lot.

He explained, "It's just...it doesn't happen all the time in my world, and..."

"I know." She leaned in like she was sharing a secret with him. "Mine, either," she said. "Not personally. But I know the score. And with cohosts, testing the waters is a natural step in the process. You see what it's like and you move on. Takes the mystery out of it. It's all just settling in to play the part."

"You're sure?"

"Positive." She squeezed his hand. "For what it's worth…it was a relatively painless growing pain."

His kiss had been a growing pain.

A painless one.

It happened to everyone. Meant nothing.

Which meant Jolene—or someone—was still on. He hadn't checked the online dating site in a few days. He'd best get to it.

He was really glad he and Natasha had had the conversation.

BETSY BROUGHT THE kids in later that afternoon, after school. Spencer had told Natasha that he and Bryant would be out on the ranch, tending to some cattle that had been trapped by a fallen telephone pole with live wire attached. The rotted pole had given way just before lunch, and a cowhand had noticed that there was a problem when it had shown up on one of the monitors in the bunkhouse. A couple of his full-timers were out there already, corralling the cattle into a makeshift pen.

Even ranching had moved into the technological world, Spencer had informed her. He had cameras all over his property.

"When do I get to go on stage?" Justin asked, all puffed up and walking with exaggerated swagger in his new cowboy boots. Justin's old pairs were all scuffed up, and Spencer had insisted on purchasing him a new pair—which he hadn't been allowed to wear outside. At all.

"In just a couple of minutes," Natasha said, grinning to herself. Betsy had left, and Natasha was waiting for Angela before she got to work with Justin. The little boy knew what to do. Natasha's concern was keeping his brain occupied enough to allow him to focus.

Tabitha tugged on the edge of her shirt. "Guess what, Natasha? An old lady likes us!"

"It's a secret, Tabby." Justin's tone had just the right amount of exasperation.

"Not from Natasha. She's our friend."

"She said it's a secret from everryyy-booddyy."

"Daddy says it's against the law to tell kids to keep secrets from their moms and dads."

"Natasha isn't our mom."

"But since we don't have one, she could be our…stepmom."

Natasha's heart was leaping and bounding

right along with her stomach as she stood there, a mere witness now to the face-off between brother and sister.

"An old lady likes us!"

As much as she was interested in, and taking in, the rest of the debate between the kids, she couldn't let go of that first line.

"An old lady likes us!"

According to Spencer, Claire Williamson was back in Washington, DC. Having agreed to wait to hear from Spencer.

But what if she'd lied? She was a lobbyist. In a family of lobbyists. Used to convincing others to think what she wanted them to think…

"What's a stepmom?" Justin asked.

"I dunno. Amanda has a new one."

Natasha could only assume that Amanda was a girl at school.

"Natasha?" Both kids were looking at her now. "What's a stepmom?" The question came from Tabitha. The little girl's hair was falling out of a ponytail that was no longer in the center of her head, if it ever had been.

Presuming that Tabitha liked it that way, she left it alone. But, as had happened pretty much every time she'd seen the little girl— other than after she'd been with Lori and

Diane, their hair and makeup crew—Natasha itched to take a brush to the long brown locks.

"When a dad marries after he has children, the woman he marries becomes a mom to his children." She pulled words out of the air, praying that Spencer wouldn't be angry with her.

"What does the *step* part mean?" the little girl asked.

"Yeah, what about that?" Justin, his little hands in his pockets, asked. He was no longer looking at Natasha, more interested, apparently, in the divot he was digging in the dirty floor with the shiny toe of his new boot.

"The *step* means the children were there before the mom." She was sweating. More nervous than she'd been before her first television appearance.

Which was absolutely nuts.

Taking Tabitha's hand, she knelt down in front of the little girl. "Tell me about the old lady who likes you," she said, hoping that she had the proper combination of happy interest and compelling adult in her tone.

"She comed to see us at school today," Tabitha said, glancing up as a camera rolled past. And then following its journey toward the stage. They'd been working on the lens...

"Who was she?"

"I dunno." Tabitha shrugged. Reached for Natasha's hair and started running her fingers through it. She'd worn it down all day.

"Where did you see her?"

Justin jumped toward them with both feet. Kicking up a cloud of dust. "She seed us," he said. "She called our names out."

"And waved," Tabitha inserted.

"Where?"

"When we got on the bus," Justin said, jumping again.

Natasha wanted to stop him. To brush off the dust. But she had to find out everything she could about this woman while she was still fresh in the kids' minds.

"How did you know she liked you?"

"She smiled," Tabitha said. "She was dressed up like church and was pretty, and she smiled."

"Yeah, and Tabby says that's when you know someone likes you," Justin added, giving his sister a not-so-common admiring glance. He punctuated his words with individual nods.

"But she didn't come toward you or call you over to her?"

"Nope." Justin spoke. Tabitha shook her head. "She just called your names."

"Yep." Justin spoke. Tabitha nodded.

"You two know that no matter how much people like you or if they know your names or even your daddy's name, you never go off with them, right?"

Justin rolled his eyes. "Stranger danger," Tabitha said. "And Daddy would take away everything we ever liked forever," she added dramatically. Justin nodded.

Natasha had to talk to Spencer.

CHAPTER TWENTY

SPENCER WAS ON the side-by-side, dragging the dead pole, secured by rope, behind him, when his cell phone rang. He had kids. He always checked.

Natasha. Work. It could wait.

Justin had had a practice scheduled that afternoon.

"Longfellow," he said into the phone.

"I think Claire Williamson is still in town."

Glancing in the rearview mirror, he saw Bryant on an identical side-by-side, back and to the left of him. He was seeing Spencer out to the road, where he'd leave the pole to be picked up, and then Bryant was heading back to help the guys herd the cattle to another field.

Not now. He didn't need Claire Williamson in his vocabulary that day.

As soon as he rid himself of the telephone pole, Spencer was going straight back to the compound. He had calls to make.

Not because of the pole, or the wire. But because while he'd been out on the property, Spencer had checked on a small orange grove his father had planted. It didn't amount to much. A couple of hundred trees. Didn't make enough money for him to consider it a viable part of the business. But it had been his father's.

And he'd seen larvae on several leaves from the light brown apple moth—a non-native invasive pest from Australia that had migrated to Hawaii and most recently to California. The bug was said to cost the state potentially millions in lost produce and controlling expenses and could affect not only fruit and produce but also many of the other trees on his property. He had to get it off his land.

"You still there?" Natasha's voice was soft. Calling to him in a way that made him want to answer, in spite of the fact that he didn't want to hear what she had to say.

"Yeah. What makes you think Claire's here?"

He was no happier when he heard a replay of the twins' conversation regarding the "old lady" who liked them.

"She didn't approach them," Natasha was

quick to add. "Or attempt to get them to come to her…"

"They know better than that." He hoped. If they didn't, they would before either of them stepped foot outside the house again.

Too bad he couldn't put Daisy Wolf on the woman's scent. Send her to school with the kids.

"Tabitha told me that you'd take away everything they ever liked forever if they did," Natasha said with a soft chuckle. Like the moment could use some levity.

And he realized she was right. It could. Claire hadn't specifically promised to go home. He'd just assumed she would. She was a busy woman. Not one you'd think would have the time to hang around a small southeastern California town.

"What are you going to do?" Natasha asked. "Call her?"

"No. She didn't do anything illegal. I still want to avoid the fight if I can. I'm going to do what I said I was going to do." He was making it up as he went, but liked the soundness of the plan as it unfolded between them. "I'm going to think about it. And call her cell when I'm ready to speak with her again."

"I wouldn't wait too long." As he'd come to expect, her advice was reasonable.

"I don't intend to."

"I'll be done at the studio by seven. We can talk more then if you'd like."

Afraid he'd *like* it too much, he wouldn't have accepted the invitation if he could have. But… "Jolene's coming for dinner," he told her.

He'd invited her over as soon as he'd left the studio that afternoon. If the kiss between him and Natasha had just been a work-related growing pain, then there was no reason to diverge from his original plan.

"I'd say that by the sounds of things, that's a good plan." Natasha's agreement solidified his own certainty to the rightness of his course.

The only reason he felt a pang of disappointment, of letdown, as they rang off was because of the bad news she'd delivered.

Not because any part of him wished a different woman would be joining him and the twins for dinner that night.

NATASHA MET JOLENE on Saturday. She took the fact that Spencer had invited the woman to sit in the audience with Tabitha to mean that Friday night's dinner had gone well and his plan to ask Jolene to marry him, to make her a part of his family, was on track.

Jolene held her hand out shyly when Spencer introduced them. She looked Natasha in the eye when she smiled. And thanked her for allowing her to attend the day's taping.

Natasha played her part. The gracious, successful show host and producer who flirted on stage with her rancher cohost. And when Spencer took her hand at one point, linking his fingers with hers, and she felt that same peculiar thrill she'd noticed when he kissed her—a sensation that swept through her like the chills—she put the whole thing down to professional growing pains. She'd never had a cohost before.

Had never had an onstage flirtation.

The whole thing had been Angela's idea. And the noticeable boost in the first week's ratings gave credibility to the rightness of Angela's choice.

And now they'd be on stage together, one segment a year, for four more years. At least. She wasn't worried. She'd adapt. She always did.

Because it was good for *Family Secrets*.

And what was good for *Family Secrets* was good for her.

"DID YOU TELL Jolene about Claire?" Standing on stage with Spencer near the end of the show, Natasha turned off her mic and asked the question. They needed shots of her and Spencer on stage while the cooking was going on—looking like they were enjoying themselves. She and her crew would clip and paste them in as appropriate before that night's airing.

He glanced at their contestants, grinning. "No."

Impressed with how quickly he'd picked up the ability to be "on" and real at the same time, with how quickly he'd grown comfortable with his role, she nodded, as though agreeing with something he'd just said.

In the red Western shirt that fit him to perfection and tight black jeans, he looked... exactly as they'd wanted him to appear to their viewers. Like everybody's fantasy cowboy.

"I'd have thought you'd tell her." Why was she pushing this? And why did she feel a momentary thrill knowing that, for now, his deepest problem was between the two of them?

Like they were best friends or something. He shook his head. "If I decide to ask her to marry me, I don't want her to think I'm only doing so because of Claire Williamson," he said. "Because I'm not. My plan was already in place."

Curious about that, she studied him. "Because…"

"It's time."

The innocuous words gave her nothing. And yet…she understood them. Life had a way of letting you know that a change was necessary. Like her funk over the past few months, culminating with the news of her mother and Stan's breakup. She'd needed to adopt a cat.

And she'd needed a new professional challenge, too, which had now come her way. Funny, that. Life knew what you needed even when you didn't.

And often had a way of providing it, too.

ANGELA CALLED SPENCER Tuesday evening to set up a time for a film crew to get some shots of him around his herd. She also suggested that he hire a firm to help him come up with branding for his beef.

When he explained that Longfellow Ranch's brand had been around for more than a century, she asked for an image she could use and permission to use it.

With the merger of two TV stations, the establishment was going to be taking on more of the responsibility of getting advertising revenue. Because ratings were up for this segment, they wanted to run a national commercial, paid for by the station, about the new venture with Longfellow Beef.

He agreed to meet with the film crew on Wednesday. And to speak with his lawyer about the rest of it.

He wondered if he needed additional legal aid. Someone in the entertainment industry. Or someone in national food distribution— beyond selling cattle.

He wondered what he should wear for filming the next day.

He didn't ask any questions.

Angela wasn't Natasha.

And Spencer had always been one to keep his own counsel.

IT WAS GOOD business for Natasha to accompany the film crew to Longfellow Ranch on Wednesday. And to make the trip even more worth the drive time, she scheduled appointments for later that afternoon with the design firm that she'd hired to remodel the Longfellow studio. The architect was driving out from Palm Desert to do a walk-through with her.

She had appointments with a couple of local businesses on Thursday, too, lining up sponsors for future episodes. Angela normally handled the local ad base, leaving the national, more moneyed clients for her, but now that they were going to be a permanent part of Longfellow Ranch for a number of years, and because Longfellow Beef was going to be a notable part of the show, she wanted to tap into local money.

Every town had it—the elite who held power. Those who, if she offered a win-win, could be counted on to support their efforts rather than fight them. Media was bound to find the town, at least for curiosity's sake. She wanted to make certain *Family Secrets* had some friends there when they did.

Filled with the familiar adrenaline, she arrived at the ranch in time to drop off her things at her cabin. Took time to open a window and let in some fresh air. And to have a glass of the tea she'd left in the refrigerator Saturday before heading back to town.

She'd said goodbye to the kids while Spencer had been introducing Jolene to Angela after the show.

She'd left without saying goodbye to her cohost.

It hadn't seemed right for her to intrude on Jolene's time.

The rap on her door was unexpected. And yet…she wasn't surprised. She'd come early. Driven up the main drive, past the house. If Spencer was around, he'd know she was there.

Her cabin was the only place they could be assured of being alone.

Not that they had need to be.

He was holding a pose that nearly tripped her heart when she opened the door. Pure cowboy in tight, worn blue jeans and a red-and-white-checked Western shirt, his thumbs hooked in his front pockets, drawing attention to the big, shiny buckle on his belt.

"Got a minute?" he asked, a slight grin shining from his eyes more than curving his mouth.

"Yeah." She sipped tea to rid herself of her suddenly dry throat.

When had he become such a consummate actor? And how had she suddenly grown susceptible to such frivolous things?

Tempted to step out onto the porch with him, she thought about someone seeing them there and drawing the wrong conclusions.

And if that someone happened to be Angela stopping at her cabin before going down to the studio, she'd make a big deal out of nothing.

She drew back, allowing him to follow her to the simply but comfortably furnished living room.

CHAPTER TWENTY-ONE

PERCHING ON THE arm of the big leather couch, Natasha shrugged. "What's up?"

"I wanted your opinion on this week's wardrobe," Spencer said, stopping just a foot away. For a second there she detected that hint of uncertain cowboy she'd seen in him a time or two before.

But no less macho cowboy.

And it occurred to her that he hadn't been posing on her porch. That he'd been the same Spencer Longfellow she'd met the first time she'd been on his ranch. And every time since.

Maybe she was the one changing.

Or...

She shook her head. Didn't like being confused.

"If that's it, it's fine," she told him, sipping again. It seemed the most prudent thing to do. The safest. Sip. Swallow. Distract her senses. "The idea for your commercials is to look natural," she told him. Her crew would direct the actual ads. And edit them. With Angela's input.

She'd have final approval when all was said and done, before the finished product was sent to Spencer for his sign-off. Generally their national sponsors had their own firms to produce their advertising. Some local ones did, too. But Natasha and her team offered their services, as well.

He was watching her. A strange look in his eyes.

She didn't appreciate feeling like a bug under a microscope. "Was there anything else?"

"I had a call from a meat packing company," he told her. "They want to sit down and talk about packaging Longfellow Beef, starting sometime next year."

She wasn't surprised. "When's the meeting?"

"Next week."

"I'd talk to more than one before I made a decision," she told him.

"They're local."

"There's something to be said for that, but I'd still talk to more than one." She'd been at this a long time. And knew that the more people you talked to, the more you learned about what you didn't know you didn't know.

He nodded.

So…they'd discuss business. As partners should. Good. She glanced at her watch— a smartwatch that showed her fifty unread emails from the time it had taken her to drive out from Palm Desert.

Showed her, too, that she had another half hour before she was expected at the studio on the other side of the half-mile compound.

"She said no." He hadn't changed positions any, still stood there with his thumbs in his pockets. So when it seemed that Spencer's entire demeanor changed, Natasha couldn't be sure if it was her imagination or something to take note of.

"Who said no about what?"

"Jolene. She said she wouldn't marry me."

The sweating tea glass slipped in her fingers. She caught it before it fell to her knee. "I didn't realize you were going to ask so soon," she said, buying herself time while she tried to comprehend why the news was so huge to her.

Even if they'd become friends as well as business associates, whether or not he married his first choice was not a life-changing event for her.

Or shouldn't be.

He shrugged. "I wasn't necessarily going to ask so soon, but I called Claire Williamson," he said. "Sunday morning while the kids were in the chicken coop with Betsy. She was back on the East Coast but had given me her cell number. She picked up on the first ring. Said she's planning another trip out at the end of October. She wants a formal introduction to the kids at that time. And to take them to Palm Desert for the night."

"You don't have to let her do that."

"I know. And I told her so. If she wants to see them, it has to be here."

"And?" Natasha was standing now, having set her glass on the coffee table and her hands on her hips. She'd spent much of her life dealing with entitled people like Claire Williamson. The woman might think she had the upper hand dealing with a naive rancher, but Natasha could help Spencer—who was far more aware than the other woman apparently gave him credit for—fight this battle.

"She conceded that, in the beginning, it would be best for the children if the visits were on familiar territory. Because they're so young."

The threat implied in those words, that Claire was only biding her time before fighting for the right to take the children for private visits in her world, was hardly concealed.

"Why is she doing this? Why now? Why the sudden interest?" She shook her head. He'd said she hadn't known about the kids, that her daughter had recently married, but…

Spencer shrugged, looking…vulnerable… again. "The way Kaylee talked about me… about the kids…there in the end…we were clearly an embarrassment to her. Dusty, small town rats, I believe were the words she used in her worst moments."

Natasha saw red. Blinked. Thought about how her mother would sit on the bench in court and remain calm no matter how horrifying the circumstances being presented. She'd asked her how she did it. Susan had said it was a matter of will. Of taking deep breaths and disassociating. A matter of focusing on the job, the law, the words, the facts and solution, not the emotion attached to them.

Natasha had been about ten at the time. And had been practicing ever since.

"But if you're a nationally known rancher

with coveted Wagyu beef…" She didn't want it to be that. But it made sense. Not that they cared about his money…it was the clout. Beef, ranchers…lobbyists could use those votes. "Did she tell you how she'd found out about the kids?" she asked. But then it dawned on her.

"The show." She should have thought of it before. But her show, *Family Secrets*, while hugely successful in its venue, was still just a reality cooking show. On a cable station. Not prime-time television. And the kids…probably just Tabitha at that point…had been on air for only seconds…

"We played up the fact that Longfellow Ranch children…your children…were guest judges."

She felt sick. Ads had been running for the ranch segment for six weeks. If the Williamsons had known that Spencer was going to be featured and tuned in to see him, to see what their daughter had married, and escaped, they'd have seen at least a mention of the kids. Of course, she'd had no way of knowing that Spencer's current life needed to be hidden from any aspect of his past life. He clearly hadn't, either, or he'd never ever have taken the chance…no matter how much financial remuneration he stood to gain.

He was looking slightly sick to his stomach. "That explains why she said that it wasn't proper for little girls to be raised solely by philandering fathers… She saw the first segment. Saw you and me and…"

For a second she started to panic. And then she focused. "We still don't know why she cared," she said slowly. "Do they suddenly want to parade their grandchildren around because they are no longer an embarrassment? Or did she really not know about the kids, and she has a genuine desire to get to know them? A desire made more critical in light of Kaylee's recent marriage and the certainty she won't have more kids?"

Studying her, he said, "I almost think it's the latter," he told her. "Unfortunately. Because that will make her a determined powerful woman on a hunt she's not about to lose."

"A mama bear," Natasha agreed.

"She said she'd just landed in the city and rented a car," he was saying. "I didn't think about it at the time, but that could imply that the trip was spur-of-the-moment. Which it would have been if she'd just found out she was a grandmother. And cared."

"She didn't approach the kids," Natasha was remembering. "As though she had their best interests at heart…"

"…and yet she couldn't leave without seeing them," Spencer added. "She said that. When I spoke to her on Sunday."

Natasha considered the facts. The consequences and potential consequences.

"You said you had a second choice in mind if the kids and Jolene didn't hit it off."

He nodded, his chin jutting slightly. His reticence could be so irritating sometimes. Didn't he get that she was trying to help him?

"So…have you called her?"

He shook his head. "I don't know her yet. I've signed up online and had responses, but so far, none that I would consider meeting, let alone bring home to meet my children."

"And Jolene said no." She still couldn't believe that one. What woman wouldn't want to marry Spencer Longfellow?

Other than the fact that he didn't love her, of course. Even she had been a little put off by his attitude about not marrying for love.

"I didn't tell you why she said no." His gaze became intense. She tried to read the message there.

But couldn't decipher it…

"Why did she say no?"

He crossed his arms over his chest. "Because of the way I look at you."

"What? That's crazy!" What was wrong with people?

"I told her it was all for the show. Told her about the stage chemistry thing. But she said a woman knows. She was willing to think about marrying me without my being in love with her because she knows me and thinks I'd make a good husband. And because she's already falling in love with the kids. But in light of the recent contract you and I just signed, she's not willing to go through with it, knowing that you and I will still be in contact."

Her heart was pounding. This wasn't her fault. "That's ludicrous."

His shrug didn't offer any solution whatsoever. They needed a solution.

"We can tear up the contract." It was between him and *Family Secrets*, which meant her. Not the studio. And if it meant the kids would have a traditional home that would keep them out of a future court battle with a wealthy and powerful grandmother manipulating them...

"No." He shook his head. "The money I'm going to make is a godsend, coming at the same time I'm faced with the possibility of an expensive cross-country battle. Without the show, I'd lose not only that money but also all of the advertising, the beef packaging... I'd go back to being a small cattle rancher with the distinction of raising Wagyu. It would take me years, the rest of my life, to get this operation making anywhere near the money that it's going to make with your help. Instead of raising my herd from scratch, I'll be able to purchase more purebreds to breed."

She nodded. Good. This was good. Her heart was still pumping like there was no to-morrow.

Now, solution...

"Maybe you should sign up for multiple dating sites..."

"And hinge everything on the hope that I get someone perfect right away?"

When every potential candidate would know about Natasha, her show and the im-pression they were giving?

She needed to think. Considered calling her mother.

The man needed a wife. Not a lover. Just a wife.

"So, I'll marry you." Everything inside her froze as the words popped out of her mouth.

Everything but the thoughts that were tripping over themselves. "It would be the perfect stop to any hope Claire could have of eventually getting anyone to believe the kids are better off with her. Who would dare take children away from America's sweethearts? Or even think about doing so? Dedicated dad, great family cooking show mom…

"We could get married on *Family Secrets*," she went on. "Have contestants provide our wedding dinner. Our cake. Everything. Think about it. It would be the romance of the year, televised nationally. Viewers will eat it up. Public perception will be set. And there's a silver lining, too. Ratings will soar, which means *Family Secrets*' value soars. And our signature beef will soar, too. It's what's called in the business world a win-win."

She was rambling. But not like an idiot. Every word made perfect business sense. It was the deal of a lifetime. And she was putting it together on the spot.

The feeling she got when she knew she was onto something big, something winning, had never been stronger.

Until she noticed Spencer Longfellow standing in front of her, mouth open, staring at her like she'd lost her mind.

CHAPTER TWENTY-TWO

HAD THE WOMAN just proposed to him? The idea was so preposterous, Spencer couldn't believe she was serious.

Or even that he'd understood her correctly.

"The next segment doesn't start until January," she said, "so it couldn't be a done deal by Christmas. But we could announce our engagement on the special, one episode, live Thanksgiving Day show. That should do the trick as far as Christmas vacation is concerned. There's no way the kids can be gone since they'll be playing such a big part in the wedding and we'll need fittings, rehearsals, scripting. They'd need to do some filming for ads and…"

The nerves in the back of his neck felt like they might snap. She just didn't stop. Didn't shut up.

There was no way he was going to let his kids be part of some kind of circus act.

"No ads with the kids." He got some words out. Considered them a victory.

She frowned at him for a minute but was blessedly silent. And then nodded. "You're right. That wouldn't be good for them. I'm still new to this whole kid thing, but don't worry. I will defer to you on everything where they're concerned."

"Are we negotiating?" He almost laughed.

Completely serious, she nodded. "Of course."

He couldn't believe this conversation was real. That he was standing in the cabin he'd lived in alone so many years before, with a woman who was so much larger than life she'd begun to believe her own hype.

"You don't negotiate marriage," he said.

"You do."

"No. I do not."

"What do you think you were proposing to Jolene?" She shook her head, spread her hands. "It was a business arrangement. You wanted her to agree to live in your home, love your children and be a partner to you. In exchange, you'd be a loyal partner to her."

"You live in Palm Desert."

"Yes. But I'll have an office here, too. A lot of couples have two homes. It makes sense that you'd stay here, with the kids, because you can't do your work anyplace but here. You need to be on your ranch. And the kids have school."

"So we'll live apart." He wasn't considering the idea. Still wasn't even sure she was serious. But it was so...outlandish, he wanted to hear her out. For future laughs, if nothing else.

"Not as far as anyone else is concerned," she said. "I'm working this out as we go, but think about it. I could live in the city during the week as needed. Commute when necessary. I'll have the office here made larger, and when I can, I'll work from the ranch. And sometimes you and the kids can come to the city. Just to keep up appearances. We can take them to shows. To the zoo. All the things parents do with kids, whatever they want. My condo has four bedrooms, so there'd be plenty of room. We could keep clothes in both places..."

She was getting way too far ahead of herself. He couldn't even imagine this scenario on some situation comedy featuring the ridiculous.

It was time to preserve his plan.

"I want a wife."

"You want a business partner."

"No, I want a wife. I want to have the same woman in my bed for the rest of my life. Someone to grow old with. And...maybe have more kids with."

Finally she'd shut her mouth. Tight.

But only momentarily. "Good luck with that anytime soon," she said. "With our keeping up our on-screen flirtation for the foreseeable future. Think of Jolene's reaction."

"A lot of actors in Hollywood are married to people other than their on-screen partners."

"You said you didn't have anyone else in mind here. So you're back to finding someone on the internet in time for Christmas."

If he hadn't been so flabbergasted, he might have admired her tenaciousness. Kind of reminded him of his own.

But he'd also remembered something else. Another threat posed by any legal battle Claire Williamson might wage against him. Discovery. If he was married, there'd be no reason to look.

If he was married to a reality TV star, even if the truth came out, he'd have enough money to protect the ranch. And probably wouldn't need to because everyone knew that stars had dirt hiding in the corners of their closets.

He'd be seen as...imperfect...but not inadequate. In the future Natasha was painting, no one would dare challenge his right to his heritage.

But...

"It's a business deal, Spencer," she said, her tone not quite mocking. "Granted, a creative one, but then, I'm a creative person. I think outside the box. A lot of times, that's where you find answers to problems that seem insurmountable."

She wanted him to believe she was for real. And she was completely outside any frame of reference he had to pull from.

"We take it like any other business deal, one step at a time. If, in the future, you meet someone you want to marry, we can always part ways."

How could she make something so wrong, so ludicrous, sound...almost plausible?

"I'll be traveling quite a bit for the show over the next weeks," she told him. "And more overall since I'll be doing two other location segments. It'll be understandable that I'll be in and out..."

He couldn't do this.

He had to make it stop.

"I want a wife," he said. "A real relationship." Did she get what he was saying?

She stared at him.

"I understood you the first time," she told him. "So…fine."

"Fine?"

"Yes. We'll go into this understanding that you want a real marriage and that I agree to those terms. I would stipulate for the record, however, that I will need time to build up to that point with you."

Blood thrummed through him. Igniting him. Shutting down his brain.

He'd never heard anything like it. Was still standing there out of incredulity. Horrified and curious to see how far she would go.

"I suggest that over the next eight weeks, we concentrate on the courtship. As I said, I'll be traveling a lot with auditions, and now scouting potential locations for future shows, but when I'm not on the road, I'll spend as much time here as possible." She was pacing, a look of concentration on her face, as though she were addressing a board of directors. "It will work well since the studio renovations will be under way, and I need to be getting to know any potential sponsors I can find locally. You can introduce me around, which will help pull me into your fold."

Fascinating the way her mind worked. The

focus, the way she brought everything to-gether, it was like…art.

Business art.

"You and the kids should come to the city, as well," she said. "Visit the condo. We'll get some photos. Nothing big. Nothing that will expose the kids. Maybe we keep them in shadow and just you and I are visible… We can work on that. I've got a public-relations firm on retainer. I'll call them."

He needed a notepad to keep up with her.

"Then, at Thanksgiving, we make the en-gagement announcement. We can have the PR firm work on the logistics. Followed by a January wedding."

The whole situation was so fantastical he almost wished it was real. Just so he could watch it happen.

"I propose a six-month period after the wedding to settle into living together, to flesh out exactly what that looks like, how many nights a week we spend in each other's homes, that sort of thing, and then, at that time, we can proceed to move forward with the relationship side."

He couldn't just keep standing there.

"We'll need a prenuptial agreement," he said. "Something that keeps *Family Secrets* and the condo yours and Longfellow Ranch and all of its holdings mine." He was playing along with her out of perverseness. Looking for the way to catch her. To show her that her idea was preposterous.

She didn't even blink. "Of course." Clearly she'd assumed as much.

So he went for the big guns. "And the kids? I retain sole custody of them."

Her pause gave him pause. She stopped pacing. Faced him. He could almost see the thoughts speeding through her mental thoroughfare.

"I don't know how that works," she told him. "I mean, legally, if I'm their stepmother, that would automatically give me rights. And...if anything ever happened to you...well, you'd rather they stay here with me than go to Washington, right?"

Bearing a tone he'd never heard before, a certain vulnerability, her words touched him like nothing else in the conversation had done.

He felt like a jerk for messing with her.

"Natasha, I'm grateful for your offer. Frankly, the exuberance with which you jumped on board has me stunned. I don't know that anyone has ever come to my aid with such... ferociousness. I'm still trying to comprehend why you'd do such a thing. But…surely…you have to see that this is crazy."

"You like me."

"Of course I like you."

"You kissed me like you really like me."

"I like kissing you," he conceded. Now was not the time to think of *that* craziness. He'd fumbled once. And been with her several times since without repeating the mistake.

"I know it's unconventional, Spencer." She was sounding more like herself, and yet… softer. In some ways, he was facing a woman he'd never met before.

He didn't like being blindsided.

"But you and I…look at us…we're unconventional."

He wasn't. That was the point. He was a reliable family man with respectable standing in the community. A successful landowner, with more than a hundred years of heritage backing him. A good father. His whole reason for wanting a wife…before Claire came into the picture…was to complete the conventional image.

Getting ready to tell her so, he got out, "I—" when she cut him off.

"You made a plan to marry, Spencer. If one woman didn't want you, you'd move down your numerical list of potentials to choice two. You want a partnership without love and all of the drama and unpredictability it brings."

Crap. Did she have an answer for everything?

Then it occurred to him to turn it on her. She'd said if he found another woman, she'd release him from their…agreement. But…

"I'm not the type of guy who'd be okay with his wife taking an interest in other men."

She shrugged. "I figured as much."

He had to rattle her. He didn't even know, at that point, why it was so important. It just was.

"You're telling me that in order to help me, a near stranger, you're willing to sign away the probability of you ever marrying for love?"

Her chuckle was pretty much his undoing. "I've known for years that that wasn't going to happen," she told him. "Look at me, Spencer."

He *was* looking. That was part of the problem. He liked what he saw far too much. And knew that other men did, too. Eventually one would come along whom she liked back, and…

"I'm…determined," she said. "Or…to put it bluntly…bossy. I'm far too good at calling my shots to give anyone else the right to do so. But here…this situation…it doesn't just help you with your two major goals in life—keeping your kids on the ranch with you, safe and happy, and growing the ranch into a business that will give them lifetime security—but it also helps me. My life…it's been missing something. Tabitha and Justin… they fill those holes."

When her words faded away, his full attention came to the fore. She'd faltered once before in this conversation. Talking about his kids. She loved them. Or was close to it.

The game had just changed.

CHAPTER TWENTY-THREE

WHEN SHE KNEW she was onto something powerful, something right, Natasha didn't give up. She was her mother's daughter. Aware of this tendency, she channeled it, as her mother always had, into something positive.

And she lived a mostly lonely life. Keeping herself apart from others who could fall prey to her strengths. Angela had been around so long not only because she was great at her job but also because she could hold her own with Natasha.

Natasha was positive that while her proposal to Spencer Longfellow had crossed boundaries of expected behavior, it was the best answer for all four of them. Spencer, the kids, her. The minute the idea had occurred to her, she'd gotten that feeling. The one that led her to victory every single time.

Still, being right didn't guarantee success—most particularly in this current matter. She couldn't force him to marry her.

Spencer had a will of his own. Maybe even as strong as hers. Angela respected him, and that was saying something.

He wasn't jumping on the idea. Worse, he seemed almost to be…laughing at it?

"Just out of curiosity, how do you see this relationship being good for the children down the road?"

Raising her head, she studied him. He was completely serious.

Sensing the possibility of a turn in the negotiations in her favor, she thought carefully before replying.

"I see them growing up with two champions in their lives, two people who love them unconditionally and who will always be there for them."

"What if we decide to end our arrangement?"

Shrugging, she shook her head. Didn't need time to think about that one. "They'd still have two champions in their lives, two people who love them unconditionally and who will always be there for them."

"What if you found out, somewhere down the road, that I have some dirty little secret…?"

"Do you?"

"Maybe."

He was baiting her. "Are you involved in anything illegal?"

"No."

"Anything immoral?"

"Of course not."

"I suspect we all have things that we don't tell the world. We're entering an unusual, perhaps lifelong, business arrangement, Spencer. Not giving up our autonomy."

The designation was key. She couldn't do it otherwise.

And suspected that neither could he. He was more like her than he seemed ready to admit, as committed to his ranch as she was to *Family Secrets*—and any future ventures she'd create if *Family Secrets* ever served its time.

The sky was her limit. Not Spencer. Or anyone else.

"You're really serious about this." He was staring her right in the eye.

She didn't blink. "I am. Believe me, I know it's out of the blue, but can you think of a reason why it isn't a good decision? Why it won't work?" Because she couldn't.

Except… "Depending on how much time I spend here, I might have to bring Lily here to live." Which, now that she thought about it, *did* work, because then the kitten wouldn't be alone so much when she traveled.

"Fine. Cats are good in farmhouses. They keep the mouse population down."

Her heart started to pound again. She thought of her mother up on the bench. The deep breath. The focus. "So, you're agreeing?" she asked when she could.

"I can't believe I'm saying this, but I'm agreeing to think about it."

She wanted his answer. "For how long?"

His grin screwed with her focus. "You got someone else on the hook?" he asked.

He knew she didn't. "If I'm going to be embarking on a project of such a scope, I'll need time to prepare. We have a Thanksgiving deadline for our announcement if we plan to forestall any viable attempt Claire would have to make to take the kids for any period of visitation over Christmas."

As always, sticking to the facts, to the logic, brought the answers. Kept the solution in clear focus. Susan would be proud of her.

Susan. She'd have to tell her mother she was getting married.

If Spencer agreed.

For the first time, she felt a note of real doubt. Saw it, not felt it. Her mother was a strong proponent of freedom. She'd lived her whole life as an example to Natasha of who she was and how to live with who she was.

Her mother was not going to approve of a marriage—any marriage—for her daughter. But only because she'd be certain that such a union could only end in disaster.

But this one wouldn't. It wasn't a traditional marriage. It was a business deal being signed in family court.

She'd just have to make certain that Susan had all the facts.

"Having second thoughts?" Spencer's words brought her back to the cabin in the desert. She saw him watching her, a strange expression on his face, kind of warm and... affectionate?

"Absolutely not," she told him. "So, when can I expect an answer from you?"

"Right now," he told her, his gaze piercing. "I agree to your plan, Natasha. I have some questions, some stipulations, but overall, I agree to your plan."

She couldn't speak. Couldn't hear anything but thickness in her ears. Like she was standing in the midst of a rushing wind.

Sucking in air just in time before she had to sit down, she forced a smile.

"I'm sure we'll both have questions," she managed. "Let's each make a list, and we can discuss them at our next meeting."

"Meeting? We're going to have meetings?"

"Regularly." That was a given. "This has to succeed, Spencer. Which means we have to stay on top of it."

He was grinning again. She didn't like what that did to her.

"When is our next meeting?"

"I don't know." She frowned. "I'm not going to do all the work here, Spencer. You can be in charge of meeting times... No, wait, I guess it makes sense that I do that, considering that I'm the one who'll be coming and going so much."

"I'll need a couple of days' notice, when possible."

"For the meetings? Or my coming and going?"

"If this is going to be your home, Natasha, you're welcome anytime. I was speaking of meetings. However, now that you mention it, I would like to be kept apprised of your schedule."

No one but Angela had access to that. Because she didn't report to anyone. Yet...his request made sense. "Okay," she said. And added, "And I'll need yours and the kids'."

"Fine."

They talked about sharing an online calendar. Spencer said he'd set it up.

She agreed.

And they both went to work. On separate parts of the ranch.

All things considered, Natasha was proud of herself. She'd had a very productive morning.

HE HAD HIS LIST. And wasn't completely hating all aspects of Natasha's plan. In some ways, it worked out quite well. They'd have their separate lives—it was clear that couldn't change for either one of them.

There'd be no messiness like there'd been with Kaylee. No recriminations or threats or defensiveness if, at some time in the future, either one of them wanted out of their arrangement.

And in the meantime…it was like he'd won the lottery. His kids would have a female influence in their lives—and he'd have his family unit, too. Claire Williamson would no longer have a leg to stand on in a custody battle when he was married. Every potential argument she'd raised had stemmed from him being a single father with a start-up cattle business and limited resources, while she could offer Tabitha the world—and a grandmother's womanly influences.

Under Natasha's plan, his business was going to soar. And yet…he gave up none of his autonomy. He was taking on a silent partner where the ranch was concerned.

Yes, the more he thought about the plan, the more he liked it. So much so that he stopped by the studio to tell her that afternoon.

She was in a meeting.

He told Angela not to disturb her.

And was glad to know that nothing had changed between them.

NATASHA WORKED TOO late to have dinner with the kids. Or to tell them good-night. It was going to happen. A lot. She knew that. And knew she was entitled to work late when needed.

Still, she was feeling a bit…deflated…as she drove slowly past the main house and down to her cabin. But figured the majority of her unease came from the phone call she had to make to her mother.

It was almost eleven in New York. Susan

would still be up. And Natasha, like her mother, was one to face difficult deeds head-on, to get them done, rather than stew about them.

Forgoing dinner, she made herself a piece of toast with peanut butter. Poured a glass of fresh-squeezed lemonade—a gift from Betsy—and sat down at her kitchen table with a notepad and pen.

Susan would have suggestions. Probably geared toward showing Natasha that she could be making the biggest mistake of her life.

She wasn't going to change her mind. But she didn't like being at odds with her mother. When you were different, as they were, sometimes each other was all you had...

"You're *what*? Did you say you're getting married? To the rancher?"

Natasha had expected the incredulity. Holding the phone away from her ear, she frowned. She hadn't expected the excitement that was raising her mother's voice a couple of octaves.

"Yes. Well...we're not officially getting engaged until the Thanksgiving live show, but yes, we will be married in January. Here on the ranch. So you'll need to clear your calendar..." She talked about dates.

"I can't believe it! Oh, Natasha, I'm just so...happy for you."

What? Well, then, "I'm just so happy you're happy," she said and proceeded to give her mother the entire rundown of her business proposition. The wins for everyone in so many ways.

Highlighting what was, for her, one of the biggest wins of all, aside from *Family Secrets*.

"I'm going to have a family, Mom, but keep my autonomy," she said. If the arrangement worked as projected, she wouldn't be alone in her old age. A retirement plan like none other.

When she'd shared all of the details, she fell silent and took a bite of cold toast. The peanut butter was still good.

The lemonade chaser was nice, too. Not too tart. Not too sweet. She'd have added a touch more water to soften the sharpness of the lemon...

"Mom? You still there?"

"I'm here."

Uh-oh.

"I thought you were pleased I was getting married." Her stomach sank as she waited for the conversation she'd been dreading.

"You don't love him."

"Of course not."

"Marriage is for love, Natasha. Not for business."

"But…"

"It's a sacred bind."

"It's a legal contract," Natasha countered.

"Because we as a society define it as such, but that's not what the personal, lifetime partnership between two people is all about."

"You love Stan but you won't marry him." She sounded like a petulant kid. Even to her own ears. And hated that her mother still had the ability to bring that out of her.

"I won't marry him because I don't love him."

Shocked, Natasha leaned both elbows on the table and stared at the veneer top, as though within the faux wood grain she'd find something that would take away the sting of emotions trying to get the better of her.

"You…"

"I'm extremely fond of Stan." Susan's voice broke. "I miss him. But I don't love him."

"You should call him."

"No. That would be selfish and unfair. I won't marry a man I don't love. It's not right."

For the first time in her life, Natasha openly disagreed with her mother. Vehemently.

"I'm going to marry Spencer, Mom. It's the right thing for both of us." She'd considered everyone involved. Saw no losses.

Not even small ones.

It was the most perfect business deal she'd ever come across. Or even heard of.

"I wish you wouldn't."

"But you understand that I have to do what's right for me."

"Yes."

She'd never heard her mother sound so sad. "You should call Stan," Natasha tried again.

"I don't love him."

The denial bothered her. Maybe that was why she couldn't let it go. "How can you possibly know that? You probably do love him. You're just refusing to see that…"

She'd overstepped. She knew it the second the words left her mouth. Holding her breath, she waited. Would it make matters worse to apologize? Or did she show more respect by waiting humbly for Susan's verbal dressing-down?

"I know because I have been in love." Susan's words were the last thing Natasha had expected.

"You have?"

"Yes."

She had to… "When? With whom?"

"With your father."

"But…"

"He left me pregnant and alone. Because he didn't love me."

Whoa.

The world had tilted. Alarmingly. Her view of her mother…their relationship…everything she'd known it to be was disintegrating right before her eyes. Her mother, a victim of unrequited love?

"Have you ever tried to get in touch with him again?"

"Yes."

"When?"

"After you were born. The day you graduated from preschool. And high school. And college…"

"What did he say?"

"Nothing. He never responded."

He didn't want them. Didn't want the woman who'd spent her whole life loving him…

"I love you, Mom."

"I know you do. And I love you, too, Tasha."

She hadn't heard that name in…years.

"I'm going to be fine." She felt like the parent all of a sudden.

"Not if you marry this man, you won't."

So some things about Susan hadn't changed. And probably never would.

"Why do you say that? You're happy. And you've lived your whole life without a partner relationship built on love." It was something she was just now beginning to see—the fact that Susan really was happy. She'd made her own happiness. With everything she had.

"You aren't me, Natasha. You're a nurturer. I am not."

"That's not true. You're a great mom. And you and I, I've always known we're exactly alike. I'm proud to be like you."

"No, we're not."

The words cut her to the quick. Pushing away her half-eaten toast, she got up from the table. And had nowhere to hide. "Of course we are," she finally said. Arguing again, because she had no other choice.

"No, Natasha. I spend my day judging people. You spend yours helping make people's dreams come true…"

Her news had shocked her mother, as she'd known it would. Disappointed her. As she'd known it would. Susan was handling it badly, was all. She'd come around. Especially after she met Tabitha and Justin.

She hoped. Though Susan didn't have a lot

of cause to be around children, and had never seemed particularly enamored by them—especially in restaurants—she'd loved Natasha. Been a good mother to her.

Getting her mother to at least agree to mark herself off her judge calendar for the time in January she'd need to be in Palm Desert for the wedding, she rang off.

Her mother's goodbye had been the same as always. Same exact words. Almost as if things were back to normal.

Natasha had a feeling life wasn't ever going to return to the way it had always been.

CHAPTER TWENTY-FOUR

SPENCER WAS ALREADY in bed Wednesday night, almost asleep, when his phone signaled a text message.

Meet tomorrow at eight?

It was almost midnight.

The kids would be on the bus at seven fifty-five.

Your office, he typed back, keeping things businesslike. He had a nice office, too, but it was in his home. He wasn't ready to have their meetings there.

Not until this *project*, as she'd called it, was firmly in place.

Though he was worn out, he sat up. Grabbed his tablet off the bedside table and added a couple of items to the list that had been growing since he'd left her that morning. Then he checked hay and beef prices. Read some news. He did everything he could to keep his mind occupied so that he didn't think about the woman who was going to be a part of the rest of his life.

WITH HER SEATED on one side of the table serving as a temporary desk in his barn and soon-to-be full-time studio, and him on the other, they discussed everything on his list. And hers.

They were going to continue on as friends in front of the kids, letting them get used to having Natasha around more, having dinner with them whenever she was at the ranch and free, spending Saturday evenings with them after the remaining three shows. They'd wait until right before Thanksgiving to tell them they were getting married.

She'd continue to stay at the cabin until they were married, at which time she'd move to a spare bedroom in the house when she was on the ranch. For the first six months.

After the *Family Secrets* segments at the ranch were over, he and the kids would spend at least one night a week in Palm Desert—or as often as he could work it out that he could be gone overnight.

They would wait until the first of November and then, before the engagement was announced, each see their own lawyers regarding the prenuptial agreement so that all was in place before they went public.

They would hold hands where appropriate. And kiss occasionally.

He would keep her apprised of any major business decisions he made. She would do the same. The small things they didn't need to bother sharing.

She would pick out and purchase her own engagement ring.

He had it all down. Even managed to fall into a somewhat comfortable routine over the next weeks as the plan fell easily into action. Other than the "family"-style dinners and the offstage hand holding, everything was pretty much as it had been.

With one major difference—he felt secure for the first time in a long time.

He called Claire. Invited her to stay at the ranch with him and the kids the last weekend in October and wasn't the least bit surprised when she opted to stay in Palm Desert and drive out. What did surprise him was that she actually showed.

And that the visit went...well. It was low-key. They'd agreed not to tell the kids yet who she was, just said she was a friend, but she seemed genuinely interested in every aspect of their lives. And while every other sentence seemed to be filled with innuendo, promises to Tabitha that she'd take her to see Washington, DC, and that she'd love it there, the woman hadn't crossed a line that would have allowed him to end the visit.

Or prevent future visits.

He told Natasha so when she called from New Orleans an hour after Claire had left.

"She doesn't know about us yet," Natasha reminded him. "Next visit, I'll make sure I'm home…"

His gut clenched at the surge of emotions rocking through him.

Home.

She'd be home. He knew what she meant. And still, the word uprooted his world.

But more important was the sense of… something warm and fuzzy and therefore god-awful that came with knowing she had his back. That a woman as powerful, as sure of herself, as confident and contained as Natasha Stevens was on his team.

The realization was sickening.

So he went and took a shower.

BY THE FIRST Monday in November, Natasha was at her wits' end. She hadn't been sleeping. Her appetite was half of what it had been. She'd been to see her doctor. Had a full barrage of tests. She was in perfect health. The Longfellow Ranch *Family Secrets* segment had wrapped up with the highest ratings ever. Sponsors were flooding in. Plans were in full swing for the live Thanksgiving Day show, featuring dishes made by Natasha from mailed-in "family secret" recipes. The judges would choose their favorite dish. The submitter of that recipe would be one of the eight contestants on the January segment of *Family Secrets*.

Because of the wedding, they were filming the first segment of the year on site. The other three would be traveling—one to Longfellow Ranch.

And she was losing weight.

Late that night, she gave in and did what she'd always done… She called her mother.

"You know the problem, Natasha," her mother said without even asking about her physical symptoms. "It's this wedding."

It wasn't.

"You've been this way your whole life. Some people get nosebleeds when they lie. You can't sleep and you lose weight when you know you're doing something that goes against your instinctive sense of right. You're making a decision that isn't good for you."

She wanted her mother to be wrong.

But some part of her acknowledged, because she was at such a low point, that she'd called because she'd known what her mother would say.

Because she knew she was right.

"It's the perfect solution," she said, sitting out in the darkness of her walled-in garden, thinking about turning on the jets in the hot tub.

The kids had been there the previous weekend. It had been too cold for them to swim, but they'd loved being able to "take a bath outside."

She couldn't ever remember a better night spent in her own home.

"If it were the perfect solution, you'd be embracing it, rather than making yourself sick with forcing it."

She knew that, too.

"So, what do I do?"

"Uh-uh," Susan said. "I can't tell you that. Only you can figure out what's at war within you, Tasha."

Then why could her mother tell her the

marriage was wrong? If she couldn't give her the solution?

Now, in addition to feeling sick, she was adding peevish to her growing list of discomforts.

"Ask yourself what you most want from life. Answer honestly and act upon it, and you will be in the right place at the right time. Ask, answer, act, and you will be happy with you." The Law of Susan.

"I have."

"And?"

"*Family Secrets* is what I most want," she said, feeling a headache coming on. "My career, being my own boss, having the outlet for my creativity, making people's dreams come true, just like you said."

She'd been doing a lot of thinking over the past several weeks. Instead of sleeping.

"You sound sure."

"I am sure."

The pause at the other end of the line could have been purposeful. Whether it was or not, Natasha second-guessed herself. Asked herself again. Listened honestly to how she felt. *"Family Secrets,"* she said.

"So, how do you act upon that?"

"I don't know." She'd never felt so utterly

alone. "The marriage, it helps *Family Se-crets*. A lot. Our ratings have always been above average, but they're skyrocketing with Spencer on the show. Viewers love our relationship. I see that carrying on, like so many family reality TV shows, far into the future. We'll show the cooking, and America will also watch the rancher and the TV host meld their lives..."

She had it all worked out.

"Then there's Spencer's beef. He really knows what he's doing, Mom. And he does it for the right reasons. Out of love for the ranch. For his family. For his heritage. He'll be a show sponsor," she said. "We'll not only advertise his beef but also get proceeds from the sales." She and Spencer had worked it all out.

In a few short weeks, he'd gone from a disbeliever to the driving force in their merger. He insisted on meetings. Pushing her for times when he could bring the kids to the city so that he was keeping up with his part of the agreement, in spite of the fact that she knew he really hated to be away from the ranch.

He'd already completed all of his prenuptial paperwork and was just waiting for her and her lawyer to do the same before setting up a meeting between the two attorneys to hash out the differences—if there were any.

He'd held her hand when they were in town together.

The only thing he hadn't done was kiss her again...

"You've said the marriage is blocking you, Tasha." Her mother's tone held warning.

Because she didn't have to marry Spencer to have him on the show. Yes, the wedding would inflate ratings. A bit of their ongoing family reality would add extra spice to the show. But the health of her show did not depend on a marriage. Spencer was already under contract for the rest of it—the continued shows, the continued hosting, the beef sponsorship.

"I know. It is."

"And you're sure about that?"

Unfortunately, she was. Absolutely. She'd asked herself so many times. And each time she thought about the marriage, she was besieged with unrest. Sometimes even nausea.

"So find what's blocking you from acting," Susan said. Her tone held sympathy. But warning, too.

And she knew. Spencer was blocking her. He'd become a good friend to her over the past weeks. She thought she'd become a friend to him, too. She didn't want to disappoint him. More than that, his kids were blocking her. She wasn't ready to dim the light they brought to her life.

But Susan was right. She had to act. Anything else was wrong. Selfish. Unfair. For everyone involved.

She'd loved becoming part of a family.

She'd been playing make-believe with herself. Asking, but not answering honestly. Lying to herself and living on quicksand.

She'd managed to kid herself until she'd made herself sick.

Her body was telling her the jig was up.

SHE WAS GOING to tell him the next time she talked to him. They'd reached an agreement to be in touch at least once a day. But the next morning, he called right after putting the kids on the bus to tell her he'd heard from Claire, who was planning to fly in the day after Thanksgiving and wanted to have the kids with her at her hotel in Palm Desert overnight. And Natasha held her tongue.

"I have to tell you, you were right." He sounded...happy? Did guys like Spencer allow themselves that? "Announcing our engagement on Thanksgiving is perfect timing. We can make arrangements to stay in the city the whole weekend instead of just the couple of days we were going to take for the PR shots. Claire can see the kids, but they'll have a home to sleep in at night—no need for them to stay in the hotel with her."

Yes, it was all working so perfectly.

Except that, for her, it wasn't.

But she couldn't tell him yet. She had to come up with another plan to cover the Claire problem—some way to protect Tabitha and Justin from being lured away from their home on the ranch—before she could break their agreement.

And she'd best do it quickly or the whole thing was going to get messier than anyone wanted. To announce the engagement and then break it off would be...catastrophic.

On Tuesday she told herself she'd have something figured out before Friday, when she was going back to the ranch for the weekend and was supposed to be moving most of her personal files to her now-complete office in the new studio. She slept well for the first time in weeks.

Maybe they could stage the wedding. For

the show. For his beef. For all of the publicity for both of them. For Claire.

But not really go through with it.

She tried on the solution. Thought it might fit. Wore it all day Wednesday. Slept okay Wednesday night. Made a note as soon as she got up the next day to call her PR firm and run the idea by them. Confidentially.

On Thursday morning, before she had a chance to get to anything on her list, her lawyer called.

She wanted to see Natasha as soon as possible.

Not liking the sound of that, Natasha, dressed in her power purple blouse with the black slim line suit she'd had on when she'd signed her largest sponsorship a few weeks before, left the studio before Angela had even arrived, driving straight to Sharon Divers's office. The middle-aged attorney met her in the parking lot, but they didn't exchange anything other than pleasantries until the two of them were seated in her office.

On a leather couch, not at the desk.

Sharon pulled a folder out of the satchel she'd carried in. Handed it to Natasha and said, "You asked me to do a thorough background check."

With an instant headache traveling up through the cords in her neck, Natasha held the folder closed.

"You found something." That much was clear.

Sharon, dressed in a gray suit with a pale pink blouse, looked so nonthreatening as she nodded her head full of short, dark hair.

"What?" She preferred to be told. As though whatever was coming would be less painful if she heard it rather than read it herself.

Was this why she'd been feeling sick lately at the thought of marrying Spencer Longfellow? Because some part of her had known something wasn't right? Had she sensed that he was hiding something from her?

"What if you found out, somewhere down the road, that I have some dirty little secret...?" He'd asked the question.

And she'd hidden from it. Or hidden it away so that it could rob her of sleep and her appetite.

"He's not a Longfellow."

Whatever she'd been expecting...some kind of criminal record, maybe...it hadn't been that.

She'd have preferred the record. People made mistakes. They made reckless choices and spent the rest of their lives being responsible to them.

But to lie about who you were?

The blood drained from her face as the next thought occurred to her. If he wasn't a Longfellow, who was he? And why was he pretending to own a ranch that wasn't his?

"Who is he?"

"He was born Spencer Justin Barber."

"When?"

She named the date. Natasha did the math. He was thirty, just like he'd said he was. She took a deep breath, as though the fact that he hadn't lied about his age made it all a little better.

It didn't.

How could he think he'd get away with this? Entering into contracts with her?

Saying he was going to marry her?

Like she wouldn't have known when they got the license that he wasn't who he said he was?

Family Secrets. She'd made him a cohost of her show. This news was going to put a blemish on a show that had been fair and true reality since its inception...

Panic started to set in. She focused on her attorney. Took a deep breath. It had taken her several thoughts down the path to get to *Family Secrets*.

This whole knowing-Spencer-Longfellow thing—or rather, Spencer Justin Barber—had been putting her off her game since the beginning.

"Tell me the rest," she said.

And wasn't happy when Sharon shook her head. "I don't know much more yet. I wanted to show you what I've got and discuss the possibility of hiring a private detective to dig deeper."

She didn't have to think about that one. She stood. Clasped the folder against her chest. Walked calmly to the door.

Turned back and said, "Dig."

CHAPTER TWENTY-FIVE

IF THE SUV coming up his drive Thursday midmorning hadn't alerted him to the fact that something was wrong, the look on Natasha's face as she exited the vehicle and headed straight toward him would have done so.

He'd been standing outside the horse barn, talking to Will, his local groom and horse trainer, about the addition of a small horse to their stables just before Christmas, when she'd turned at the T just beyond the house.

Turned away from the studio. Like she'd been looking specifically for him.

"We need to talk," she said, barely managing a polite smile in the direction of the young man from town whom she'd met during her initial tour of the ranch.

With the calm that had come over him since Natasha had convinced him that her harebrained idea was the answer to his prayers, Spencer led her down to the creek. The woman he'd called his mother had had a bench installed there years before because she liked to listen to the water while she read.

What made Spencer choose the location now, he didn't know. He just wanted Natasha away from anyone who might overhear them.

"What's up?" he asked when he sat and she didn't.

Facing him, standing over him, she dropped a folder in his lap. She'd pulled it out of the satchel on her shoulder.

He was noticing every little detail all of a sudden.

Opening the folder, he closed it again almost immediately. He didn't need to read what the pages bore.

He also didn't need to be a mind reader to know that, despite her earlier assurances, his dirty little secret wasn't his alone.

She was taking ownership of it inasmuch as she was going to use it against him.

He should have known she, like Kaylee, was too good to be true.

"Who is Spencer Justin Barber?" Her voice was calm. He detected no accusation.

No hint of the friend he'd thought she'd been, either.

"Obviously you know the answer to that."

"I might have doubted," she said, a hint

of…something…in her voice. "But the *Justin* gave it away. You pretend you're someone you're not, but you name your son after the person you were."

"Something like that."

"I think I deserve an explanation."

She really didn't. He'd told her he had a secret before they'd finalized their *business* arrangement. That had been her chance to pursue the matter.

But there was no point in being a jerk about it. And he was going to need her cooperation.

How he was going to get it, he didn't know. That depended on what she was planning to do with the information she had.

"How much do you know?" he asked.

"I know that you're Spencer Justin Barber." She said the name like it was dirty, too. He waited for her to say more.

Looked up at her when she didn't.

"That's it?"

"Yes."

He could lie to her. Or rather, tell her some of the truth but not all of it. For several long seconds, he considered his options.

He'd been lying since he was six years old. It came naturally to him. He'd long since known he'd do anything for his kids…

"Where are the Longfellows?" Her question led him into an explanation—the part he'd been planning to give her anyway.

"Sadie Longfellow was the last of them. She died shortly before I married Kaylee."

"So…did you work here? You said you lived here when you were in college." She was frowning. Not quite meeting his eyes.

He wanted to haul her down beside him and shut her up with a kiss that would make her forget that anything else mattered.

But knew, even if they were a real couple, he'd never do that.

"I've lived here my entire life," he told her. "I was born on this ranch."

Her gaze was piercing, and she pinned him like a fly to a board. He didn't flinch. Or feel the stabs, either.

At least, he didn't want to. Told himself he wouldn't for long. He'd been through the pain of loss before. Survived. Every time.

Her sigh told him she was losing patience. And he remembered that he might need her help. Would definitely need her help. Claire Williamson couldn't know what she knew. Not unless Natasha was still going to marry him.

A circumstance he was strongly doubting.

Doubting, too, whether he even wanted her to—aside from the Claire Williamson threat. He didn't mind marrying a woman he didn't love—one who didn't love him. But he did care about tying himself to someone who didn't see in him the man that he was.

Yes, he'd withheld information. But he'd offered it.

"Sadie and Gerald Longfellow were not happy together. They both loved the ranch. They loved each other. But when Sadie found out they were unable to have children, she was never the same. I didn't know all that much about it when I was a kid."

He'd found out in pieces. Mostly from Sadie herself. When she'd begged him to be who he wanted to be...

"My mother died giving birth to me," he continued. "My parents had been living in one of the smaller cabins, and that's where I lived with my father until I was six."

"Then what happened?"

"A couple of weeks before I was due to start school, my father and Gerald Longfellow died in a crop dusting accident."

All true.

"Sadie inherited the ranch. She had no close family. Wasn't able to have children, and suddenly, she's got this little boy without parents…"

"She took you in."

"Yes."

It was a fairy tale. Not dirt.

"She adopted you?"

"No." To do that she'd have had to present his original birth certificate. Along with his parents' death certificates. There'd likely have been other things involved—not the home checks of the modern day, but certainly she'd have had to petition the court.

She'd never researched it.

"She enrolled me in school as Spencer Longfellow. I don't know how. Maybe back then her word was good enough. Maybe she lied about documents or had some made up. I have no idea about that part. She told everyone that I was her son. The town you know today didn't exist back then. We were all bused over an hour to a first-through-twelfth-grade school when I first started. For many of us, it was the first time we'd ever met each other. You think life on the ranch is secluded now. It was its own little world back then…"

"I don't think it's secluded now." She sounded defensive. "And I'm sorry that I jumped to the wrong conclusions."

He had a feeling Natasha Stevens didn't apologize very often.

She sat down. Close to him.

And that was when he knew he had to tell her the whole truth.

"SADIE LONGFELLOW GREW up in the foster-care system."

Natasha had been waiting for an acceptance of her apology. Hoping that all would be well between her and Spencer. Which made no sense since she knew she couldn't marry him. She didn't have an alternative plan for the Williamson threat yet.

When he finally started talking after several minutes of silence, she had no idea where this was going. She waited to find out.

If he thought he owed her...he didn't.

"From what I understand, it was something of a fairy tale the way Gerald fell in love with her. He not only married her but also made her the matriarch of what was one of the biggest ranches in the area back then. For the first time in her life, she had a home of her own. She was going to have Gerald's children, be the mother of a real family and... find what she'd been missing her entire life.

A sense of identity. Belonging. Emotional security."

His voice was soft. Kind. She liked listening to it.

And liked that he was sharing this part of his past with her. Liked knowing him better.

"When she found out she couldn't have children, everything changed. She changed. She had an emotional breakdown, and though she recovered enough to keep up appearances, to be completely self-sufficient, she'd grown...hard. She never laughed. Or showed compassion. That's the only way I ever knew her, but I was told by an old groom that she used to laugh all the time. That everyone loved her and she loved them back. I was about ten at the time. He'd found me crying in the barn."

She looked over at him—this big, strong cowboy.

He was leaning forward, his elbows on his knees, looking at her. As though waiting for her judgment.

"Why were you crying?"

He nodded. Seemed to be making some kind of decision. Natasha hoped it was in favor of answering her question. She waited some more. Heard the water in the stream just in front of them. But watched him.

With fall having come and gone, there was little growth around them. Just dust and brownness. Rock and...him.

He sat back. Glanced at her again. And then toward the creek.

"My father was a thief."

He'd shocked her again, this man who'd seemed so straightforward.

With a sense of foreboding, she listened.

"Like a lot of ranchers, Gerald Longfellow didn't trust banks. He kept his money, a lot of it in gold pieces, in safes on the property and in the house. My father, who'd worked on the ranch since he was a kid, spent years stealing from him, bits at a time, sums that grew larger as my father's gambling addiction got worse. By the time Gerald found out, he'd taken a quarter of a million dollars. And gambled every dime of it away."

Natasha focused on the facts. On her way to the solution she felt certain was going to be necessary. Ask. Answer. Act.

"Gerald could have prosecuted him, sent him to jail, but he wasn't that kind of man. He understood that my father had a problem. He offered him a chance to get help, to fix his life, to make restitution. Had legal papers drawn up whereby my father agreed to work at Longfellow Ranch for nothing but room and board. No wages. Just free labor. Free room and board. He'd pay back his debt but have no cash to squander. Gerald would provide for my needs until the debt was paid, or until I turned eighteen."

"Gerald sounds like a guy I would have liked."

Spencer nodded. "When I knew them, they were both men I...liked." He glanced her way, grinned and then sobered immediately. "Who'm I kidding? I idolized them both. I thought they were best friends."

"Maybe they were. Maybe that's why Gerald made the deal he made with your father."

She wasn't sure where this was going. But the insight it was giving her into her business partner was invaluable.

"The legal agreement stated that neither my father nor his adult heirs could receive a dime of Longfellow money, including ranch profit, until the debt had been paid in full."

The ax fell.

Quietly.

And lay there embedded in the dirt beside the stream.

SPENCER NOTICED THE change in Natasha immediately. She was a smart woman. A businesswoman who would immediately begin to catalog possible problems and ramifications.

He'd known when he'd told her the truth what he was exposing himself to.

The only thing he couldn't figure out was why he'd done it.

"I didn't know about any of this until I was thirteen." He was determined to finish the story he'd started. "From my very first memory of living with Sadie, the first night I moved into her home when I was six, the night that Gerald and my father died, she let me know that I was living on borrowed time. She said that Spencer Barber wasn't good enough to do all of the things she expected me to do, and that's why I became Spencer Longfellow. She told me, every day before I left for school that first year, that if I didn't look and act good enough, I could lose everything. That I'd have to go live with strangers in a strange place. I think at first she was just panicked. Later it became a way to control me.

"In her own way, I believe Sadie cared about me. She just couldn't conquer her own demons. And maybe I kidded myself about that. Maybe she was incapable of feeling love. She'd been raised without it."

"Your name...was it legally changed?"

Good. She was sticking to the facts. Exactly what he'd have expected out of her. What he needed from her.

"Yes, as the paperwork in your folder shows."

"Did Sadie have a will?"

"Yes."

"And she left you the ranch?"

"When I was thirteen, Sadie showed me a copy of the legal agreement between my father and Gerald Longfellow. I'd been getting mouthy, fighting back against her constant barrage of telling me I had to earn my right to be a part of Longfellow Ranch. I'd told her that she had no right to talk to me like I was less than she was. She'd said something about her having to make certain that she wasn't letting Gerald down, that she was raising me to be worthy of Longfellow heritage, and not one who would take from it as my father had, and it all came out from there."

He could have remembered it word for word if he tried. But had no desire to.

He hadn't answered the real question she'd been asking.

"No one but me...and now you...know

those papers exist. But they're there. If someone looks hard enough, they'll find them."

"Then what?"

He looked at her. "I don't know. When Sadie was alive, they were legally binding. I know that much. I worked like a dog but never had a penny in my pocket. She gave me a credit card for gas and essentials. She trusted me."

"A trust well-placed."

He'd kept meticulous records of every purchase he'd ever made. But liked that she didn't doubt him again.

"After she died, I found out she hadn't included the document in her papers. I could let the document die with her, in the hope that it never came to light again, or I could bring it to light and see how the chips fell."

The choice he'd made was pretty obvious.

"I'd spent a lifetime lying," he said.

"You were taught as a grief-stricken little boy, by the sole semblance of family you had left in your life, that lying was the only way you'd be safe, have family or a home."

She had his back.

For the moment.

"You asked me if Sadie left a will."

He could feel her staring at him.

"She left the farm in trust...to me." He looked at her then. "Right now I am the living tenant and have sole say in the running of the business, but I am not technically the owner. Yet. I have to show a profit until I am thirty-five, and then the ranch is mine."

"So the document between your father and Longfellow is no longer legally binding."

She focused on the best part. He nodded.

"She honored her husband's wishes by making you prove you wouldn't squander the ranch before it becomes yours."

He'd understood that, too. And nodded again.

"I'm assuming you've shown a profit every year?"

"I have. But that doesn't change the fact that this could come out," he told her now.

"You aren't a Longfellow and technically you don't own the ranch. You might not have legally committed fraud, but you look fraudulent. And you're the son of a crook. As far as the show and Longfellow Beef are concerned, it's a PR nightmare."

He knew Natasha was worried when he heard her statement.

Which escalated his own growing concern. If only he'd been satisfied just to show a small profit each year, he could have quietly turned thirty-five in a few years and been home free.

But no, he'd gotten greedy. Had to make it big. Had to have the best beef. He'd brought Longfellow Ranch into the limelight. And if public perception turned against him for his lies...if he lost money because of it...

He was not going to lose his home. The ranch. Ruin Tabitha and Justin's future. Their security.

Their very identity.

He couldn't.

No matter what he had to do...

"I think that you should let me talk to my lawyer." Natasha's voice broke into his ruminations. Rescued him for the moment. "She can make discreet inquiries. I'll find out where everything stands. We can't make a decision until we're fully informed."

He nodded. And wished he'd never met her.

"We could just leave it alone," he suggested, without any real oomph. She wasn't going to do that. And he didn't blame her. He wouldn't expect or even ask her to.

"*Family Secrets* is involved now," she said. "The ease with which my lawyer found the name change means that anyone who digs will find it. And to anyone looking for dirt on you, the name change will be a red flag, throwing up questions as to why…"

If Claire found out…

He stood. "It's best that we face this now," he said. "I need to be armed. I can have my own attorney look into it…"

She was shaking her head. "He's local, Spencer. Let's keep this one step away from you, from the kids, if we can."

One step away. Her plan was sound.

But he didn't like her doing his work for him. Didn't like the idea of anyone in his business. Period.

But for Justin and Tabitha…he'd do anything.

"Call your lawyer," he said.

And walked away.

CHAPTER TWENTY-SIX

NATASHA DROVE BACK to Palm Desert. She had an early afternoon meeting with Sharon. They were going to do this in person.

And as quickly as possible.

The Thanksgiving show was only weeks away. She needed time to rescript it without the engagement, to rescript the coming year's themes and content.

To rescript her life.

But after no more than a cursory glance-over, she didn't think about any of that as she drove for endless miles in what was seemingly the middle of nowhere.

Everywhere she looked, she saw Spencer as a little boy, alone in the desert. As a teenager, learning to drive and seeing beyond the ranch. As a college boy, traveling this very road. He'd lost so much. Starting with his mother at birth.

He'd never known the nurturing love of a mother.

Then, at six, to lose both men who were father figures to him.

To be raised by a woman who, no matter her motivation, had been cruel to him. Withholding the one thing he'd needed most—love and affection.

And shortly after her death, his young wife had left him—letting him believe his country ways were an embarrassment to her elite and powerful family.

Somewhere along the way, tears appeared on her cheeks.

No wonder Spencer wasn't open to love again.

In so many ways, he was like the woman who'd raised him. Striving for the things that had seemed forever out of his reach—acceptance, belonging. Security.

And, like her, he'd prevented the possibility of further hurt by refusing to love again. The only difference between him and Sadie—and it was a huge one—was that he loved his kids. With every ounce of love inside of him.

It was no wonder to her now why he clung so tightly to his ranch. To the legacy he would pass on to his children. No wonder he got antsy in the city—or anytime he was away from the ranch overnight.

It was also no wonder why he'd had only a loveless marriage to offer Jolene. Or any woman. Except for with his kids, Spencer Barber Longfellow wasn't capable of giving his heart away.

NATASHA HAD SAID she'd call as soon as she knew anything. Spencer spent all day Wednesday out working fences. With more than two thousand acres to cover, there was always fence line needing repair or adjustment. Parts of the property still had Gerald Longfellow's old wooden fence posts. Spencer wasn't going to tear them down until he had to. So he painted them when necessary, treating them with waterproofing so that they'd last another lifetime. And he restrung the fencing that ran between them.

Mostly, those jobs he did himself.

As a penance. And a reminder.

He wasn't sorry for what he'd done. Wasn't sorry he'd kept up the lie after Sadie died. The ranch had been trusted to him. He only had to work hard and make it pay for it to be his solely and completely. If not for him, Longfellow Ranch would have fallen out of the hands of anyone who loved it, knew its history or cared about its heritage.

He'd done it for Gerald as much as anyone. For the man who'd saved his father from jail, and in so doing had given Spencer not only a home but also a father. Gerald had made a decent man out of Frank by staying by his side, taking away all the means by which he could feed his gambling addiction, being the friend who had his back. Because Frank had been willing to do the work. To earn the second chance.

Gerald had made an honest man of Frank. He'd helped him buy back his soul.

Spencer was a couple of miles from the compound, painting a post in the cool November sun, when his cell phone buzzed just before two.

"The agreement between Gerald and Frank was null and void upon Sadie's death."

She didn't even say hello.

He appreciated her more in that moment than ever before.

"And there is nothing overtly illegal in what you've done. You have the legal right to represent Longfellow Ranch in business dealings. Which is what you're doing. Your name is legally Longfellow."

She was confirming what he already knew.

"Our problem isn't a legal one," she continued without giving him a chance to speak. "It's a public-relations land mine."

He'd known that, too. When it came to selling beef, reputation was everything. A hit, even a temporary one, could render him destitute—one year's lack of profit was all it would take.

And if he had no home, no job… Claire would swoop in and take his kids.

The thoughts had been pounding him down all afternoon.

He stroked his brush against the wood his father's hands had cut. Standing on the ground his father had dug to bury the pole. And looked at the hundreds of others just like them, neatly aligned for as far as he could see.

All hand-cut, hand-placed, by his father.

"Is there anyone else who might know that Sadie told you about the agreement?"

"I have no way of knowing that."

"But you said that no one but you and Sadie knew about it."

"As far as I've ever known, that's true. But

she might have told someone when I was a kid that there was an agreement regarding my inheritance. Someone could have overheard her going on at me about it…"

He couldn't guarantee that no one knew…

"And what about the trust? Who knows that you are only a living tenant until you're thirty-five?"

"Again, I have no way of knowing for sure, but as far as I know, only the attorney and I. And he can't divulge anything."

"Sharon suggested that we just leave this alone. And hope that Claire, or anyone else, fails to find what I found."

He could continue to live the lie. Again. For just a few more years.

Relief swept through him. He'd do anything for his kids.

He looked at the long row of perfectly straight posts. Thought about a man who'd given up his freedom to make good for his son. Frank had died an honest man.

What he'd left to his son was the example of hard work. Of giving everything you had to do the right thing. To protect and provide for your children.

"I'm not going to lie anymore," he said. "You found it easily. I've had warning."

He couldn't read into her silence.

"I'll get back to you," she said.

And the line went dead.

SHE CALLED AGAIN less than an hour later.

With paintbrush in hand, he stood upright, gazing at the horizon.

"I haven't been to my PR firm yet. I've been here talking to Sharon."

Her lawyer, still.

The sun was shining so brightly it hurt. Giving way to skies perfect in their pristine blue. Together they seemed to be a spotlight on his shame.

Could he breathe easier or not?

"There is a way to make this whole thing go away."

He froze, one hand holding his phone to his ear, the other hand dropping his paintbrush. "Legally and aboveboard? Officially go away?"

He knew her well enough to figure that was the case.

"Yes."

"Okay. Whatever it takes. I'll do it."

"As a living tenant and eventual recipient of the trust, you could sell the ranch."

The expletives springing to the fore were

unspeakable. He'd thought, for a brief second there, that she'd had some hope to offer him. Something new.

"I cannot sell my ranch."

"Actually, you can, though I understand that you don't want to."

He frowned. Feeling a permanent headache coming on.

"You could sell it to me, Spencer. And then I can sell it back to you. We would have to wait until you turn thirty-five so it doesn't give the appearance of something underhanded between you and me, and we'd have to discuss sales amounts…"

He shook his head, disappointed again. She was sweet, trying so hard on his behalf. And that sweetness was actually making this all a little easier. But it didn't solve the problem.

"If you buy the ranch, the money goes to the ranch, not…to me. I wouldn't have the money to buy it back."

"You've got the money I paid you for *Family Secrets*."

"You paid the ranch."

"I also paid you to cohost. That was for your services, Spencer, not the ranch's."

She was right. Both ways. He had some money of his own. It wasn't nearly enough.

"The best solution is for me to buy the ranch. And when you turn thirty-five, I will sell it back to you."

He was becoming his father.

Had already been his father, if he took a good hard look. By living the lie of being an owner instead of a living tenant, by pretending all these years that he was a Longfellow in more than name only. Natasha was giving him a chance to buy his soul back.

"Yes."

"Yes?"

"Yes."

"Yes, what?"

"I agree to sell you the ranch and then, when I turn thirty-five, to buy it back from you. Under one condition. You put the ranch in a trust with my kids as heirs and make me a living tenant."

He was grinning. Looking at the horizon in a whole new light.

Longfellow Ranch was finally, legitimately, within the reach of his children.

Natasha talked some more. About paperwork, official hoops to jump through. He listened. Was completely amenable.

He surveyed the land with new eyes. Legitimately belonging to Tabitha and Justin. Paid for. By blood. Sweat. And hard work.

And when Natasha ended their conversation, he threw his phone into the air, dropped to his knees, kissed the ground.

And wept.

CHAPTER TWENTY-SEVEN

SHE'D MADE A sound business decision. Found a way to give Spencer what he needed, a way to keep him bound to the show. She still hadn't dealt with his vulnerability to Claire due to being a single father.

Nor would he have the *Family Secrets* money he'd been counting on to fight Claire, if need be.

She'd saved his ranch, yet by ending their engagement, she'd be cutting him off at the knees.

But she couldn't marry him. Her inner self continued to make that quite clear. The idea of the marriage made her sick every time she thought about it. It wasn't right for her.

As soon as she finished with Sharon, she drove straight to her public-relations firm. Jenny Teague, who had been with her since the beginning of *Family Secrets*, had told Natasha she'd be waiting for her no matter what time she arrived.

She told Jenny everything. It was the only way Jenny could do her job. From the planned engagement, the on-air wedding. Jenny already knew about the initial business arrangement Natasha had made with Spencer, had been part of the team that had designed the ads they'd used to promote the Longfellow Ranch *Family Secrets* segment. She filled her in on the second phase. And then the most recent developments. Her plan to call off the engagement, Spencer's trouble, and the plan to continue to have him on her show, and Longfellow Beef as a sponsor, for the next four years. She told him she would be purchasing the ranch and putting it in trust for Tabitha and Justin. And that she'd agreed to sell it to Spencer on his thirty-fifth birthday.

She left out nothing. Because if there was anything out there anyone else could discover, Jenny needed to know it first.

"I'm sorry" was the first thing Jenny said. She wore her navy pants and jacket like she was made in them.

Normally one to inhabit that same poise, Natasha felt uncomfortable in her power purple blouse and black suit. She was wrinkled. Her shoes still had farm dust on them…

"Sorry for what? None of this was your doing."

Gesturing with one hand, Jenny leaned toward her. "For the broken engagement."

They were sitting in a conference room, sharing a corner at the end of the table. "Oh, no," Natasha quickly assured her. "It was purely a business decision on both our parts. I just have to figure out how not to leave him in the lurch where his ex-mother-in-law and his kids are concerned," she said. "But that's not pertinent here. I need to know what pitfalls might be ahead as all of this legal stuff gets taken care of. I want to make certain that *Family Secrets* isn't impacted in any way. At least, not in a negative way."

She should have tried to eat more of her take-out lunch on her drive from the ranch. She was lacking in energy.

As always, Jenny had taken notes as Natasha had talked. She'd made columns, drawn arrows.

On the bottom corner of the page, she'd made a list. She took a few minutes to look over the legal pad and then pinned Natasha with a glance that told her she wouldn't like what she was going to hear.

But that she'd be hearing the truth.

"The only way to ensure that *Family Secrets* is not negatively impacted is for you to drop all association with Longfellow Ranch," she said. "And most particularly with Spencer Longfellow."

"But…"

"I know, you just agreed to buy his ranch, but since you just left Sharon's office, nothing has been made official," she said.

"I…"

"The initial segment is done," Jenny said. "The original plan was to have him be no more than a memory in your past, as far as the show was concerned. You can still do that. If, at some point, you want to stage an engagement and wedding, I think that would be great. It would really work, given the family emphasis of your show. But you should pick another actor to play the part."

"I…"

"This whole buying his ranch and then sponsoring his ranch's Wagyu beef…it could look like nepotism. Or at the very least, like the cover-up it is. You know his reputation stands to be hurt, and most likely impact his ability to show a profit this next year. Most particularly since he doesn't have a solid hay crop to fall back on. You know the guidelines of the trust. By buying his ranch, you make yourself implicit in the fraudulent face he's been showing the world. There's nothing illegal here, but it will definitely impact your reputation and the clean family branding you've worked so hard to develop for your show."

Jenny was making her sound like she didn't have a business brain in her head. "The original plan was that we'd be married, so a marriage of the two businesses would be a natural next step…"

"I understand. But now you aren't going to be married. Now it looks like favoritism for your cohost, or worse, it could look like you're swooping in and cashing in on someone else's misfortune."

Her head hurt. She really should have eaten.

"That's the smallest part of it, anyway," Jenny continued. "You've got a guy who not only faces possible difficulties with his highly respected, rich mother-in-law but also has admitted to pretending to be someone he is not. Pretended to be the son of a respected rancher, when he is the son of a thief. Who pretended to own a ranch when he is, at this point, only a living tenant."

"He hasn't committed a crime."

"You and I both know that what matters here is public perception and reputation. The whole reason you pay me is to protect that for you. There is enough here to make Spencer look like a creep."

Spencer was most definitely not a creep. Natasha knew that Jenny was only playing devil's advocate.

Which was, as the woman had just said, what she paid her for.

Still… "He's not a creep, Jenny. In fact, he's the greatest guy I've ever met. Can't we do something to show the world the man he is, so that if the rest of it gets out, people sympathize with him?"

"We could. But you risk the negative impact on *Family Secrets*. This is a tough one. A rich guy who knowingly defrauded you when you signed him on to your show as Spencer Longfellow, son and heir to Gerald Longfellow, generational ranch owner—and all to get where he is now, with a lucrative beef deal… There's really no way to spin that one."

Natasha wasn't going to take no for an answer.

The knowledge came to her with such clarity, she didn't question it. She didn't really have time to. Jenny was awaiting her direction.

The woman worked for her. She'd do as Natasha asked her to do.

"So what if we lead with it?" Susan had always said to confront, not hide. And her mother had been right about pretty much everything else she'd ever taught Natasha. "What if we tell the story of the boy he was. Of the way two men worked together to beat an addiction. About the man Spencer grew to be because of it."

"You sound really fond of him."

"We're friends."

Jenny studied her. And then shook her head.

"What?"

"We've been working together, what, five years?"

"A little more than that, but yes. Why?"

"In all that time, you have never, not once, ever, continued to pursue a single idea after I've told you that it could have a negative impact on the show. And this one…it's got more potential to blow up in your face than anything ever has, yet here you are, pushing it at me."

She was.

And just like that, when faced with the facts, looking for a solution, she knew what she'd been blocking. Knew why she'd been so out of sync since the cowboy had come into her life. Knew why she couldn't marry Spencer.

She was in love with him.

A man whose lifestyle, whose needs, were diametrically opposed to hers.

A man who was incapable of loving her back.

She couldn't marry him knowing that. To her, marriage was a pact of the heart. Made by two people who were in love.

Once again, her mother had been right.

NATASHA DIDN'T CALL after her meeting with Jenny Teague. Spencer didn't fool himself— he knew that wasn't good.

No PR firm was going to advise that Natasha attach her show to a man who'd knowingly misrepresented himself.

Bring in a wealthy, powerful family fighting him for his kids, and he was a crapshoot at best. A nightmare in reality.

Life was a crapshoot.

Truth was, you never knew what was going to happen. Or what you'd do about it when it did.

But you could guess.

And he guessed it was possible that Natasha would renege on every deal she'd made with him.

Family Secrets was everything to her.

He understood that.

Longfellow Ranch was everything to him.

Now she knew why.

He supposed that if she did leave him high and dry, he could sue her for breach of contract for the four-year deal.

But he wasn't sure what he stood to gain by doing so.

He supposed he could take his kids and move to... Alaska.

He hated being bandied about. Being at the mercy of others.

He'd been that way his entire childhood.

He'd promised himself it would never happen again.

And there he was. Waiting to hear where his life would blow next.

When he didn't hear from her Thursday morning, he put the kids on the bus, notified Betsy that he was going to be off the ranch, asked her to meet their bus if he wasn't back and set his truck on course for Palm Desert.

He knew individual cacti along the way. Mountain shapes, peaks and valleys. There really were a few things in life that didn't change. At least not rapidly enough for a man to notice in one lifetime.

When he was almost in the city, he called Natasha's studio line. In the beginning, it had been the only number he had for her.

She picked up after the second ring.

Agreed to meet with him.

After that brief conversation, he could tell nothing about her state of mind—or her intentions.

Parking the truck where she'd instructed him to, he went to the far west door on the south side of the building, punched in the code she'd given him, took two turns down long hallways filled with closed doors and busy offices and came to an impressive-looking glass wall with her name on it.

Pushing through the door, he walked past what had to be Angela's office out front, through to Natasha's kingdom.

In black dress pants and a white button-down fitted silk top, she stood as he came in.

The lavish office, with its thick carpet, expensive couches and counter bar, looked good on her.

Her unsmiling expression did not.

In fact, if he hadn't known better, he'd have thought she looked…nervous.

"Have a seat," she said, indicating the chair in front of a mahogany desk that matched the size of Gerald's back home. His now.

He sat. Noting that he'd been ushered to an all-business seat, not a more personal one, like the couch.

Again, he didn't blame her.

Just noticed.

"What's up?" Hands crossed on the desktop, she faced him.

"You didn't call. After the meeting with Jenny."

She nodded. "I know."

"I figured we had some things to discuss."

"So you just left the kids, the ranch, drove all this way to...have a talk?"

"You drove out to the ranch yesterday morning for the same reason." He thought for a moment. "And the kids are in school. Betsy's on call and will meet the school bus if I'm not back in time."

She nodded. "Good."

Her approval pleased him.

Or maybe it was that she'd thought about the kids...

Maybe it was that he was at her mercy and...

"I want to end our engagement," he said.

"Or rather, to change our minds about having one."

The relief that flashed immediately across her face was unmistakable. As professional as Natasha was, and a consummate actress to boot, she didn't give much away, unless you caught her in the first seconds of her reaction when she heard something that got to her.

When he'd figured that out, he didn't know.

But he'd used it to his advantage. He'd been right in his assessment of their situation. She was going to renege on him.

Again, he didn't blame her.

But he just couldn't let himself be rejected again. From now on he was going to drive his life rather than hide from it.

No more lying.

"Why?" she asked.

He hadn't anticipated the question. Not following her obvious relief. He'd predicted her acquiescence, a professional parting of ways, something along those lines.

To be followed by his own trip to his lawyer to find out where he stood with the rest of his life.

"What?" he asked her. When you didn't have an answer, you answered with a question.

"I asked why you don't want to marry me."

"Because…" Another brilliant response.

"I'm afraid that ending our engagement is not possible." Not even a supposition, that response.

"Why not?"

"Because I've got too much invested…too much at stake…and I'd have to…sue you for breach of contract."

What?

The look on her face was odd. As though she wasn't any more sure of herself than he was of himself. But then, they were both kind of in uncharted territory.

And he still had Claire to deal with. He had no ideas there. And only until Christmas vacation to figure out something solid. He already had Thanksgiving covered, thanks to Natasha. If he and the kids weren't staying at his place, he could always use some of the money she'd paid him as cohost to rent a hotel room.

Not knowing where his future lay, if he lost the ranch due to non-profit, he had to use his money sparingly.

"I met with Jenny, and I believe we've come up with a plan that will minimize damages the most for all concerned."

Minimize damages?

He sat there, stunned, as she told him about the negative impact risk he'd become, confirmed by her public-relations team after a full meeting the night before. And when Natasha had refused to back down, to concede that bringing him on or having any more to do with him was the wrong choice, they'd come up with a plan that they thought would give them the best chance to counteract any negative effect.

"The best part is, it takes care of your situation with Claire, too. At least for the next couple of years."

He was still waiting to hear the plan.

"They propose that we get engaged as planned. That we move forward with our merging of *Family Secrets* and Longfellow Beef in terms of sponsorship, that we continue with the four-year location filming plan on Longfellow Ranch. With my purchase of the ranch. With all of it, actually, except the actual wedding."

He wasn't going to get ahead of himself here. Wasn't going to let even a hint of hope in. Sure as hell wasn't going to relax.

But he'd listen…

Except that she wasn't saying anything

now. She was looking at him as though she needed something from him.

He had absolutely no idea what that would be.

"Long engagements are common in today's world," she finally said, her expression changing to the professional one he was most used to. "They also allow an unwritten escape clause. If, at any time, my association with you were to become too dangerous, in terms of the integrity of *Family Secrets*, I could always break it off and gain public sympathy for what I've been through. And you and the ranch would still be protected through the trust I will have set up naming Justin and Tabitha as heirs.

"I would still continue with our proposed living arrangements. I would be as much a part of the kids' lives as we discussed, for as long as they want me in their lives, regardless of what eventually happened between us. It is believed by my attorney and PR firm that an engagement, especially one as public as ours would be, would be enough to deter Claire from gaining any support in any attempt she might have wanted to make to take the children to Washington, DC. Without Claire looking into your past, there is no reason to expect your past to reappear."

Her lip seemed to have developed a little bit of a twitch. Would occasional kisses still be part of the agreement? The inane thought popped into his mind. And didn't leave as he willed it to.

"The engagement would also be enough to put a stop to an appearance of nepotism in terms of merging our business interests. That is to be expected among fiancés."

It was clear her people had worked with her long into the night.

When had she been planning to let him in on the proposal?

"I'm to assume that at some point, in, say, a couple of years, or maybe four, when our contract expires, when I've repurchased the ranch, one or the other of us will break the engagement?"

"That is the expectation. Yes."

"So...it's all still a go. All of it. You just don't want to marry me."

She took a moment to answer and then said, "Correct."

He had the most ridiculous urge to haul her across the desk and hug her as tightly, and for as long, as he possibly could.

Instead, he stood and reached across the desk to shake her hand.

And then turned and walked out of her office.

CHAPTER TWENTY-EIGHT

NATASHA DIDN'T EAT much on Thursday. And didn't sleep well, either. She packed for the weekend at the ranch, because she'd already committed to going and had arranged for a couple of her camera people to be there getting shots of her and Spencer in and around her new office and studio.

As she'd done for the past couple of weekends, she put Lily in her carrier and took the kitten with her. Lily seemed happier at the cabin than she was in the condo.

Natasha had found her solution. She wasn't marrying Spencer. She was saving him from Claire. Her show was protected. His ranch problems would fade away as though they'd never been.

And she would somehow get over loving him.

Her mother had found happiness without her father.

She knew it could be done.

Spencer hadn't batted an eye when she'd told him she didn't want to marry him. He'd seemed no more upset about her refusal than he'd been about Jolene's.

Because he wasn't going to be emotionally invested in any woman. Ever. She was becoming convinced that, just like Sadie, he wasn't capable of that kind of emotional give-and-take.

She understood.

All that remained was for her to find her own way to happiness. And then to act.

THE ENGAGEMENT ANNOUNCEMENT went off without a hitch. Spencer played his part. Rather enjoyed doing so. Apparently there was more of an actor in him than he'd supposed. The kids had been told—though he'd also told them that engagements were just trying-on periods. That sometimes clothes didn't fit and you ended up not keeping them.

He hated that he'd felt the need to liken Natasha to garments, but more, he hated the idea of misleading his kids into believing that she would someday be their mother.

"Step," Tabitha had corrected him when he warned them that it might not happen.

"What?" He and the kids were having ice

cream outside, wearing heavy winter sweaters. They'd wanted to make ice cream. He'd read that accompanying serious news with something positive made it easier for children to accept.

"Natasha told us all about steps," Tabitha said. "It's someone that only becomes a mom when she marries a dad." Her cone, though soggy, was pristine. Unlike Justin's cone, which was almost saturated with dripping ice cream.

Spencer missed Natasha. As soon as they'd done the Thanksgiving show, and they'd hosted a submissive and respectful Claire Williamson at the condo for a couple of hours together as a family, Natasha had left for location scouting. She'd been gone a week.

And he missed her.

So much that he told her so when she called that night. True to her word, during their original negotiations, she made sure that he always knew where she was. And they talked every day.

"What do you mean, you miss me?" She sounded almost angry. And he figured he'd crossed into territory too personal to fit their business model.

"I'm sorry," he said. "Still feeling my way here."

"What does that mean?" She didn't sound angry anymore. Or even defensive. Just... tired.

In his downstairs office, he stared at the chair his father used to sit in when he met with Gerald in his office. "This whole...figuring out who we are, what we are and what we're not. As you said in the beginning, it's unconventional. I guess we need a new provision."

Daisy Wolf was house-trained now and sleeping upstairs in the bathroom between the twins' rooms, keeping an eye on both of them. He missed having her downstairs with him in the evenings.

"And that is?" Natasha asked.

The new provision?

"That if ever one of us does something that makes the other uncomfortable, or if one of us is uncomfortable for any reason, we need to talk about it."

She didn't respond right away. Now that he was thinking about what he'd just put forward, he figured it was pretty much mandatory if they hoped to succeed in pulling off this venture.

They had a right to have a business engagement. But they had to do it right. In a way that minimized the possibility of anyone getting hurt.

"Agreed."

He sensed there was more that needed to be said. Or maybe he just wanted more. Either way…

"So…let's talk," he said.

"Is something making you uncomfortable?"

Now that she mentioned it…

"You've talked about your mother. Originally she was going to be joining us in January for the wedding. What does she know about our arrangement?"

"Pretty much everything. She'd like to join us for Christmas, if that's okay with you."

He hadn't been certain they'd still be spending it together. Some of the holiday, yes, but not necessarily Christmas Day itself.

Although it would appear odd if anyone were to see her in Palm Desert without him and the kids…

"It's fine with me. I look forward to meeting her. What's your preference in terms of location?"

"Excuse me?"

"Would you rather have Christmas Day at

the condo or on the ranch?" He had to ask. They were partners. And he owed her.

"I assumed it would be at the ranch. Kids should celebrate Christmas morning at home…"

He hadn't had a lot of memorable Christmas mornings. But he'd made certain that Justin and Tabitha did. Every year.

"Okay, good," he said. Another hurdle settled. "So…what about you?"

"Nothing's making me uncomfortable."

"I don't believe you."

"Excuse me?"

"You said you want this to work." He knew pushing her was dangerous.

"I do."

"You've been…different. Ever since you met with Jenny Teague the day I came clean about my past. You were fine when you left the ranch. Normal, for you, for us, after we met with Sharon. But then, after Jenny, you didn't call. I had to come to you even to find out what was going on, and something has been different with you ever since."

There. Let her deal with it. He was tired of trying to figure it out. Tired of worrying that everything was about to blow up on him again.

He was done hiding.

And waiting. Done living on a prayer that everything would work out.

"You sure you want the truth?"

"Of course."

"Be careful what you ask for."

Now he had to have it. "I want the truth."

"While I was sitting in Jenny's office, hearing myself insist on working out a plan that included you, rather than dumping all association with you as she suggested, I realized that I'm in love with you."

He didn't know gulping was more than an expression until he did it. Reaching for a canister that had been on the shelf since before Sadie died, and contained whiskey that was as aged, he removed the lid and took a sip.

Almost convinced himself that she hadn't just said what he thought she'd said.

"I know your feelings on the matter," she continued. And while he welcomed the return of his old Natasha, more than she'd probably ever know, he wanted her just to stop talking.

"I accept your choice not to love again. And, frankly, have accepted the fact that you probably are incapable of doing so."

Was she challenging him? It wasn't like her. So he figured she was giving him the truth he'd asked for.

"Am I wrong about that?" she asked.

And now he had to give it back to her.

His first instinct was to lie. His second and third instincts that followed were exactly the same. But he'd made a promise to himself, a silent vow to his father, who'd turned his life around, to Gerald, who'd given him the chance, and to his own children. He would not lie. Or hide.

"No, you aren't wrong."

She wished him good-night. And hung up.

NATASHA CALLED SPENCER the next night as planned. And every day that followed, too. She was a businesswoman.

And *Family Secrets* was vital to her.

He was part of her business world. A boon to *Family Secrets*—assuming nothing about his father's theft, and his own subsequent subterfuge, didn't get out.

With Claire contained, if she remained contained, there was not a lot of risk of the old agreement coming forth. It hadn't in all the years since Sadie passed away. There was no reason for it to do so.

As long as Natasha stayed engaged to him. And if she didn't—the ranch sale was going through. Sharon had told her Spencer's lawyer had just approved the final papers for the trust.

If the truth ever came out in the future, after they broke off their engagement, the public would most likely sympathize with her for getting away from him in time. It would appear that she hadn't known about his past until it came out.

Frankly, she was tired of thinking about the whole thing. About running her life based on Jenny Teague and Sharon, on Angela and PR and legal "teams."

She wanted *Family Secrets* to succeed, as badly as always. She knew full well she wouldn't be happy without the show. But she had her own family secret now. She was in love. She wanted to marry the man she loved. To raise his children. To have more with him. She wanted…normal.

She'd agreed to settle for so much less.

And for the first time in her life, she was afraid of failing.

She needed her mother. And so, that first week in December, she flew to New York and called it a Christmas shopping trip.

She checked possible sites for location shooting. Liked one. And followed up with a day with lawyers, working up a proposal to take back with her.

Mostly, she ran home to lick her wounds.

They didn't heal.

THE PAPERWORK ARRIVED for the sale of the ranch—making, at worst, Justin and Tabitha heirs of Longfellow Ranch. He signed immediately.

With the torn envelope still in hand, he pulled out his phone and called her.

She didn't pick up.

He took the kids to town for hamburgers and malts that night to celebrate—though they had no idea about what. And as he drove home, he did so with a new feeling. That he was driving to *his* home that night.

It had taken until he was nearly thirty-one years on earth, but he'd finally become legitimate.

SHE COULD HAVE HAD it all. The marriage. The kids. A shared life with the man she loved. Spencer had been willing to marry her all along. She was the one holding back.

On the long flight back to California, Natasha stared out the window at cotton candy clouds and pristine blue sky, at life on the outside.

And knew, as tempted as she was to give in and take the easy way out, she couldn't settle. She could not marry without love.

She'd reached the decision weeks ago. Hadn't swayed from it since. But this time, flying back into her life, the choice was final. Irrevocable.

She was never going to marry Spencer Longfellow.

She'd been holding on without realizing it. As though something would change. She would. Or he would.

But he wasn't. She wasn't. They weren't.

There were some things you just could not control. Or make happen. No matter how fiercely you believed in them. Wanted them. Would work for them. She wasn't all-powerful.

Letting go was hard. Even when you were letting go of something that hadn't even happened.

Letting go also brought a measure of peace.

And truth.

She would find a measure of happiness. She would make her life count. She would laugh.

Just as Susan did.

She was going to become her mother.

There were worse things.

But, like her mother must have done all those years ago, she couldn't help but acknowledge one thing.

Something inside of her had just died.

CHAPTER TWENTY-NINE

SHOPPING FOR CHRISTMAS was completely different that year. Spencer went out with abandon. He'd already purchased the horse for Tabitha. At Natasha's suggestion, he'd gone back and bought one for Justin, too. As she pointed out, as much as they grumbled, the kids did everything together. They were best friends.

And he would make every effort to keep them close. He and Natasha both knew what it was like to grow up alone. What Tabitha and Justin had was…priceless.

Natasha again. Everywhere he went, everywhere he looked—most particularly in his own thoughts—Natasha was there.

Not because she pushed herself in. Or was even around nearly as much as he'd once thought she would be—like Christmas shopping with him, for instance. Instead of going together to shop for the kids, they were each doing their own shopping and wrapping.

He didn't know why he couldn't take a step without seeming to take her with him. But he'd slowly grown accustomed to having her there.

And when he started to get uncomfortable with his fascination for his business partner, he'd try to reason away his obsession. The woman was gorgeous. What guy wouldn't think about her?

They were engaged to be married—and had to keep up appearances of such in more than just a business sense. It was natural he'd have her on his mind.

She had his back. Not since he was six years old had he felt that assurance. Or known what that was like.

Not even with Bryant. Because he hadn't let himself get that close.

Bryant didn't know Spencer wasn't a Longfellow. By the time they met, he had been one. Bryant had thought, as most everyone did, that Spencer was Gerald's son. That was how Sadie had passed him off.

He'd been born on the farm. Other than the doctor who'd delivered him, who had long since passed away, who was there to have known outside their secluded little world that he wasn't Sadie's son?

But Natasha knew. Everything. And she had his back.

She'd risked *Family Secrets* for him.

She'd given him the one thing he'd been unable to give himself—himself. She'd handed life to him.

Her friendship, her caring, had given birth to a new man. One he'd been born to be.

When he realized that he'd been standing in the same aisle of a toy store for nearly twenty minutes, and that he couldn't remember one thing he still needed, he left the store.

He was in Palm Desert. Natasha was at the ranch with the kids. Making Christmas cookies, of all things.

He didn't think he'd ever had Christmas cookies baking in his home before.

He wanted to rush back.

To join in.

But they had another new agreement. He had to keep his distance from her whenever he could. This was her special time with the kids.

He had to do more than just stay away. He had to find a way to…

Natasha had given and given. She'd had his back over and over. And what had he done for her? Other than help show ratings that hadn't been hurting to begin with?

In the end, he went home anyway. He couldn't not. His family was calling to him in a way it never had before.

The call scared him. Life and death scared him. So much he wasn't sure he'd be able to answer it.

When he got to Longfellow Ranch, he didn't go to the main house. Natasha was putting the kids to bed that night.

He parked the truck at the cow barn. And then he took off. Starting at a run. Slowing at some point to a walk. When it started to get dark, he sat for a while. Facing life. And death. Meeting them head-on.

All that he'd lost. All he could lose.

He shook like a baby. Maybe from the cold. Maybe not.

Eventually he stood and started walking again.

He'd made no conscious decisions. Other than, maybe, to acknowledge that his choices had been taken away from him.

Maybe to let them go.

NATASHA WAS TIRED. Ready to rest now that the kids were sleeping soundly.

She was sad that Spencer hadn't come in the house in time to have cookies and milk with Tabitha and Justin before they'd gone to bed.

She'd heard his truck come up the drive hours ago, but he hadn't stopped at the house.

Whether he was out with the cows or just… out…she didn't know.

And couldn't care.

Her heart was open to the kids. Wide open. It was open to her mother. To Angela. To her *Family Secrets* family.

Not to Spencer.

That was how she survived. She closed the doors that led nowhere.

Long talks with Susan in New York had helped her see that.

She could watch television. Didn't want to have to avoid Christmas specials that inevitably led to warm, fuzzy family moments.

She'd have her own moments. At the *Family Secrets* Christmas party. With her mother and the kids on Christmas morning.

Spencer would be there, too. Just not in her warm, fuzzy moments. He'd be the friend who happened to stop by before she got there and stayed until after she left. Or something like that.

When the house started to close in on her, she left Daisy Wolf inside with the kids, pulled on her sweater coat and moved outside to the deck. It was still in the low sixties. This part of the California desert rarely got down to freezing, even in January. She felt the chill, though.

She wasn't sure, at first, if she was just hearing things when a strum wafted through the air. Still not used to the quiet of a night that allowed even the softest sounds to travel, she tried to make out what she'd heard.

Some kind of bird? Wind?

It came again. One strum. And then two.

Afraid to move, though she couldn't say why, she sat completely still. Waiting.

A couple of chords followed. Called to her.

Spencer was out in the darkness. Playing his guitar.

Remembering that night months before, she knew it had been the night she'd begun to fall in love with him. She'd been so hurt that he didn't want her to be friendly with his kids. Hurt beyond what a producer would feel toward her employee.

The kids had already had a part of her heart then. That quickly. She'd never known love could just…happen.

That it could descend without warning. Take possession so quickly and completely.

Soft chords filled the air now. She wasn't sure if they were coming closer. Or if he was playing louder.

As though in a trance, she stood. Followed the sound.

Once she was in the yard, she knew where the sounds were leading her. Back to that first night. His father's truck.

Only now she knew it was Frank's truck. Not Gerald's.

Knew, too, why the truck was still there.

He missed her friendship. He'd told her so. She missed his, too.

Walking closer, slowly, so slowly closer, she wanted to be able to be friends with him.

Wondered if time could take care of that.

She could see the truck. Could see a shadow of the man sitting atop it, strumming his guitar. She recognized every nuance of his shape in the darkness. The tilts and angles.

Her heart would know him anywhere.

And then she heard his voice. As though he knew she was there. And he was speaking to her.

"'But it's your world now I can't refuse.'"

She froze. Just stopped cold.

She knew the song. Anyone growing up in her generation had to have heard it. Country-music lover or not.

Garth Brooks, the singer and songwriter of that piece, was a legend.

And this particular song… Women all over the world longed to have a man sing it just for them.

Or at least, Natasha always had.

He was singing about having a lot to lose.

No. For the first time ever, Spencer Long-fellow had nothing to lose.

But he continued on. Calling to her. He called his life his own. Was in control. Until she'd come along.

Now he was shameless in his love for her. Just like the song said.

Like he was saying.

He didn't have original music. But the music he sang spoke for him. She knew that now.

Natasha started to back away.

There was just one problem with all of that.

He wasn't singing to her, calling to her. He didn't know she was there.

She'd let her heart get away from her. Get in the way of her focus. She took a deep breath with every backward motion she made.

Focused on facts. Spencer's growing up. The lack of nurturing he experienced. His inability to…

He wasn't on the truck anymore. She'd watched his shadowy frame slide down off the hood. He was still singing. Softly. Hadn't missed a beat. The same song. A second time. But with every line he sang, he took a step closer. Matching hers.

For every step back she took, he took two steps forward. Until she just quit stepping back.

And he stopped singing.

SPENCER DIDN'T SAY ANYTHING. He didn't have any words to give her. Or the ability to deliver them.

Not without his guitar and another man's song.

"Spencer?"

She needed something from him. He held up his guitar. Held open his arms. And knew complete and total happiness when she came into him, wrapping him up tight.

"It might take me a while," he whispered into her hair, just above her ear.

"The song. Do you relate to it?"

She didn't loosen her grip on him. Or look at him.

"I do." An admission about a song he sang. He got it out.

"Who do you think of when you sing it?"

That was easy. "You."

"Then you go ahead and take as long as you need, Spencer. Take forever. Just don't stop singing your song."

She was crying. He could feel the shudders against him.

Inside him.

And he was crying, too. Just a couple of tears. Filling his eyes. Not falling. Tears of joy. Of thankfulness.

And that was when he looked up and saw the twins...gazing down at them from the second-story window of Justin's bedroom.

His son who couldn't fall asleep—and the twin sister who always had his back.

Their grins seemed to spread across the state of California. Justin gave him a thumbs-up. Tabitha nodded. She looked like she was crying, too.

There was nothing more to say. No plans to make. No agreements or agendas or paperwork to tend to.

Just raw, naked truth exposed.

Bared and fragile souls finding each other.
His lost cowboy heart had finally found
its way home.

* * * * *

*Be sure to check out the other books in
Tara Taylor Quinn's FAMILY SECRETS
miniseries:*

*FOR LOVE OR MONEY
HER SOLDIER'S BABY
Both available now from
Harlequin Heartwarming.*

*And look for the next FAMILY SECRETS
story from Tara Taylor Quinn, coming
soon!*

LARGER-PRINT BOOKS!

GET 2 FREE LARGER-PRINT NOVELS PLUS 2 FREE MYSTERY GIFTS

Love Inspired®

Larger-print novels are now available...

LARGER-PRINT BOOKS!

GET 2 FREE
LARGER-PRINT NOVELS
PLUS 2 FREE
MYSTERY GIFTS

Love Inspired®

SUSPENSE

RIVETING INSPIRATIONAL ROMANCE

Larger-print novels are now available...

WESTERN WP PROMISES

YES! Please send me **The Western Promises Collection** in Larger Print. This collection begins with 3 FREE books and 2 FREE gifts (gifts valued at approx. $14.00 retail) in the first shipment, along with the other first 4 books from the collection! If I do not cancel, I will receive 8 monthly shipments until I have the entire 51-book Western Promises collection. I will receive 2 or 3 FREE books in each shipment and I will pay just $4.99 US/ $5.89 CDN for each of the other four books in each shipment, plus $2.99 for shipping and handling per shipment. *If I decide to keep the entire collection, I'll have paid for only 32 books, because 19 books are FREE! I understand that accepting the 3 free books and gifts places me under no obligation to buy anything. I can always return a shipment and cancel at any time. My free books and gifts are mine to keep no matter what I decide.

272 HCN 3070 472 HCN 3070

Name	(PLEASE PRINT)

Address	Apt. #

City	State/Prov.	Zip/Postal Code

Signature (if under 18, a parent or guardian must sign)

Mail to the **Reader Service:**
IN U.S.A.: P.O. Box 1867, Buffalo, NY 14240-1867
IN CANADA: P.O. Box 609, Fort Erie, Ontario L2A 5X3

* Terms and prices subject to change without notice. Prices do not include applicable taxes. Sales tax applicable in N.Y. Canadian residents will be charged applicable taxes. This offer is limited to one order per household. All orders subject to approval. Credit or debit balances in a customer's account(s) may be offset by any other outstanding balance owed by or to the customer. Please allow 4 to 6 weeks for delivery. Offer available while quantities last. Offer not available to Quebec residents.

> **Your Privacy**—The Reader Service is committed to protecting your privacy. Our Privacy Policy is available online at www.ReaderService.com or upon request from the Reader Service.
>
> We make a portion of our mailing list available to reputable third parties that offer products we believe may interest you. If you prefer that we not exchange your name with third parties, or if you wish to clarify or modify your communication preferences, please visit us at www.ReaderService.com/consumerschoice or write to us at Reader Service Preference Service, P.O. Box 9062, Buffalo, NY 14240-9062. Include your complete name and address.

WPBPA16R

LARGER-PRINT BOOKS!
GET 2 FREE LARGER-PRINT NOVELS PLUS
2 FREE GIFTS!

HARLEQUIN®

super romance®

More Story...More Romance

YES! Please send me 2 FREE LARGER-PRINT Harlequin® Superromance® novels and my 2 FREE gifts (gifts are worth about $10). After receiving them, if I don't wish to receive any more books, I can return the shipping statement marked "cancel." If I don't cancel, I will receive 4 brand-new novels every month and be billed just $5.94 per book in the U.S. or $6.24 per book in Canada. That's a savings of at least 12% off the cover price! It's quite a bargain! Shipping and handling is just 50¢ per book in the U.S. or 75¢ per book in Canada.* I understand that accepting the 2 free books and gifts places me under no obligation to buy anything. I can always return a shipment and cancel at any time. Even if I never buy another book, the two free books and gifts are mine to keep forever.

132/332 HDN GHVC

Name _____ (PLEASE PRINT)

Address _____ Apt. #

City _____ State/Prov. _____ Zip/Postal Code

Signature (if under 18, a parent or guardian must sign)

Mail to the **Reader Service:**
IN U.S.A.: P.O. Box 1867, Buffalo, NY 14240-1867
IN CANADA: P.O. Box 609, Fort Erie, Ontario L2A 5X3

Want to try two free books from another line?
Call 1-800-873-8635 today or visit www.ReaderService.com.

* Terms and prices subject to change without notice. Prices do not include applicable taxes. Sales tax applicable in N.Y. Canadian residents will be charged applicable taxes. Offer not valid in Quebec. This offer is limited to one order per household. Not valid for current subscribers to Harlequin Superromance Larger-Print books. All orders subject to credit approval. Credit or debit balances in a customer's account(s) may be offset by any other outstanding balance owed by or to the customer. Please allow 4 to 6 weeks for delivery. Offer available while quantities last.

Your Privacy—The Reader Service is committed to protecting your privacy. Our Privacy Policy is available online at www.ReaderService.com or upon request from the Reader Service.

We make a portion of our mailing list available to reputable third parties that offer products we believe may interest you. If you prefer that we not exchange your name with third parties, or if you wish to clarify or modify your communication preferences, please visit us at www.ReaderService.com/consumerchoice or write to us at Reader Service Preference Service, P.O. Box 9062, Buffalo, NY 14240-9062. Include your complete name and address.

HSRLP15